ANNIE'S WAY

Sisters of Haworth Moor Series Book One

Eve Everdene

Copyright © December 2022 Eve Everdene

The right of Eve Everdene to be identified as the author of the work has been asserted by her in accordance with the Copyright, Designs and Patents Act 1988.

This ebook edition first published in 2022 by Eve Everdene.

Apart from any use permitted by UK copyright law, this publication may only be reproduced, stored or transmitted, in any form, or by any means, with express prior permission in writing of the Author or, in the case of reprographic production, in accordance with the terms of licenses issued by the Copyright Licensing Agency.

All characters – apart from the obvious historical figures – in this publication are fictitious and any resemblance to real persons, living or dead, is purely coincidental.

CONTENTS

Title Page
Copyright
Chapter One — 1
Chapter Two — 10
Chapter Three — 19
Chapter Four — 29
Chapter Five — 35
Chapter Six — 43
Chapter Seven — 48
Chapter Eight — 57
Chapter Nine — 65
Chapter Ten — 79
Chapter Eleven — 92
Chapter Twelve — 101
Chapter Thirteen — 108
Chapter Fourteen — 114
Chapter Fifteen — 124
Chapter Sixteen — 131
Chapter Seventeen — 140
Chapter Eighteen — 148
Chapter Nineteen — 152

Chapter Twenty	161
Chapter Twenty-one	171
Chapter Twenty-two	181
Chapter Twenty-three	191
Chapter Twenty-four	201
Chapter Twenty-five	208
Chapter Twenty-six	214
Chapter Twenty-seven	218
Chapter Twenty-eight	225
Chapter Twenty-nine	236
THE END	245
Join my mailing list!	247
Books By This Author	249
If you enjoyed this book...	251

CHAPTER ONE

Haworth – May 1814

Annie lay in the long grass, her eyes screwed tightly shut against the brightness of the sun. Her hand swept the earth around her and finally found William's shoulder. "Stay here with me late into the evening, don't go yet", she whispered as she turned on her side and peered at him through one squinting eye. She observed him as he dozed, his chest rising and falling rhythmically, his mouth slightly open. She knew he would soon gather his things and leave her again; a lump rose in her throat at the thought. Annie longed for the day when there would be no more parting, once and for all. *Not too much longer,* she thought, *surely he won't make me wait much longer.*

A curlew called to them across the moor, returning them to their senses. William stirred from his nap and groggily retrieved the pocket watch from his waistcoat. "By Christ Annie! It's almost 6 o'clock, I had better get on or...". Annie cut him short with a deep and lingering kiss, holding tightly to his arms as if to hold him down - to stop his inevitable departure. He gave a drawn-out moan as he returned her embrace, caressing her cheek and allowing his lips to open slightly at the pressure. "*God, it makes me feel but a lad again when I'm with you Annie*". He pulled away and surveyed her, smirking, "and so bonny to boot, I bet I'm the envy of every man in the West Riding".

"Well, maybe if anyone knew about us, aye", she said sulkily. "I want to start telling people Will. Feels like we've been courting forever, I hate sneaking about like this". She crossed her arms, carefully surveying his face for a reaction. "I'm fed up of meeting out here on't moors, I get cold...". She was cut off by William grabbing crudely at her chest, "Who wouldn't with their skirts around their waist, you naughty girl!", his tone was mocking and she felt cheapened, not for the first time. "Come now Annie", he chuckled, sensing her disappointment. He pushed her away and rose to his feet unsteadily, stretching the afternoon out of his joints. "I'm due at the Black Bull to speak with Mr Hague any moment, and then there is the ride back to Keighley". He didn't want to keep the Landlord at the inn waiting again. Mr Hague did not take kindly to lateness – and his was business that William could not afford to lose.

Annie stood up beside him, crestfallen. "He's there all evening Will, why does it matter what time you arrive? And besides, there's only you to buy spirits from around here, he's not going to travel out for them - is he? Not with Mrs Hague ill again, anyway..." she trailed off, realising he had already turned his back to her and was walking down the pathway towards his horse. "Did you give any mind to what I said last week then?" she ventured tentatively, stumbling after him on the uneven ground. "Only, it's been six or seven months we've been meeting. Why don't you come to meet Tab and Joe at home, I think they would be glad to meet you". He spun around and pulled her roughly towards him by the waist, "Aye, but then I wouldn't be able to have you all for myself, would I?!", he cried, nuzzling into her neck. She recoiled at the sensation, finding the tickle of his moustache thoroughly unpleasant. "I could come to visit at your house then", she reasoned. "If your sister is any better".

"For heaven's sake Annie!" William interrupted – finally losing his patience, "Do you ever stop going on about your bloody family, my *bloody family*? I'm a busy man - I'm kind enough to make time for you, don't keep demanding more!". His eyes narrowed as he turned again to his horse and untied the reigns from the fence post. "Come on Neddy, let's be away now". He walked in pace with the giant creature side by side as Annie followed on behind longingly. She wished him more considerate. Not once had he offered her to mount Ned and ride to the edge of the moor to save her legs, and her legs had been much more tired and troublesome recently. All of her had been tired and aching over the last few months. She pushed the thought from her mind: "I'm sorry Will, I know you are good to come all the way to see me, only, we have talked about marriage and I want to be able to start organising things. I'll need time to send for Lottie from Scarborough, that's all.".

He shook his head and kept his eyes trained on the floor in front of him. "Annie", he exhaled, "you know things are not that simple. Not with Maria unwell, you know she relies on me. It's my duty as her brother to care for her, you wouldn't want me to neglect my duties, would you?". Annie instantly felt ashamed of her persistence. Of course, he was right - she too knew the importance of siblings, especially after Mother and Father had died. *I really should have more patience with him,* she thought. It stung when he was not enthusiastic about marriage like he once was though. She recalled the first time they had met, walking across each other's path by the waterfalls in November. How bold he was in calling out to her, offering her a drink of whiskey from one of the bottles in Ned's saddlebag. *It's freezing girl,* he'd said. *Take a drink here with me before you catch your death.* She had thought him so handsome and revelled in the attention of a more sophisticated man, a more experienced man, who she had judged to be at least ten years her senior.

It was only four days after that first meeting that they had made love for the first time, both of them stood up, Annie's back pressed against the cold and damp stone wall that ran alongside the graveyard, not even three-hundred yards from the cottage. Annie was terrified of being caught, they could have been stumbled upon by any number of people at any moment, but she could not have refused if she wanted to. It had felt utterly inevitable. Annie cast her mind back to that, his passion and devotion had been intoxicating. But that deed had punched a hole through the bucket, with William's love and respect for her slowly but surely flowing out.

"I'm sorry Will, I don't mean to be a nag", she tried in vain to make herself seem relaxed and aloof, scrambling to please him again. She grieved the earlier days, when he would squeeze every last second out of their time together, delighted to see her, delighted to *touch* her. Something had shifted recently though; she could feel it in her gut. He came to visit less frequently now, and when he did meet with her, he was distracted and curt. *Well, he's curt after he's had his way with me, of course,* she thought bitterly. There was a great distance between them, and nothing Annie did seemed to draw him any nearer.

"When will you be coming back to see me again then?" - they had reached the narrow passageway beside the Black Bull and Annie was already sick with grief at his departure. "Next week perhaps? If you come on the Sunday again after church I won't be at work and I can spare almost the whole day...". William rubbed his knuckles firmly across his forehead in exasperation; "Right, Sunday then".

"D'ya promise me Will?".

"*Yes Annie*, I promise you". He spoke to her like one would speak to an irritating child.

"Will you send me a letter before then? I do miss you between visits, and what with me not having an address to write to you...".

"Jesus help me, *yes Annie*, I will write to you. And you know why I don't give my address...".

"Your sister, I know", Annie replied, glumly.

They both fell silent as Mrs. Goodwin passed them, not wanting to fuel any more gossip than there already was. William took the opportunity to hitch Ned to his usual post. "After next week I am away to North Yorkshire for a month or so, maybe more. We're coming into the busy season and I need to secure my contacts up at the coaching inns and country estates", he said quietly. "Many bottles to be sold, money to be made". He fiddled with the bridle at Ned's mouth, distractedly. The thick silence hung in the air. Annie wanted to say something about her suspicions, she truly did - but she chose to tell him the news next Sunday instead; maybe he would seem happy and in love with her then, like he used to. She was sure his affection would return, as long as she did not press him. What was another week anyway? And besides, Jenny always said, *you only tell a man when you're certain*, although, who knew how much longer she could go on waiting before her swelling belly told tales on her.

"So after next Sunday, I won't see you for I while I suppose?", she prompted, crestfallen.

"Ba-bye my darling," William called quietly to her over his shoulder. He was already walking across to the pub, too far to hear the question, and he would be upset if she followed. He did not like it when they were spotted together. Tears stung Annie's eyes, such a familiar sensation nowadays. She swallowed hard and turned away, giving a ragged outward breath, preparing herself to return home, late again, to the questioning of her sister. As she did, she felt it once more. That strange sensation in her womb, *the quickening* Jenny always called it. Annie knew, more certain this last week or so. No rags to soak for five months now. She needed an answer next Sunday, that was for certain. *As soon as he knows it will all be different,* she comforted herself. *Then there will be a proposal, and a wedding to follow very quickly after.* She mused about when would be best to tell the Reverend so he could prepare to read the banns. *Perhaps at work, the following Monday,* she decided. *After he asks me proper.*

~

As Annie raced past the herb garden and up to the door of the cottage, she heard her brother-in-law Joseph call after her. "Annie! Where the hell have you been? It's gone 7 o'clock.

Your sister's furious - so mind yourself". Joseph shook his head and returned to his chickens. The meetings with William were beginning to cause tension at the cottage. Annie wondered if Joseph knew somehow, about her secret. She shuddered at the thought and hurried on past.

She pushed the heavy wooden door open and saw her sister Tabitha bent over the range, her long black hair tied back under a bonnet to protect it from the steam in the kitchen. She was boiling the pot for some tea, banging the spoons and caddy around to make her frustration obvious. "Tab, I'm really sorry, I went to visit the church after service and I saw Jenny at the parsonage and we forgot the time", she said, breathlessly. "I'll make it up tomorrow, I know I've loads to do. I promise, the garden and the range tomorrow, honest. And the washing. Here, I'll do that". Annie tried to grab the caddy from Tab's hand but it was snatched back and slammed down on to the table.

"You and Jenny aye? You and Jenny were busy at the parsonage until gone seven tonight - is that it...?". Tab narrowed her eyes and examined Annie's face. Annie knew that tone; her shoulders dropped as she realised she had been caught in a lie. "... The same Jenny I saw on her way up to visit her daughter at four o'clock?". Tab had her arms folded across her body, dish rag gripped tightly in her hand. Her cheeks were bright red, half from the fire and half from anger, Annie suspected.

"'Ere, I know exactly where you've been", she continued. "I'm warning you now girl, you want to keep away from that man before something happens that you can't get out of". She turned back to the stove. "He's nowt but a peddler Annie, a no-good bloody *cheapjack!*".

Annie's stomach dropped – she was terrified to tell Tab already, dreading the disappointments and the shouting and the heartache it would cause. It made her all the more certain that things would need to be righted with Will before the confession could be made. What could anyone do about it if there were to be a marriage anyway? That would surely make it acceptable.

They we so absorbed in each other that they didn't notice Joseph sitting down at the table beside them. "Girls, enough thank you!" he said firmly, glaring at them both. "Let's not have quarrelling now". Annie sat herself down at the table with a heavy thud and stared down at her hands, twisting her skirt into knots. She felt like crying when she noticed how her skirt bunched around her middle when sat down, emphasizing the budding roundness. Restless, she leapt up again and busied herself, putting another log in the grate and then poking absentmindedly at the embers underneath it. She wanted more than anything to tell them both straight out and just be done with it. *At least then the burden would be lessened*, she thought.

"Have you heard anything much from your uncle, Joseph?", Annie tried to change the subject and soothe the tension bubbling away between them in the small kitchen.

"Aye, he's not too good unfortunately". Joseph took a long sip of his scalding tea, "I was hoping to go up to visit soon but Whitby is a long way away. And what with summer coming, it's not the best time for – well…" he gestured vaguely at the small leaded window, preoccupied with his brew. Beyond it sat their small farm, the neat rows of vegetables, the fragrant herbs and rich fruit trees, their pigs, sheep and milking cows. The clucking hens that pecked around the garden pathway. Joseph was born in this cottage and the home farm his parents had established while they were still young and healthy had proved fertile and productive.

"I can always do more here Joe, if it would help?", Annie offered, taking comfort in being useful. "I'm only working for the Reverend on Mondays and Tuesdays, I'm sure I could watch over things here too… if you were called away for a bit, like".

"Ha!" Tab gave a snort of disbelief. "You're going to run things here when we don't see hide nor hair of you from dawn 'till dusk some days!" She opened her eyes wide in exaggerated disbelief. "I'll believe *that* when I see it".

"Well you *will* see it Tab, I won't be out late again for a month at least", Annie said sharply. All this talk had touched a nerve with her, reminding her of William's sudden departure and cold mood. "He's away week after next anyway, up North for a while", she muttered, suddenly self-conscious. Tab softened, noticing the tinge of sadness in Annie's voice.

"Ah I see, well in that case you can make yourself useful here". Tab gently squeezed Annie's arm in a show of harmony, the argument over for now. The sun outside was setting, casting a warm orange glow through the room that illuminated the dust particles and smoke from the fireplace. The sun on Annie's face made her look even more beautiful, Tab noticed. *Just like when she was a little girl, just like my Samuel.* Her golden hair was a halo around her pale face, made almost luminous by the evening light, loose from its plait and untamed where she had been lying in the grass. Annie was the one who had needed Tab the most, not like Charlotte - the youngest sister of the three – who was so independent and quick. Annie had needed to be mothered, and Tab was devoted in her role as substitute.

"Let's see how things go". Joseph tore at the bread he had been handed by Tab and chewed on it hungrily. "I don't like the idea of you alone here like that Annie, what if something were to happen?".

"I've got Abraham fifty strides away if I need someone, I'd be alright".

"Abraham has his own business to attend to, he can't be up here doing your work as well".

Annie was desperate to prove herself capable, she felt a tremendous pressure to grow up, to be as strong and able and organised as Tab was. Lord knew she would need to be taken seriously soon enough anyway. She drained her tea and ate a piece of cheese and some bread that Tab had reluctantly prepared for her. That troublesome exhaustion suddenly found her again, enveloping her like a heavy woollen cloak. "I'm not half tired, I might go to bed", she said to no one in particular. "I'm dead on me feet".

"Aye, go to bed girl, you look done in", Joseph agreed, looking up at her with a warm smile. Joseph was the peace-keeper in the house, kind yet firm, he was a wonderful stand-in father for Annie and she suspected she would need him more than ever soon enough. Annie felt a pang of jealousy that Tab had been so lucky; she and Joseph knew each other as infants, they grew up together around these familiar moors and fields. She had known his integrity, his honesty and his gentle nature years before they wed. It was tried and tested over many summers. He was well respected in Haworth, broad and dependable. He'd had no shortage of options, but he would consider none but Tab.

Annie went through to the back room where her bed was, carrying a jug of warm water from the range. She was due at work in the morning and desperately needed her sleep - it was getting harder for Annie to keep up when working at the parsonage. She didn't want to finish, not yet anyway, she adored Jenny the housekeeper and the Reverend Charnock. But Jenny was getting older and was relying more and more on Annie for the heavy work, work that could soon prove troublesome.

As she undressed and splashed the warm water over her face and neck, she wondered what would become of her. Underneath all her clothes and the binding wrapped tightly around her belly, she was becoming round and full. Being undressed and confronted with it made her feel dizzy and breathe fast, like she could faint. She dropped into bed, screwing her eyes shut and willing herself to sleep, before the worries took hold of her again.

CHAPTER TWO

Annie leant over the wall of the pigsty with one hand on the small of her back. The stone was cutting into her other palm but she felt that if she took her weight off it, she might stumble and fall. Quickly then, same as most mornings, she was sick - bringing barely anything up, tears streaming down her tired face and stomach seizing involuntarily. She tried to stifle the retching and coughing, tried to be discreet and so far, it seems to have worked. Some mornings she was forced to find a different spot, depending on who was about. She couldn't bear the smell of the privy first thing though, so it was often out with the animals or into a hidden bucket under her bed, to be emptied out when she was alone. She straightened herself up slowly, giving her back time to adjust, and squinted into the early morning sun.

A blackbird sang loudly nearby as she surveyed the little farm, the crisp air helping with her nausea. She closed her eyes and drank the freshness of it in, taking deep breaths in and out until the sickness subsided once more. The sound of footsteps broke the peace and she opened her eyes to see Joseph rushing over to her, the geese darting out of his path. *Just my luck,* she thought.

"Annie, what's wrong love? You alright?". He took hold of her arm gently and looked into her eyes with concern. "Shall I fetch Tab? Have you got a fever?". His rough cool hand pressed into her forehead, nearly knocking her backward.

"Must have eaten something spoiled yesterday, that's all", she said nonchalantly, pulling her head away from his hand; she didn't like his scrutiny and questioning but Joseph wouldn't take the hint.

"You look right drawn and pale", he went on, "I'm on my way to see the Reverend now about fitting some pews for the church, why don't I tell him you're not well enough to work?".

"Joe honestly, I'm alright - don't fuss!". She gave a forced smile. "Jenny needs me, it's laundry day. Besides, I just need something to eat and a brew, breakfast will be waiting for me at the parsonage now". He did not look in the least bit convinced.

"I really don't think you should. I hope you don't mind me saying, but you've not been right at all recently. Why don't you get yourself back into bed and I can have Tab fetch the doctor to have a look at you? Or at least ask Jenny this afternoon, see if she has a remedy that might help".

"No!", Annie shouted, grabbing his hand to stop him from leaving. They were both taken aback by her abruptness. If the doctor came, that meant an examination and her secret would be instantly discovered. "Listen, don't tell Tab but, William gave me some pie yesterday afternoon - I thought it smelt a bit funny at the time, might just have been off like", she whispered conspiratorially.

Joseph nodded his head almost solemnly and looked towards the cottage where Tab was building a fire in the range - "don't worry, I won't mention it girl. Last thing we need is Tab thinking he's trying to do away with you", he chuckled. They both knew Tab hated William with a passion. Annie knew why, though the two had never formally met, Tab had heard enough about his reputation from the gossips in the village.

"Look 'ere Annie", Joseph said awkwardly, "if you needed to tell me something, I can be a good listener. And know that you have my confidence, I needn't share your business around all and sundry". Annie was so moved by his gesture that she felt tears prick her eyes and her lower lip wobble slightly, she bit it so it wouldn't betray her distress. She wiped at her sour mouth and clammy face with her apron to refresh herself and turned away from him, embarrassed.

"I'm going to get a cup of water and then I better leave for work. I don't want to keep Jenny waiting today, we want to catch the good drying weather". She walked past Joseph briskly before anything more could be said, but heard him follow along behind her.

"I'm heading down to the church anyway, need to measure up for the wood. I'll walk with you. You go have a drink and I'll just feed the hens".

~

Joseph and Annie walked together in comfortable silence. Their cottage sat just south of St Michael's and All Angels Church on the edge of the moorland. You only needed to pass through the graveyard and out of the little iron gate on the south side and you were almost home again. Annie loved her home because it was outside of the village itself. Not many folk passing, just peace and quiet all of their own. They were an island there, away from prying eyes, just as she preferred it. And behind them - the great expanse of the moor.

Joseph busied himself in the graveyard, gathering bluebells and forget-me-nots into a small bundle and laying them on a plain little grave. Annie observed him curiously, he was not a man of great sensitivity and yet this display of tenderness seemed to come very naturally to him. *Married nine years and only Samuel to show for it,* she reflected. The poor little thing had lasted only a short year before he was taken away again – with a fever, four years ago now. It took him so quickly; he was right as rain one night and dead the next.

"Here lies the body of Samuel Naylor, who departed this life on the second of November 1809, aged one year", Annie read out absent-mindedly. As Joseph was tending to the grave the Reverend Charnock called out to them both from over the headstones. She realised she was twenty minutes late for work and began her apologies but the Reverend halted her with a raised hand. "No matter Annie, no matter", he assured her. "I'm not here seeking you out, I merely wanted to speak with our Mr. Naylor here about the pews".

The Reverend was small in stature - barely as tall as Annie, with a shock of bright white curly hair combed back neatly and set with grease. Every day he wore his black suit with woollen frock coat and high white bands around his neck, a uniform that made him instantly recognisable as a man of the cloth. Annie had never seen him without his delicate round spectacles balanced on his nose, shielding the sparkling grey eyes that saw everything, even the soul itself. He was *eccentric*, that's the word the villagers used. Annie wondered whether that was due to his advancing age but Jenny said he had always been *odd*, even as a young man.

Joseph rose and shook the Reverend's hand enthusiastically. "Good to see you Reverend, come, let's have a look at the damage, see if we can't repair the old ones first".

Annie left Joseph to his carpentry and hurried up towards the side entrance of the parsonage. A beautiful building, sat at the very top of Haworth, it was of modest size but always busy with worshippers; other members of the clergy, academics, friends and Reverend Charnock's now-grown up sons. Annie had never known another place like it, she felt at home amongst its comforts and sense of peace. She passed through the scented gardens, damp in the morning air, and reached up to undo the latch on the door when it was wrenched open, taking her by surprise. There stood Jenny, grinning at Annie's fright.

"What time do you call this?" Jenny giggled. Despite her sixty something years, Jenny could often be more mischievous than many of the children in the village. "Overslept again by any chance?". She flung the door wide open and stepped to one side impatiently, "Come on in then". The fire was already crackling in the range with large bubbling pans of soapy water on top. The air was thick with steam and the harsh scent of the homemade housekeeping soap that Jenny used to wash the bedclothes and garments.

"Oh Jenny, I'm so sorry, I got up a bit late and lost track of time feeding the animals". She rolled her eyes for effect, "You know what our Tab's like if I don't do all my jobs in the morning. Feels like I'm making excuses to everyone recently, I just can't keep up with anything", she said with a deep sigh. Jenny wrinkled her nose and looked her up and down, "Have you eaten something this morning? You look *grey*. Sit down!". She pulled the chair out from under the table and gestured firmly to Annie. She wanted to protest, to get away from yet more questions about her health and start stripping the beds. But despite it being only half past eight she was already weary - so she relented. "Get this down you love", Jenny said as she dropped a plate of porridge and stewed gooseberries down in front of her. "Let's start as we mean to go on". Annie ate the food gladly, the only noise in the kitchen then was the bubbling pans and her spoon tapping on the bowl. Jenny was busying herself making tea and setting two cups on the table, a signal that work could wait.

"Your dress is coming along nicely - it will be ready in time for the dance. We'd better do a fitting soon, just t'make sure it's right...", Jenny took a sharp breath, "don't mind me saying Annie, but you're looking a bit *full* these days. Jenny let the comment linger in the air between them, watching Annie's face for a reaction. "Any idea why that might be?".

Annie furrowed her brow. "No no, it must just be me eating more. I've been eating like a horse recently - Tab's been doing them fruit pies again...". She dared to look up at Jenny to see if her lies had had the desired effect.

"Annie, have you seen much of that William lately?". Jenny's distaste was evident but her tone was kind all the same.

"Aye, I saw him only yesterday. Just for a bit though - he's very busy at present. As it happens, he's away on business in North Yorkshire week after next. Good money to be made, he says". She wasn't sure who she was trying to fool more with her casual tone, Jenny or herself.

"Have you told him?", Jenny asked, straight out. Annie gave a sharp laugh and shrugged her shoulders enthusiastically. "Told him what? There's nothing to tell, is there?". She dropped her chin to her chest defensively and continued to eat, slower now.

"About the baby, Annie". Her face was riddled with concern.

Annie refused to meet Jenny's gaze but her breathing was shaky and the spoon trembled in her hand.

"What *baby*? I don't know what you're talking about. I'm just getting fatter, that's all!". She gave a high-pitched laugh but it emerged as a strangled sob.

"Please don't lie to me", Jenny whispered.

Annie buried her face in her hands despairingly. "How did you know?", she muttered. With her blushing face hidden away, Jenny could barely make out the words.

"I've had my suspicions a while, but this morning I can see it in you. I just knew…". She held the dishcloth to her forehead and shook her head in pity, "well, God help you Annie, God help you. It's true".

Sobbing, Annie started to plead with her, "I know I've done wrong. Please don't be upset with me, *please.* No one knows Jenny. And no one is going to know until I can tell Will and get all this straightened out".

"Oh Jesus, he doesn't *know?*", Jenny gasped. Annie held a finger to her own lips and gave a desperate *shush.*

"Please Jenny, *no one* knows, not Tab, not Will, not Joe. No one.

It's really early anyway. That's why I haven't told Will yet", she lied.

"So there must have been talk of marriage - yes? Yes?", her eyes were searching for an answer.

"Well, obviously, I said I wouldn't do *that* unless we were going to get married...", Annie protested.

"So he's asked you then?".

"...Well, he said he would give it consideration!", Annie wailed. As she explained the situation to someone else she could hear how stupid and reckless she sounded. His coldness, the change in his behaviours, fewer days together – he must have noticed her changing body, he *must* know. The fear began to creep over her again, that tightness in her chest that ended with her gasping for breath.

"Well what on earth are you going to do about this then Annie? When are you planning on telling Tab? *Tonight* I hope!", she cast the dishcloth down on the table in defeat.

"She's going to be heartbroken, isn't she? She hates him Jenny, honestly, she doesn't even know the man and she hasn't a good word to say about him".

"I imagine she will have worse to say after this". Jenny grabbed Annie's hand and looked her deep in the eye. "Do you hand on heart believe him to be coming back to marry you?".

"He loves me. He said he loves me and that we will marry. I believe him", Annie said slowly and firmly, repeating the mantra she said to herself endlessly.

"Ha! Was this before or after he got in your drawers?".

"I'm telling him when he comes up on Sunday. Then he'll ask me, won't he?". The two sat in uncomfortable silence, Annie wishing for a sign of approval or reassurance from Jenny, but it didn't come. "We better get on with our work", Annie said biting her lip. "I don't want to get you in trouble with the Reverend".

Jenny sighed heavily and pulled herself to her feet with the edge of the table. She had seen her fair share of unwed mothers in her time. She was Haworth's resident midwife and there weren't many people in the village she hadn't seen enter the world. Of course, she knew that carrying and birthing the baby was the easier part for an unmarried woman... what came after that would be hellish. It was a sin like no other, one that made itself known to the world with little chance of concealment.

The two trudged up the main staircase with a large wicker basket and between them stripped the bedding from the Reverend's bed in uncharacteristic silence. Annie gathered the discarded pillowcases from the floorboards and retrieved the worn shirts that would need a good soak from the cupboard. "Please don't tell Tab, will you? Or Joseph". Annie wrung the linen in her hands with nerves. "Just give me time to do it, it needs to be at the right time when it's all sorted with Will. But not now, not with Samuel's birthday coming".

Jenny rushed across the room and slammed the bedroom door shut. "Will you watch your mouth in here Annie, do you want people to work it out?", Jenny hissed. "How far gone are you, would you say?".

"I don't know, can't be very long, can it? Surely not", Annie mumbled.

"Why are you asking me? Don't look to me for an answer". Jenny sat down heavily on the bed in resignation while Annie stood in the corner of the room next to the window, wide eyed, chewing at her nails.

"Try to think, when was the last time you had your monthly?".

"Three months ago, I think – must have been early February", Annie lied. "You know I'm not regular". She knew if she told her it had been five months back that it would worsen things still. She would go straight to Tab and tell her, surely, worried even more by the looming date and her inevitable discovery. "Three months ago - that's all. I'm sure of it. I can't be more than that". Annie's cheeks flushed with shame, she hated lying to Jenny and had done it so rarely, not since she was a child.

"When are you going to tell her?".

"I'm going to wait until Sunday. I'll tell her on Sunday evening, once I've told Will and got a proposal. I won't leave it any later". Annie clasped her hands together and begged, "Just let me sort this out Jenny, alright? By Sunday it will all be sorted".

Jenny crossed the floor slowly to Annie and took her face in her two warm hands gently, yet firmly. "Promise me that Annie, because if you do not, you leave me in a very difficult predicament", her voice was sad, with a note of resignation and her grey eyes were damp with tears, "and I will have to take matters into my own hands, for your sake". Jenny took a deep breath and confirmed - "By Sunday?".

"By Sunday", Annie agreed.

CHAPTER THREE

It was much warmer when Annie left the parsonage that afternoon. Unsurprisingly, it had taken her and Jenny a lot longer than usual to get through their work. On other days they would have their jobs finished by two o'clock, but as Annie traipsed back down past Samuel's grave, she heard the church bells ring out half past four. Still, she always worked two days in a row at the parsonage, so anything forgotten today could wait for tomorrow - although Jenny had seemed reluctant to entrust Annie with the donkey work she normally did, like lifting the big pans of hot water and carrying the soaking wet linen. As she shuffled, Annie quietly prayed that Jenny would not determine her useless and decide to end her employment. Not until Annie was able to straighten out the more pressing matters in her life at least.

Before she left, Jenny had given her some remedies wrapped in a big cheesecloth from the well-stocked pantry. A large jar of candied ginger, some chamomile tea and a strong-smelling balm to rub on her chest and under her nose when the sickness struck. She said if the nausea did not pass soon, she was to tell her they would try something a little more potent. Annie clung onto the bundle; it represented the motherly love and support that had been sorely needed over the last few months. The relief was immense knowing that Jenny would keep her confidence - a problem shared may not be a problem halved, but it certainly seemed to weigh less.

So deep in thought was she, that a loud yell from nearby made her jump and drop the bundle to the floor. Luckily, the jar of candied ginger was so well wrapped that it did not break when it landed on the grass to the side of the path. She spun around to see Abraham standing behind her, a way back up the track. Next to Abraham, of course was Pip, the giant wolfhound - his most faithful and constant companion. The two were never without one another since that day Abraham returned with him from Bradford, years ago now.

"Now look what you've bloody done", Annie grumbled, retrieving her dropped bundle from the verge. "You know I can't bear to be crept up on". Abraham came striding over with a look of confusion on his face. "What's got into you? Bad day at work? You're late finishing anyway", he said, craning his neck to see the church clock through the full branches of the oak tree. Annie felt flustered by the interruption, she really did not feel like speaking to anyone at that moment - but she did feel guilty for snapping at Abraham all the same. She tried to tuck her hair back under her cap where it has been shaken loose, tendrils sticking to her damp forehead after her hard work over the steaming tubs.

"Sorry, I've had a long day and I was late this morning too. What've you got there?", she gestured at the leather pouch in Abraham's blackened and calloused hand.

"Joe asked me to forge a set of nails for him, he has some work up at the Balfour Estate in a fortnight or so. Got many more to do for him yet like, but thought I'd start him off", Abraham said with a chuckle, "You know what he's like when he gets going, he'll be through that job in no time".

"Oh aye, I know", Annie nodded in agreement.

"'Ere, I brought this for you Annie, I know you like them". From his back pocket he produced a gnarled and worn horseshoe and held it out for Annie to admire as Pip did his best to knock it from his hand with his curious nose. He often brought trinkets for her, nothing fancy or costly mind, but thoughtful things.

After all, they had long been close friends, the three Crossley sisters, Joseph and Abraham, all born here in Haworth and close in age, although, some into better circumstances than others.

Annie took the horseshoe in her one free hand, the other hugging the bundle to her waist. "Thank you Abraham, that's cheered me up greatly you know. Another for my collection - this one can go above the barn door", she exhaled and dropped her shoulders down, resigning herself to having company. "Come on with me then, you can leave the nails at home for Joe". The three began to stroll towards the cottage, Annie setting the slow pace with Abraham and Pip falling into step.

"So how's work? How's your father?", Annie asked, making conversation despite not caring much for the answer.

"He's been a bit off colour this week, I've been at the fire more and more recently. Might be time for me to take over the smithy soon. Not like I can't manage it, I've work coming in from all over the West Riding", he nodded self-assuredly.

"Well, Joe seems to think highly of you anyway... as a blacksmith like, not as a man", she retorted, giving him a cheeky wink.

"You little piglet!". He gave her a playful shove in the arm, managing to get a laugh out of her.

"I tease you of course, it was only the other day I heard Mary-Anne in the store telling people how you were the best about. *Oh and so young and handsome too!*", she mimicked, which made Abraham crease with laughter. "You forget about Mary-Anne", he said, "she's about fifty years older than the girls that usually catch my eye".

They both sauntered into the cottage. Abraham threw the packet of nails down on the wooden table and sat himself in the rocking chair by the empty grate. "No Tab today?", he asked, looking around for her.

"No, she'll likely be late, she's out visiting what's-her-name, the widow". Annie went into the back room and stuffed the candied ginger underneath the bedding in the large oak coffer. She didn't want any questions arising.

"Do you fancy some chamomile tea? It's good stuff, from the parsonage". She waved the packet in the air to tempt him.

"Better not, I was going to carry on up to the waterfall, let Pip have a swim. I've been promising him all week". At this, Pip lay his head in his master's lap and panted expectedly. "Why don't you join us - nowt to do here, have you?"

It was true, on working days Annie didn't have much to do in the evenings. She had seen to the animals that morning and would do the lion's share of her work through the rest of the week. And just strolling and laughing with Abraham had already lifted her spirits considerably. "Go on then", she said. "But I can't be all night mind".

~

The water was cooling on Annie's skin. Despite the breeze and it being only May, she was hot. She was warm every day now, with the hot flushes coming periodically. It felt so refreshing to swim and float in the wide pool while listening to the water bubbling nearby. Abraham had been in too, fighting playfully with Pip and throwing a stick for him to swim to, but now he was lying on his side on the bank, propped up on one elbow as Pip paddled alone.

She left her heavy woollen skirts on the bank and went in just in her slip - the same way she had since she was a child. Nobody ventured out that way over the moors without good reason anyway, so Annie and Abraham were always safe to swim and frolic as they pleased.

"Ere", Abraham called out to her "What do you make of your visitor then?".

Annie bobbed down under the water then shook her head vigorously as she came back up, enjoying the sensation. "What visitor?", she asked.

"Haven't you heard? When Joe came to the forge to ask me for those nails this morning, he told me that he'd had a message and you were all having a visitor. Well, might be having a visitor I suppose".

"Oh? And who's that then?", Annie said, as she swam lazily to the bank to hear him more clearly.

"Edward Brigg", he said with a grin, "He's out, by all accounts, and nowhere to go for a season".

"Who's that when he's at home?", she shrugged, with a vacant expression.

"You remember", Abraham prompted, mindlessly pulling up tufts of grass around him and sprinkling them into the breeze. "Ed, he must be the same age as your Joseph, they came up together at the church school - boisterous little thing, joined the army, *you know!*"

"Hellfire", she said, raising her eyes to the sky, recalling his face from all those years ago. "Edward Brigg. What, coming up to see Joe is he?".

"More than a flying visit was the impression I got, think he needs somewhere to stay for a while, what with his mother gone now and his brother across in Ireland. Coming home isn't he - the only home he's really got anyway". He paused to whistle for Pip to stay close. "You know him and Joseph have always been good friends, kept in touch all these years. He's alright really, I always got along well with him. It'll be nice to see him". He shifted on the ground and propped himself against a tree trunk, crushing the red campions that Annie had been admiring only moments before.

"He can't", Annie said indignantly. "We haven't the room. Besides, I don't want some ruffian soldier hanging about the place". The worry was flooding back, it had given her a couple of hours respite but it was never far away. The next few months would be critical, the pressure of a stranger about the place could destroy her chances of surviving them with any shred of peace. Joseph would feel let down enough by news of her illegitimate child, the last thing he needed was an audience.

"Well that's up to Joe, I'm sure. Anyway, like I say, he's not so bad. I remember him quite the clown, might a raise a smile from you anyway - although he's a soldier, not a miracle worker". Annie splashed water over the reclining Abraham, giggling.

"Speaking of raising a smile", she said, swimming over to the shallows and climbing gingerly out of the water on the slippery green stones, "any word from Lottie recently?". She tried to dodge Pip as he darted around her legs, making her more unsteady still. "Don't look!". She gestured for Abraham to turn away as she walked back over to her discarded clothes at his feet, arms crossed over her middle, concealing her belly.

"As it happens, I got a letter the other day - you?".

"Oh no, I don't hear from my own sister half as much as you. Although, who knows the content of those letters, must be very encouraging to make Lottie practice her writing so often ey?", Annie teased.

"Get off with you, you know it's not like that", he protested, betrayed by his reddening cheeks.

"You carry on working hard and making a good living, you could afford to have her leave her position and marry you! Sure she would prefer scrubbing your floors to Lord Saunderson's", Annie mused. "I wouldn't mind living on the sea front like that though, would you?".

Abraham shrugged, non-committal. He would never outright

confess, but everyone knew. Everyone except Lottie it seemed.

Annie stood over Abraham, dressed again now, with her hands on her hips. "Come on, let's go, I'm getting cold". Pip had already begun to trot back down the trail, sensing the fun was over. "I want to get back and find out what's going on with this Edward", she said gazing back towards the cottage.

Abraham dusted off his trousers, "I'll walk you back".

~

Tab stirred the pot of lentil soup as it bubbled on the range, then leant across to the salt pig, taking a large pinch. "Annie, lay the table for me please", she said over her shoulder as she dropped the salt in. Annie rose dutifully from the table where she had been sat cutting the bread, and gathered three shallow bowls decorated with delicate blue and yellow flowers from the shelves of the substantial oak dresser. They had been a wedding present to the Naylors from the Reverend.

"Why is your hair all damp?". Tab suddenly seemed to be looking at Annie for the first time that day, until then preoccupied with the supper.

"I went to the waterfalls with Abraham after work", Annie said, "He needed to bring these bits for Joseph anyway so we walked up together". She nudged the leather packet with one of the bowls, sliding it out of the way of her place setting.

"Ah, I *see*. And how's Mr. Eccles today?", she asked smirking, "In close contact with our sister I presume?". The two dissolved into laughter together, Annie savouring the sound - it seemed to come less and less nowadays.

"Oh aye, heard from her but last week, so he said - not much to report". She caught Tab's eye, "That would be fit for our ears, anyway!", they creased into giggles once more.

"What's going on in here girls?", Joseph asked, as he came

through the door, eyeing the bread hungrily. "A private matter or may I join?".

"Annie here is just keeping me abreast of my own sister's condition, via our friend Abraham, naturally". Tab was in good humour that evening, and despite their teasing, it did please her to know that Abraham and Lottie kept correspondence. Tab thought a lot of him, and she was happy that Lottie might have a trustworthy and loyal admirer.

"He left these for you Joseph", Annie said, passing over the nails, "and look!", she presented the horseshoe with a flourish. "You can use one of your new nails to hang it above the barn for me", she stated, cheekily.

"Get off wi' you, you've arms yourself, have you not girl? These nails are for the honourable Mr Balfour and his estate, I'll have you know", Joseph said, mocking the gentleman's proper accent.

"Speaking of gentlemen", ventured Annie, "Abraham tells me we're having a visitor, is that right?". She ladled spoonfuls of the soup into the bowls in front of them, it was so thick it was more like a stew.

"He's worse than an old biddy, gossiping like that", Joseph grumbled, looking at Tab.

"Give over Joseph, we were going to tell her tonight anyway", Tab said, "Do you remember Edward Brigg? He lived up on Sun Street before he went in for the army?".

"Not particularly, although the name rings a bell".

"He's been away serving King and Country for twelve years, and he's out for a season. Joseph said he could come to stay here with us and help with the farm". Tab dipped her bread in the soup and bit down on it quickly, talking again with her mouth full. "You know we need the help Annie, truth of it is we can't afford to keep on as we are. Lottie's already had to take a position in service and I would hate to lose you too. But the farm needs to bring more money in Annie. And quick".

Annie sat sour faced, pushing the lentils around with her spoon. Knowing there would soon be another mouth to feed made her feel terribly guilty. "Well where's he going to sleep though? You two are upstairs, I'm in the back room. Are we to stick him in the barn?".

"He can sleep in here, there is room for a cot under the window. He won't have many personal affects; there is a spare trunk he can use anyway", Joseph said. He had thought through the arrangement carefully.

"Oh, so I am to be left downstairs with a man I don't know, during the night?", Annie said dramatically, staring at Joseph.

Tab banged her spoon down onto the table and interrupted her. "Don't be so damn ridiculous please. We urgently need the help here; we must get a better yield this summer. We're desperate, Annie". Tab's eyes pleaded with her. "We don't want to have to sell the small holding and this might just be our answer, for this year at least".

"Aye, I understand", Annie relented. She was deeply disappointed with the news, but did not want to stand in the way of her family finding its feet again.

"And besides all that!". Joseph's booming voice was amplified by the low ceiling. "It is our *Christian duty* to attend to those in need, is it not? Edward has been a good friend to me since childhood, and in his hour of need the least we can do is offer him safe lodging. That's the end of the matter as far as I am concerned. He will be here within a week". He was so rarely strict with them like that, so rarely defensive, that both Annie and Tab were stunned into silence. The atmosphere was so serious that when the girls caught each other's eye, they spontaneously dissolved into sniggers.

"Well at least… at least, if he is not comfortable down here…", Tab covered her mouth with her apron, almost unable to speak through her laughter, "He could always share the bed up there with *you* Joseph!", the two were howling now, leaning back in their chairs, shoulders shaking in mirth.

"Bloody stupid girls, the pair of you", Joseph muttered, rolling his eyes while he mopped up the last of his soup with a crust.

CHAPTER FOUR

Saturday came, and Annie felt more and more doubtful that she would see William again as the week went on. She worked on the farm until half past three, when she had thoroughly had enough. After that, she had contemplated going to see Abraham, but in the end felt she would rather be alone.

Annie traipsed over the moors for what felt like an eternity, turning her situation over in mind. She was desperate for an answer by tomorrow at the latest, then she could come clean. Whether the news was good or bad, she could come clean to Tab and Joe and arrangements could be made. She fretted over how they would react, a marriage to man like William would be terribly disappointing to them. But to be pregnant with no father to be seen for miles around would be an altogether different matter.

She sat down on a large jutting rock and glumly threw stones into the rushing stream below her, where they landed with a plop. Her relationship with Tab and Joe as she knew it was soon to come to an end and she was not ready. All Annie was sure of was that Edward Brigg was bound to make things infinitely worse by hanging around.

As she scanned the village from her elevated position, she noticed the church and recalled with a heavy heart the last time she had seen William, how he had been rushing to his meeting at the Black Bull. An idea occurred to Annie. *What if I were to get his address from Mr Hague? He must have it! Then if he does fail to come tomorrow, I could write to him. Or perhaps pay him a visit with*

Joseph... Before she had chance to consider it any further, she began marching back towards the village.

The inn was dark and smoky, it took Annie's eyes a few moments to adjust from the brightness of the sunny spring afternoon. There seemed to be a great deal of soot on the once cream walls, and she suspected it was the layer on the windows that stopped much of the light entering. Annie felt most out of place in the inn, she had only ever been in a handful of times before, and never without Joseph. As she scanned the room, she was relieved to find it was only Mr Hague behind the bar and an old man bent almost double on a stool in the corner, his ale half empty on the table in front of him. The fewer people there to overhear, the better.

"Afternoon Miss Crossley, what can I do for you?", Mr Hague asked gruffly. He was polishing glasses with a dirty rag which only served to smear them further. "Pint of ale for the lady?" he laughed loudly at his own joke, jolting the old man in the corner from his slumber.

"Not quite", Annie said, observing the still-filthy glasses he was lining up on a high shelf above the bar, "I won't trouble you, I just came for an address for that bottle supplier you use... the one from Keighley. I don't recall his name", she lied, trying to sound casual.

"And what on earth would a girl like you want with that?", he asked, smirking.

"I've been sent by Jennifer Brown, the Reverend will be having guests over the summer and she wishes to place an order". Annie lifted her chin and puffed out her chest. "She wanted to know if you could let her have it".

"I don't. I just deal with him 'ere when he passes through Haworth I'm afraid. Although tell Jennifer, should she need anything I can sell it to her - if I have enough in't cellar like". He sniffed, waiting for a reply. "Anything else I can do? Or...".

"I will tell her, Mr Hague". And with that, Annie turned to leave, wracking her brain for anyone else who might know more about William.

"Oh dear, oh dear", Mr. Hague whistled and shook his head, knowingly. "There'll be no shortage of girls across Yorkshire trying to track that bastard down, I'm sure of it", he said, as he watched her shut the door and walk away past the window. "No shortage at all".

~

Feeling defeated, Annie had no choice but to return to the cottage. Her stomach was rumbling and she felt thirsty, but she had been too shy to ask for a drink on Joseph's slate. She intended to go home, have her tea and then excuse herself to bed by eight o'clock at the latest, although she was tired enough to fall asleep there and then.

The small window at the front of the cottage glowed in the dusk as smoke billowed from the chimney. Annie noticed a large pack leaning next to the door and she wondered if Abraham had called, *but why would he bring...?* Then it dawned on her. The booming voice she could hear inside was not Abraham's. It was a stranger's. Edward Brigg had arrived several days early.

The loud laughter and chatter from the cottage danced around the fragrant garden accompanied by the sound of Tab banging pots in the kitchen. There was a nip in the air and as she opened the door the warmth of the fire rushed to greet her, putting her at ease. She had not noticed the hour but it was already 7 o'clock and she found herself ravenously hungry.

'Wondered where you had got to... get and lay the table Annie'. Tab waved her wooden spoon at the range with a wide grin, signalling that supper would soon be ready. She glanced over to the two men sat by the fire, Edward in the rocking chair. He had one foot on the hearth and was pushing himself gently back and forth. When he laughed, he tilted his head back and roared without a shred of constraint. The noise grated on Annie and she turned away to hide her disappointment. It felt odd setting four places, the table had to be pulled away from the wall to accommodate the extra seat - a bulky chair no one could recall the origin of, seemingly a fixture as old as the house itself.

Soon after, Edward had sprung to his feet and Annie could sense him hovering next to her.

"You must be Annie", he said in a voice so low and gruff it almost sounded hoarse.

"I must be", she replied, not bothering to meet his gaze.

Edward laughed to himself, not discouraged by her cool reception. "I remember you as a girl", he continued, head cocked to one side, observing her with a smile.

"I don't remember you", she replied curtly. Although this was a lie, now he was in front of her again, she remembered Edward Brigg very well.

"Annie!", Tab hissed a warning across the kitchen. Annie rolled her eyes and turned to face Edward, softening a little.

"How was your journey here?", she asked, trying to be polite. He was stood so close to her she had to crane her neck to look him in the eye. He had altered so much since the age of fourteen. He had grown broad and strong, now at least a foot taller than her. His face was weathered and creased, but his light blue eyes still sparkled the way she remembered.

"Comfortable, thank you Annie", he said quietly as he took his seat at the table.

Edward complimented every aspect of Tab's dinner and her cheeks blushed deep pink as she looked down at her plate demurely, smiling in reply. She had not had chance to prepare a more decadent spread due to Ed's early arrival. But nevertheless she had cobbled together a respectable offering; fresh bread, pork pies, homemade cheese with jams and chutney, along with some leftover fruit pudding.

"There will be something much better tomorrow", she waved her hand over the spread dismissively, "It looks like you're in need of it! Does the army not feed its soldiers well?", Tab giggled as Edward chewed ravenously, barely stopping to take a breath.

Annie was disgusted by his table manners. Admittedly she had seen a lot worse, but the way he talked with his mouth full and leant over others to take more before he had even swallowed made Annie shiver.

"You might say that", he replied. He shifted in his seat then and cleared his throat, turning towards Annie. "I apologise for my lack of grace Annie, both manners and food can be scarce in the army", he said, sensing her revulsion.

"Yes, and what of the army? Are you done with it all together or did you say you intended to return?", Joseph asked.

Edward laughed but Annie detected a hint of discomfort in his reply. "Oh. No, I certainly intend to return, this is just, *extended leave.* I've served twelve years, if I re-join in six months I get a nice bonus, you see". He scanned the faces at the table, frowning slightly. "Wouldn't get it if I stayed on directly...", he trailed off and returned to his bread and cheese.

"Well, you'll be a great help to us here", said Joseph. "We're happy you've come, in't that right Annie?".

"Aye, I'm sure it will do the farm plenty of good", she answered dutifully.

"That it will!", Tab chimed in enthusiastically. "I have a feeling our fortunes are about to change quite rapidly".

~

Annie did not get chance to go to bed early as she had wished that night. Instead, she stayed up late with the others, listening intently to Edward's stories about daring escapades and far-flung lands, and to Joseph and Tab reminiscing about how life used to be in the village, before they were married, when Edward was still here and close family were still alive.

As she nodded in her chair, sleep creeping up on her, she tried to reassure herself about the meeting with William the next day. Tomorrow night she would have to tell Tab and Joseph about the wedding, the baby, all of it. She was fearful knowing they would be displeased but almost thankful for the welcome distraction that was Edward's arrival. *At least if I move to William's house in Keighley*, she mused, *the farm will still benefit from the extra pair of hands – for this year at least.*

CHAPTER FIVE

"Are you coming to church this morning or not?", Tab asked, peering around Annie's bedroom door. It was already half past eight and Annie was still buried beneath the covers. She hadn't slept well that night due to nerves, and didn't feel like being anywhere else but bed. "Come on, Sunday Service starts at nine, make haste please!". Tab slammed the door behind her. Annie waited until her footsteps sounded more distant and sluggishly crawled out of bed, not wanting to chance Tab springing back into the room and catching her without her bindings.

She pulled the lengths of fabric out from under her thin mattress and deftly wrapped them around her middle, each morning the process took less and less time as her technique grew more accurate. Annie splashed the remainder of last night's water from the basin over her face, pressing on her puffy and tender eyes, willing away the swelling. Her reflection in the looking glass was unrecognisable. *I look like an old hag,* she thought harshly, upset by her appearance. The idea of facing William like that made her feel even worse. Especially since not hearing a word from him all week, as he promised. She had waited with bated breath every day, but no letter arrived.

As Annie shuffled into the morning light outside the cottage, Tab looked at her in shock. "Annie, have you not slept?", she asked.

"Not very well", Annie replied, "It's the cut grass or the blossom or something making my eyes bad again. I'll take some honey for it later on", she mumbled.

"Hm, better had".

"Come on girls", Joseph cried out from further down the track where he was stood talking with Edward, "we'll be late again at this rate". The women trotted to catch up with them and Annie was left red in the face and panting by the time they arrived at the south gate. They rushed through the graves toward the open door, the last of the parishioners to arrive. "Good morning, my little dove", Tab whispered to Samuel as they passed his tiny resting place, just as she did every week.

The Reverend had been preaching for what seemed like an unusually long time and Annie was starting to feel more and more unwell with each passing psalm. She felt hot, unbearably so, sweating under her bindings and heavy skirt. She didn't know if it was the tightness around her middle or her nerves that made her feel like she was gasping for breath, but the pins and needles in her face were back and her hands were trembling so much she dropped her hymnal to the floor. She didn't dare reach down to retrieve it so she left it there by her feet, scared that if she moved, she would be joining the little leather book on the cold flagstones.

Tab's elbow dug into her arm, snapping her back to the present. "What're you doing? Get up!", she hissed. Annie was embarrassed to realise she had missed her cue to stand for the hymn. She grabbed on to the pew in front of her and hauled herself to her feet, little strength left in her legs to stand up unaided. Tab tilted the open hymnal dramatically towards her, so that she might find her place and join in.

"What's the matter?", she whispered giving Annie a puzzled look, but Annie could not answer for the sensation had come again. The heat in her belly, the acid in her throat. She was going to be sick, right there in the middle of Sunday service, in front of the whole village. Annie pushed Tab's hymnal out of the way and squeezed past Edward and out of the pew, muttering vague apologies. She was only just out of the door when the vomit came.

After the retching had begun to subside, she felt a firm hand on her arm and was comforted to find Jenny stood behind her. As they walked slowly to the low wall close by Annie leant heavily on her, clinging to her arm through the thick shawl willing herself not to faint.

Jenny untied the ribbon under Annie's chin and quickly pulled her bonnet off, then stood for a moment in front of her, fanning her with a book taken from the church.

"Are you alright love?", she asked with concern.

"Aye, I'll be grand in a moment, just felt really hot and sick, had to get out", Annie said sheepishly, her eyes closed tightly against the bright sun.

They were interrupted then by Tab, who had slipped out of the church at the end of the hymn.

"Annie! Whatever's the matter? Everyone's in there wondering what's wrong with you". Her tone was light-hearted, she did not want to cause Annie further distress, but her worry was ill-concealed. "I'm sorry, I shouldn't have made you come this morning if you were no good". Tab shifted her weight from one foot to the other, feeling quite useless with Jenny already there. "Shall we walk you home? We can each take an arm. Or do you need Joseph to carry you?", she tried to coax a response from Annie who was sat quite silent and grey on the wall, concentrating on her breath, trying to stop any resurgence of sickness. "Annie..?". Tab prompted again, gently.

"It's her nerves, that's all", Jenny said, smoothing over the confusion and concern. "She told me all about it at work this week. I've seen it hundreds of times in girls her age". She nodded sagely, trying to stamp out Tab's brewing suspicions.

"She hasn't been right for a while", agreed Tab, shaking her head in pity at Annie crouched in front of her. "Have anything to calm her down?", she gestured towards the parsonage, to Jenny's jars, bottles and packets, her carefully blended cures and remedies.

"Oh aye, course I have". Jenny proffered a hand in front of Annie's face and helped her to her feet. "Leave her with me, I'll sort her", she told Tab authoritatively.

"I'll have to, I'm afraid. Joseph and I are headed over to Oakworth to visit with Mr and Mrs Spencer. We've put them off for a few months now. As long as it *is* just nerves Annie?". Annie did her best to summon a smile and nodded in agreement.

"Just nerves Tab, that's all".

"Alright, well Edward isn't joining us - I have told him to stay behind today and rest, I think he needs it. He will be around if you need anything. We'll be back late on". She returned to the service then, giving Annie a weak smile as she opened the heavy door.

Annie and Jenny walked together up the slope to the side entrance of the Parsonage, but as Jenny unlocked the door, she realised Annie had not followed. "Annie! Come on love, let's get you sorted".

"I've got to go Jenny, haven't I? I've got to go to meet him". Annie was whispering despite all the other church-goers filing out of the church and away towards Main Street, well out of earshot. She started to walk unsteadily without waiting for an answer. "I'm sorry Jenny, but I really have to", she said over her shoulder, unsure if she had even been heard.

~

The quivering call of a nightjar stirred Annie from her uneasy slumber. Pain radiated through her body as she lifted her face off the rough grass and rubbed her eyes, trying to get her bearings. She shivered violently, her clothes were damp and clinging to her skin. Pushing herself up to lean against the wall of the abandoned farm house, she tilted her head back and stared up to the dark grey sky visible through the broad holes in the roof. Droplets of rain falling through, bathing her face and dripping down her neck.

"Will?", she cried weakly, peering into the gloom for any sign of him. "Will? Please Will, are you there? Where are you?".

There was no reply, just the sound of rain falling onto the ruin around her. He still had not come. It was already evening, and he had not come. He had not written to her that week, and *he had not come*.

Annie whimpered as she climbed to her feet unsteadily. She stumbled through into the other room of the old dwelling, half expecting to see William sat there, patiently waiting for her to awaken. Instead, an empty room. *This is where we always meet,* she thought, *there is nowhere else he would have waited for me. It's always here.*

She passed under the archway and out into what used to be the yard, enclosed on all four sides by dry stone wall. Annie circled the building, leaning on the wall for support. There was no sign of William. She was alone there and she had been alone there for the past nine hours at least, by her reckoning.

That feeling, stronger than ever now, forced Annie down to her knees. She felt as though she was suffocating, gasping for each breath. She dug her fingers through the long grass and down into the earth, squeezing and curling her fingers, as if to hold on to life itself. *I'm dying. I'm going to die right now, out here on the moors,* she panicked.

"He didn't come. He didn't come!", she shouted into the gloom, her voice carried across the moors without a soul to hear it. Then, a feeling grew in her chest until it took over her completely; it was over. William would not be coming this Sunday or any other Sunday. It was heart-breaking and heavy and knocked her sick, but ultimately, she knew it. The gut feeling was true.

~

"Oh, thank God". Annie almost collapsed with relief when she reached the front path back at the farm. With so much on her mind she had forgotten about Edward's very existence, and was shocked to find him sat alone at the table reading a letter by the low light of the rush lamp in the otherwise silent cottage. He turned to greet her, but his face fell when he saw Annie's dishevelled form. She stood trembling in the doorway, her clothes wet and muddy. It was clear she had been crying, her face was blotchy and tear stained and her breath was jagged.

Oh. I forgot you would be here, I thought the cottage would be empty…".

"What's happened to you?", he interrupted bluntly. "You're soaked to the bone".

Annie didn't reply and remained stood in the doorway.

"…Are you alright Annie? You look frozen. Have you been out all day in the rain?". His chair scraped across the stone floor as he stood to get a better look at her. "Sit down, sit down here", he pulled the rocking chair close to the hearth and threw on more firewood which hissed and popped.

"I just fell asleep on the moor and didn't realise the time, that's all", she replied flatly.

"You look upset…".

"I'm not. I'm just cold".

Edward nodded and sensed it was best not to pester her any further. "Let me make you some tea". He fumbled through the dresser for the caddy, as the kettle sat over the flames. "Why don't you go through and get into some dry clothes while the water boils?". He gestured to her door with a nod of his head.

She took some of the warm water through to her room in a bowl and slowly washed her body with the lavender scented soap that she rationed so carefully. She pulled on a fresh nightgown from the coffer at the foot of the bed and brushed her hair roughly, not stopping when she came to the knots, the stinging and pulling was a punishment for her foolishness. Then, staring blankly into the looking glass she noticed her lips were blue, so she went through and sat in the rocking chair close to the fire, a large woollen blanket wrapped tightly around her.

"Is that better?", Edward asked as he poured the tea and handed a scalding cup to her.

"Yes, thank you". She stared down at her feet in their thick stockings, embarrassed that Edward should have seen her so undone.

"You shouldn't be out alone in the dark like that, not over the moors", he said quietly from where he sat at the table. "It's not safe for you".

"I know. Thank you", she replied sarcastically. She didn't look at him but instead stared into the dancing flames. "I'll not wait up for Tab and Joe", she said as she stood up sharply. "I need my bed – good night Edward". She rushed across the kitchen and into her little room, closing the door firmly behind her.

Edward remained at the table, confused. Something had happened out there in the gloom and the rain, but he didn't want to press her. He leant back in his chair deep in thought. *Just leave her to it Ed. More trouble than they're worth anyway, women.* He gazed into the fire and noticed her steaming cup sat on the hearth where she had left it. He shook his head dismissively and turned back to his letter, yet found himself unable to concentrate. With a sigh he relented and before he knew it, he was knocking on her bedroom door.

Annie was lying in a ball on her bed, sobbing silently into her pillow when she heard it. "Can I come in?", Edward's gravelly voice carried through the door. She wiped at her face furiously and sat upright.

"Aye".

The door opened and the yellow light from the fire and lamp flowed into the room, illuminating her on the bed.

"You forgot this. Don't let it get cold, it will do you some good". He placed it carefully on the little table next to the bed where she sat. They looked at one another awkwardly, before Edward cast his eyes down and made for the door.

"Thank you", she called after him. He gave a thin smile and nod, and shut the door behind him with a thud.

CHAPTER SIX

"Well, I can't believe his nerve frankly, Annie. I think that's downright disgusting to treat a young girl like that. I'll have him bloody strung up should I see him strutting about Haworth again – I shall call for the magistrate!". Jenny was polishing the little silver candlesticks in a frenzy, aggravated by Annie's retelling of the previous day. "And you were there 'till dusk? Raining, with no food, in your condition?". She stared pointedly at Annie's middle. "He's got some nerve".

"Well, he didn't know *that* part I suppose", Annie said despondently.

"He knew you were out there in't rain, waiting for him! Besides, I think he knows more than he lets on".

"Something might have happened to him".

"Aye, a change of heart most likely".

The two sat in silence for a few minutes, tending to the silverware and sipping on their tea.

"At least you've got the measure of him now I suppose", Jenny sighed. "Your Joseph's going to hang him when he finds out".

"Suppose something *has* happened though, to his sister or something like", Annie ventured. "What if that's why he never wrote and didn't come yesterday".

"Oh aye, the sister, I forgot. The reason he has to sneak about and hide and can't give you an address to write to him at". Jenny rolled her eyes, far too experienced to be conned by his excuses. "What is it, his sister or his wife? What sort of man lets his sister run his affairs like that? It's cowardice is what it is".

"Oh please Jenny, don't go on. I feel foolish enough as it is".

"I'm sorry love. I do fret about you though, you know that". She took Annie's hand from across the table and gave it a comforting squeeze. "How are you feeling today? You shouldn't have come in if you're still fragile".

"I'm knackered, truth be told. He's really hurt me this time". Annie blinked tears away, her lower lip shaking.

"It's not nice at all my love. But once people know, it will be better, I promise".

"Perhaps telling people won't even be as bad as I imagine. There's nothing to be done about it now, anyway". She peered through the kitchen door and down the hallway to ensure there was no one there to listen in.

Jenny fetched the velvet lined cutlery box from the groaning dresser and started depositing each piece back in its place, a cloth in hand to avoid any fingerprints. "So when are you going to do it, Annie? You promised me you'd do it last night. You're going to have to say something soon".

"Well that's the problem". She twisted the polishing cloth in her hands nervously. "I don't want to spoil things for Tab and Joe, what with Edward here now. They're really hopeful he can help save the farm".

"I don't doubt they'll be furious at first, but it won't change anything with Edward, will it? Besides, they will come round to the idea. You're not the first woman in the village and you certainly won't be the last! I've delivered a great number of babies with no father about in this village alone!".

"But what if they have to send Edward away?".

"And why would they do that? You're having a baby Annie, you haven't been stricken with the plague. You will all have to find a way to muddle along. Worst comes to worst, Edward can stay with me for a while and still work the farm during the day. It won't come to that – you'll find Tab softer than you think".

Jenny left her work on the table and filled up a tea kettle with fresh water. "Think we better have a brew, don't you?".

Annie nodded as she wiped at her damp eyes with the corner of her apron, tears threatening to spill over at any moment. She picked up the wooden cutlery box to return it to the dresser, when her shoulders suddenly sagged. "Oh Jenny, imagine how cruel folk are going to be when they find out, I'll be a laughing stock". She placed the box back down with a loud thud, distractedly.

Jenny rushed to Annie's side and held her in a hug, "Now, listen here. Folk can be cruel, yes, but I know you will manage. You have someone else to think of now, someone more important than every other person in this village put together".

"I will Jenny, I promise, I'm not going to let you and Tab down".

Jenny gave a tired sigh and held Annie even tighter. "We had better get to the floors Annie. Come on! You'll have to fetch your tea with you".

Trying to make up for lost time, the two women worked much harder and faster over the next few hours, barely chatting, both focused on the task at hand. The furniture was polished, the cobwebs brought down with deft flicks of a feather duster, the floors were swept and scrubbed. Jenny used to do all this, and often more, by herself in her younger days but now she relied on Annie and started to worry about being left without help. She did not want to have to advertise for another girl from the village, not able to think of anyone even remotely suitable. She hoped there would be some months left yet before she would need to deal with any of that business.

"So how are you finding it having Edward there". Jenny was satisfied enough with the amount of work done to allow for some conversation again.

"Well, I very much wish he *wasn't* there, but all things considered, not too bad. He's working with Tab today on the farm while Joseph is knocking up those pews for the Reverend. D'ya know, he was really kind to me last night when I got back from the moors. Didn't tell him anything of course but he could see I was in a state. Made a pot of tea for us and everything".

"He's a good lad, Edward. As I'm sure you will come to find", Jenny said with a knowing smile.

"I hope you're not suggesting anything", Annie said with sharp, dismissive laugh. "Even the thought of men makes me feel violently ill now".

"It never stays that way Annie, believe me. You will get over this one day. And you won't want to be alone forever, it gets lonely".

"And what sort of man would look at me twice after this?".

"You'd be surprised Annie. There're good men out there with enough love for you and your child. But anyway, no more talk of love affairs. You've a long time before you want to get mixed up in that sort of thing again".

"I am embarrassed that he will find out about the baby though. Don't want him thinking I'm *that* sort of girl". Annie looked worried as she emptied the dirty water from her bucket out of the back door.

"'Ere, don't be daft", Jenny said, trying to comfort her. "He won't because he will have gotten to know you by then. Anyway, he's there to work on Joseph's farm, not make judgment on your morals. I wouldn't give it a second thought, he will be away to the army again before you know it".

Annie nodded, somewhat comforted, "Aye, that's true enough".

"Besides", Jenny said with a smile, "If he's as I remember him, he's really not all that bad Annie. He was a bit of a ruffian, but who could blame him, coming from a home like that. Don't expect too much from him after twelve years in the army. But you never know – you might find him a good friend after all this".

"I doubt it Jenny", said Annie in a withering tone, as she turned from the doorway and returned to her work.

CHAPTER SEVEN

Edward was not in his bed when Annie went through to boil water for her tea, despite the hour being very early and Tab and Joseph still at slumber. The sun was just rising, casting a pleasing light across the kitchen and there was a cold nip in the dry air. She pulled her shawl tightly round herself with one hand, protecting herself from the chill while wearing just her long sleeve nightdress – baggy enough to disguise any shape that may be apparent underneath. With the other she carried the pail round the side of the cottage to collect water for the house.

She was startled when she found Edward stood next to the pump, stripped to the waist, splashing water over his head and broad shoulders, scrubbing vigorously. Annie thought he looked strong – his muscles were well defined and his body was covered in all manner of marks and scars from his time away in conflict. She paused to watch him for a second, unsure whether to creep back into the house and wait, or to carry on forward brusquely. Steam rose from his back into the early morning air, and she found herself soon mesmerised by him. His body was not soft and slight like William's.

He was quite breathless as he finished his ablutions and held onto the pump for a few moments afterwards, when he caught Annie in the corner of his eye.

Make a habit of watching men from around corners, do you? Is that how you find enjoyment, eh?", he teased her with a wicked smile. As he turned to take his shirt from the pump handle, Annie caught glimpse of vermilion and purple – an interruption in the vast, even-toned expanse of his back. He pulled his shirt on quickly, shielding himself from her prying eyes. She did not query it – too embarrassed to let him know she had been looking. A feeling like the one she had when William first called out to her, first stroked her cheek and lifted her skirt took hold in her chest. She stamped it out immediately, angry with herself.

"I don't make a habit of it, no, even when there are strange men loitering about the place, half dressed", Annie retorted, rolling her eyes. She dropped the pail under the pump with a clatter, then gestured for him to move so she could collect her water.

"'Ere, you let me see to that", he began to pump, though he seemed to find it much more exhausting than Annie would have, which surprised her.

"Are we having a brew then?", he asked with a warm smile. Annie suddenly felt very exposed in the thin cotton nightdress, the shawl had slipped off her shoulders slightly and she could see Edward glancing discreetly at her neck and chest. She hurried back into the house without answering, leaving him to carry the water in after her.

After the tea was made they both sat at the table cradling their hot cups, Edward smoking his clay pipe. He looked out of place in the cottage, large and cumbersome in the small wooden chair.

"It didn't matter where in the world we were", he recalled, "brewing up was the first thing, every morning". He shifted in his chair nervously, waiting to see if she would relent and talk to him. He sensed her discomfort around him and felt disappointed. He had been relieved to find himself this position with Joseph and Tabitha but now he felt distinctly unwelcome.

Annie's eyes widened when he mentioned travel. "Where in the world...? Have you been a lot of different places then?", she questioned him, cautiously. Annie loved to open the numerous books in the small reading room at the parsonage and admire the illustrations of faraway lands and exotic plants and animals.

"Oh aye", he nodded, drawing long on his pipe, "I've seen it all, me; France, Italy, Egypt, Holland, Ceylon, God – all sorts! Even India, though yellow fever nearly carried me off there".

"I've never even heard of most of those places". Annie forgot herself for a moment and let a glimmer of admiration shine through her tough exterior. She turned her body towards him in her chair, keen to learn more. "Have you been in lots of battles then? Have you done lots of fighting?".

"Ha! You could say that. Aye, I've done my fair share – that's for certain. I think the King owes me a personal debt by now...".

"Did you kill many men?", she asked excitedly.

His smile dropped and he tapped his pipe slowly on the table, trying to muster an answer. "It's a necessary evil in war, Annie. Probably best not to discuss unpleasant matters like that with a young lady, ey. Wouldn't want to bring any misfortune upon us, would I?", he said gently.

She gathered the empty cups from the table, dissatisfied. "I'm not of a delicate nature, Mr Brigg. Not like the wives of Lords and Officers I'm sure you're more used to. I'm a country girl – I know the mechanics of life and death from the animals".

Edward laughed loudly and startled Annie, "The wives of Lords and Officers! I think you may have me misunderstood Miss Crossley. They wouldn't let a man like me within fifty feet of their wives. In fact, it's been a long time since I've had chance to speak to any ladies, really. I'm a bit out of practice".

At that moment Joseph came down the steep staircase in the back left corner of the main room, from where he and Tabitha's bedroom sat up in the eaves. "Well, you won't find a better lady in Haworth than our Annie", Joseph said, nudging her in the arm, trying to diffuse the tension hanging in the stale air.

"I'm away to the church now, the pews should be finished today. Annie, please show Edward the way things are done around here before you set off to work. Tab has deliveries to make and so will be out much of the day too, I'm afraid".

"Aye, I will do Joseph". Annie answered respectfully. He lifted his cap from the hook next to the door, "And Ed, don't take any cheek from this one!". He winked at Annie and she forced a smile at his joke.

Ed rose from the chair and took a long stretch towards the ceiling. "I'll not have any messin', don't you worry!", he replied, smirking playfully in Annie's direction.

~

Edward was thoroughly impressed by Annie going about her work. He had seen women working *hard* before, in the ports carrying huge loads of equipment or buckets of catch, in the cities with their cavernous tubs of soaking laundry; but Annie was a different girl when put to work. She was capable, serene and deft. Lifting loads quite ably that he would have bet a week's wage she couldn't get off the ground.

"Do you enjoy your work here then?", Edward asked.

"Aye, that I do", Annie replied, lifting a bale of hay down off her barrow and throwing it over the stable door.

"How long have you been here with the Naylors then?".

"Since my mother died. My father was already gone you see,

so I didn't have anywhere else".

"My sympathies, Annie". Edward meant it too; he was no stranger to loss.

"It was a long time ago now", she said, swinging a bucket of pig feed over the sty wall and sprinkling it evenly along the other side. The three pigs came lumbering over promptly, their breathing noisy and disruptive. Edward did not have much to do with animals bar the rats and mice that populated every military station, and he was quite enchanted with the little farm and its workings.

"How long ago, if you don't mind my askin'? Only, I remember your mother and father, from before I left".

"Seven years ago Mum went, and Dad the year before". Annie let her eyes linger on his for more than a fleeting moment, savouring the brief tenderness. He was trying very hard with her despite her coldness and she was almost sorry he had to put up with her.

"How old are you now Annie?", he struggled to work it out from his patchy memories of her from childhood.

"I'm twenty-one this year. You?".

"Twenty-seven just turned".

"You look much older", she said, without a hint of jest.

"Well thank you! I understand that to mean I'm a man with much experience". He lifted his clay pipe and took the tip between his teeth firmly, not once breaking his gaze on Annie.

"You've had a hard life", Annie smirked. "Anyway, have you ever milked a cow before?".

"This may surprise you Miss Crossley, but we don't really attend to cattle in the army". Edward was out of his depth. As Sergeant Brigg, he was used to overseeing a platoon of over fifty men with an iron rod. He was comfortable in control, a confident and decisive leader. But *this* was altogether different. He cursed himself; he was here to assist Joseph, not to impress *her*.

"I suppose there is a lot of things they don't teach you in the military", she said, smiling in his presence for the very first time. "You're in my world now, don't worry, I'll keep you on the straight and narrow", she said over her shoulder with a grin as she walked toward the cow shed, gesturing him to follow.

She flicked the stout three-legged stool next to the back end of one of their cows and sat herself down on it, hitching her skirts so as not to tread on them.

"I'll show you first, then you try your hand alright?", Edward nodded in compliance. "Ere, pass me that milk pail then", she took it and placed it under the cow's udders and squeezed, gently but firmly – top to bottom in a pulling motion. Edward was taken aback with just how much milk came squirting into the pail with a pleasing echo. "Like that! You see what I'm doing, yes?", she looked behind her to gauge his reaction, and his face made her dissolve into giggles. "Edward you look terrified; come, crouch down here next to me and look properly", she offered.

"Right, very well", he said, though Annie noticed he looked somewhat pained as he lowered himself to his haunches, and at the last moment he needed to grab onto her shoulder roughly to steady himself. "Oh, excuse me", he muttered, "lost my balance there". She continued to milk in silence, with just the metallic spray of the milk hitting the pail.

"Are you getting the idea now? Just imagine your hand is the calf's mouth". It all seemed so natural to Annie, who had seen lots of new mothers and their babies together, lots of animals nursing their young.

"Annie, I wouldn't have a clue about that now, would I?", Edward looked puzzled but refused to be deterred. "Go on then, let me have a try". She sprang up and he took her place on the stool and took hold of the udder firmly.

"That's right!", she said delightedly, as he started to coax milk down. "Don't be afraid to be firm, you won't hurt her", she said. He was producing about half the milk Annie was, but she seemed pleased all the same. "You'll have to do this every evening, alright? I'll do it first thing but I'm often busy in the evening what with other work – it gets busy here in summer".

"Right-ho", he replied, relieved at being able to do it.

They trailed about the rest of the small holding, the crop fields, the stores, the chickens, with Annie gesturing about and giving him a flow of instructions. Luckily Edward was used to picking things up quickly, a very important quality in his line of work. *I'll earn my place here, even if I'm not as capable as I once was;* he shuddered, willing the thought from his mind.

"That's it for now", she said abruptly, her cold demeanour returning. "I don't know what you need to do today though...", she shrugged at Edward, a gesture that confirmed his lessons were over and he was free to go.

"Right then".

"I've got to get to work".

"Alright... shall I walk you?".

"I know the way, Mr Brigg", she said flatly.

"Well, I need to go into the village anyway, need some things that I couldn't bring with me – I'm walking that way" he persisted. *William had been persistent at the start too*, she thought, and then felt cynical and hurt all over again.

"Well, I'm leaving now", she said.

"Alright, well I'm ready when you are Annie". Edward wouldn't take his eyes off her, even when she looked only at the ground or out onto the moors. It wasn't unpleasant, but it was intense.

"Fine, fine", she relented. "Come along then", she started walking away without confirming he was still behind her, down the pathway toward the church. As they passed the low stone wall that she had leant against while William took her urgently for the first time, she blushed deep red. *Imagine if he knew*, she thought, *if he knew my secret*.

They came to a stop at the church, a strange atmosphere hung between them with neither knowing what to say. Edward glanced around the graves nearby; "I don't know which one is Mum", he said, the thought just occurring to him as he looked over the sea of uneven headstones.

"Oh. You couldn't come back, could you – for the funeral? She's over here Edward, just come this way", Annie said compassionately, the hurt of losing her own mother still heavy in her heart. They walked silently a short way through the jumble of graves, tightly packed against one another in the small church yard. "This one". It was modest and unobtrusive; his brother had funded it as Mrs Brigg didn't have a penny to her name at the end. He felt guilty then. Of course it couldn't be helped; she had passed away quickly while he was far off in France, the word only reaching him long after the funeral. He had not cried. Edward had learnt very young that crying was no use.

"Right then. Thank you". He said stoically, staring blank faced at the little marker. "Don't be late for your work then. How is Jennifer Brown anyway?", he asked absent-mindedly, still focused on his mother's grave. "Tell her I'll be along to check on her soon enough".

"I think she's managed well enough without you these past twelve years", Annie shot back coolly, already on her way.

CHAPTER EIGHT

Edward felt quite lost in Haworth. He had spent the first fourteen years of his life here, he knew the streets and alleyways and faces like the back of his hand. But he was lost – without his regiment, fellow soldiers, routine and his *cause,* he was lost. With Joseph and Annie at work and Tabitha making her deliveries he was at a loose end; not yet knowledgeable enough to be of much use at the farm in the absence of the others. Joseph had told him to spend the day at rest or visiting old friends, to settle back in to village life, so Edward decided to kill time until there was company back at the cottage once again.

He passed by The Black Bull with his head lowered. He wondered if Mr Hague was still there, not wanting to get caught up with him for what would be the rest of the day, talking about his Father and the old times. Mr Hague's son had been killed in the West Indies, but Edward did not feel in the mood to commiserate. He walked down Main Street, chuckling to himself at the surprise on people's faces as he passed by them. He was a ghost returned to the place of his birth; no one had expected to see him again. Not in this lifetime anyway.

"Good morning", he greeted Mrs Goodwin. He could see she recognised him, she had been squinting at him as they approached one another on the street but her memory failed. "Edward... Brigg... Do I really look so different?", he prompted with a tired smile.

"Good God!". She flung her hand up to her mouth. "I didn't think we would be seeing you back here on these streets. How are you? Are you well?", she took his face in her warm plump hands. She was happy to see him, of course, knowing his family well when he was little and his mother still fit and well and his father still decent. He did detect a hint of pity in her eyes though. "You look so old and grown, Ed. Are you back with us for good then? Back here so we can look after you?".

Being taken in kind hands like that reminded him of being a boy and he was shocked by the feeling that sprang up in his chest. It made him feel vulnerable.

"I'm here for the summer at least, six months most likely. I've done twelve years, if you could believe that".

"Six months! Wonderful. It will be so good to have you around again. Where will you stay though?". Mrs Goodwin looked down towards Sun Street, to his childhood home that now housed another family. None of Edward's family were left in Haworth.

"I'm up with the Naylors, I'm lending a hand with the work at the small holding while I'm on extended leave. Soon to return though, in time for winter I'm afraid".

"Oh, the Naylors, yes. Lovely girl, Tabitha – always has been. Her sister though…". She stared at Edward waiting for a reaction, trying to understand if he saw Annie in the same light that she did. "Just watch that one, that's all I'll say. I'm not one to gossip Edward, as you well know but that girl, well, I have seen her *around the village*". Edward remained blank faced, intrigued. "With others whom I don't recognise. *Men*. Men from out of town". She shook her head in disappointment. "I'm not one to chatter though, and it's none of my business".

Edward had to suppress his laughter. Edith Goodwin had always been like that, a nosey and interfering busy body. He didn't interrupt though, because he was so intrigued by what she was telling him.

"I wouldn't know thankfully", Edward quipped "I have only

just arrived on Saturday eve". He felt the need to change the subject, not wanting to hear another word about these other men. "I have some time on my hands, so I am on my way to visit Charles Eccles at the forge".

"Aye yes, I remember you all now, such good friends as children. I can picture you as a boy Edward. It nearly carried your mother off when you left, mind. She was devastated, a shell of a woman. Fourteen years old and leaving for the life of a soldier". Mrs Goodwin shook her head in sympathy. "But boys will be boys, as I told her".

"Yes, we will be", said Edward curtly, annoyed at the reminder of his mother's hurt.

She leant in close once again, as if to share a secret, "Charles' brother - Abraham. He's another one. She's messing about with him all hours of the bloody day and night. Folk have caught them, you know. Swimming together on the moors – naked as the day God made them", she whispered dramatically, shaking her head. "Disgusting".

Edward couldn't help but laugh at the thought. He remembered the two were so close as children, inseparable really. Perhaps it had blossomed into more, but he somewhat doubted it. He felt a pang of envy that they were still free and young enough in spirit to play and swim and frolic as they did as children, he felt so old and battered in comparison.

"I wouldn't concern yourself there Mrs Goodwin. Surely if there were anything to it, the whole village would know. They are marrying age now, of course. I doubt there is anything to hide".

"And you? Is there a wife in tow or a sweetheart waiting for you somewhere?", she grinned, hungry for information.

"No", Edward shook his head with a neutral smile, "sadly not". He was not yet used to saying no. His voice almost betrayed him, catching a little bit at the end. He coughed firmly to clear the lump in his throat. "I'll let you get on Mrs Goodwin. I know you are a busy woman". He nodded his head respectfully and took off quickly towards Sun Street.

Although he had walked the long way round specifically to pass his childhood home, he felt like he did not want to linger there when he reached it. There was a woman visible in the doorway whom he did not recognise, and she was calling to her children down the street. The house looked different, like he was viewing it in a dream where everything is familiar and yet feels wrong. A chicken pecked and scratched near her feet and she kicked at it swiftly, "Damn thing". Edward realised he was staring at her then and looked away quickly. No, there was no one left there, now he was certain. He was struck with a great pain in his chest then, it was so strong and so sudden that he felt weak and had to put his hand out and steady himself on the wall opposite the house.

The same woman reappeared. "You need a chair? You don't look well, are you alright?", she said brusquely, hanging back still with a look of suspicion.

"I'm quite well, thank you", snapped Edward, feeling embarrassed. He did not like to show any weakness. The memory of his little sister dying in the cramped bedroom had returned to him, crisp and clear and just as agonising as the night it happened. He had not remembered it until he returned there, the street and the house and very *smell* of the place dredged it up from the back of his mind. Edward thought of her now and again; the little red-haired girl, *God, how old was she?* He struggled to recall. She must have been three, maybe four years old, the memories of her had faded and been replaced by other triumphs and losses over the years. *And what was I? Six?*

He couldn't bear it any longer and propelled himself forward, gasping for breath. He willed himself not to consider the matter again. It had been years since, years filled with violent deaths and the stink and the enemy and disease. Why did it hurt him now? He had seen so much worse. Soon the pain began to subside and left only an echo as he carried on towards the blacksmiths.

~

The large double doors to the smithy were wide open and Edward saw his friend hammering on the anvil, his face and long leather apron were filthy from the smoke. "Charles!", he called out as he approached, excited to see an old friend. To his surprise, the man that turned to face him was not his friend Charles but his younger brother Abraham.

"Oh! Excuse me Abraham", said Edward, "I'm looking for your brother; is Charles here? It's Edward, Edward Brigg".

"Aye, of course! Joseph said you were coming". Abraham wiped his blackened hand on his apron and proffered it enthusiastically for Edward to shake. "Charles is out in Halifax though, sorry to say it. He's got work on up there. Although he'll be back next week for a few days, if you're still with us of course".

"Yes, I'll be here awhile, six months at least I reckon. Good to see you Abraham, are you well?".

It threw Edward momentarily, although logically he knew that Abraham would have aged in his absence, he was still surprised to find him working at the fire. He half expected the ten-year old he had left behind, the spirited and playful younger brother of his friend. The Abraham he saw in front of him now was a strong and confident young man, body conditioned by heat and hard work.

"I am very well my friend. The Lord has been good to me and I cannot complain. And you? Many adventures and travels, I'm certain of it!".

"Aye, no shortage of adventure. Although it's certainly good to be back home. To have a rest, like".

"Are you leaving the army then, or do you intend to return?", Abraham asked stoking the fire.

"Oh no I'll be going back, don't think I could survive out 'ere now. Don't know anything else, do I?", Edward laughed at himself. Soldiering was his only skill, but he let his mind wander for a moment. How nice it would be to have a forge or a farm or to be a carpenter. To have a wife and a cottage and a few bairns on the rug in front of the fire. But no, it wasn't to be. Come hell or high water he would be returning to the service.

"So what brings you back now?".

Edward rubbed at his stubble roughly, "Twelve years is the minimum service, I can finish now if I wanted to. But if you go back after six months or more you get a nice bonus for resigning. You don't get that if you stay on through; makes sense to have some leave and earn a bit out of it, you see".

Abraham had never heard of the arrangement before and did not reply, just nodded along.

"It's new". Edward reassured him. "Came in after Napoleon".

Abraham drew a deep breath and shrugged, "Makes no odds to me, great to have you. It will be like old times! You, Joe and Tab, Annie and me. We'll have a cracking summer. And the dance is coming up, who knows, you might have chance to meet a girl". Abraham laughed and winked at Edward, who grinned in return.

"I won't know my luck 'till I try, will I? What's new with you? Last I heard you hadn't married".

"Ah no, not me. Not interested in all that yet, a wife can be a burden. I'm happy working and making my fortune here", he gestured around the workshop.

"There was a time our Joseph were convinced you and Lottie would be engaged, you know", Edward said. "Oh aye, he used to write to me about it, said Tab was saving up towards fabric for a dress at one point", he teased, gently punching Abraham in the arm, sensing he had said too much.

Abraham stuck out his lower lip and shook his head. "I doubt it my friend. Besides, she's away in Scarborough now, working in a big house for some Lord. Still see her now and again but like I said, not interested in all that". His lie was unconvincing.

"Well, at least you chose the sweet natured sister". Edward rolled his eyes. "Tab's a great sort and always has been. But bloody hell, her sister Annie!".

Abraham laughed awkwardly, "Don't be fooled, she's alright really, our Annie. Don't know what's got into her recently though. She's had a cob on a few weeks now".

"Shame n'all. Such a pretty girl, but hellfire – it's clear she in't happy with me about the place".

"Wouldn't surprise me if it had anything to do with that bastard forever sniffing about her". Abraham leant against the wall and looked pensively out of the doors and into the quiet street beyond.

"Old Mrs Goodwin did say she's been seen hanging about with men. Your name came up too mind". They both laughed at the thought of her suspicions being so wrong. "So what's the story there then?".

"Oh some salesman from out Keighley way apparently. Annie wants a husband of course, it's natural. But he in't right for her though, older than her by a fair bit and a right snake, so I hear. I don't like the man myself Eddie, don't trust him. He'll drop her like a stone once he's had his fill, I'm sure of it".

"Oh 'eck, trouble brewing then".

"Trouble brewing for sure". Abraham clapped his gloved hands together. "Must press on anyway, no rest for the wicked".

Edward rose from his seat on the bench. "Of course, don't let me stop you now", he said as he made for the doorway.

"'Ere", Abraham called after him, "Why don't you come with us to Keighley tomorrow if you've nowt on. I need to collect some tools – come see how it's changed".

"Who's us?".

"Me and Annie, we go up there often. It's alright for a morning out, she's after some bits for a dress".

Edward considered it for a moment. "Aye, go on then lad, I will. Tomorrow then".

"Tomorrow, Ed".

He cursed himself for agreeing as he walked back up to Main Street. He hoped Annie wouldn't sulk all day – he should have just let the pair go alone and stayed behind to work. *Then again,* he thought, *could be a chance to win her over if I play my cards right.* He made his way back to the cottage to wash a shirt for the trip, not wanting to let himself down by being scruffy.

CHAPTER NINE

"What did you have to invite him for?", Annie hissed to Abraham who was sat next to her in the front of the cart.

"Come on, be friendly Annie. I don't know what's got into you lately, you've been right awful these last few weeks". He gave her a pleading look while still trying to be discrete, shielding himself from Edward sat behind him in the back of the cart.

Annie turned away in a sulk; the bouncing of the wheels was unsettling her stomach again, which was already a knot of nerves. She thought the trip out would take her mind off the dreaded conversation with Tab and Joe that evening but so far she was still preoccupied with worry. With a huff, she reached into her pocket for the pieces of candied ginger she'd had the foresight to bring along. "Want one?", she held her open palm out to Edward. He looked taken aback by the gesture and gladly accepted. "What is it?", he asked, already tossing it into his mouth. She laughed at his trusting nature. "That could have been anything I just handed to you there, and you ate it", this made her laugh quite a bit and Edward couldn't help but join her, perplexed at her sudden delight.

"Too trusting for me own good, aren't I?", he stared coolly out into the passing countryside, enjoying the sound of her laughter and the horse's hooves rolling across the moors. The sun was bright but it was not yet warm, especially not so early in the morning. Edward breathed deeply. The air was fresh and crisp, the ginger spicy on his tongue. He had dreamed of moments like these so many times through the last twelve treacherous years.

When the battle was too terrifying to bear, or the rations too scarce, or the nights too dark and cold, he took himself back to Haworth. Back to the moors on a fresh morning in May and now he was here, it felt like a dream.

"Have you missed home?", Annie had turned in her seat to face him now, her arm draped over the back of the bench anchoring her in place.

"Dreadfully, aye. Although it's barely home any longer I suppose". Edward closed one eye against the brightness and savoured the moment.

"Just say if you want another ginger", Annie offered, and then left him to his peace. It seemed to her he could do with a rest.

Soon enough, Abraham and Annie heard quiet snores from Edward who had been lulled to sleep propped up against the side with a folded sack behind his head.

"He must be knackered, the old dog", said Abraham, gesturing to him with a bob of the head, not wanting to let go of the reigns.

"He's not sleeping well, I don't think", Annie replied.

"Where is he sleeping?".

"Under the window in the kitchen. It's warm in there but he's only got the old bed that Lottie had. The one that was in my room before".

"Doubt he even fits in that, the size of him! Bet his feet hang off the end". The pair huddled together, shushing each other's sniggers.

"I wouldn't know, would I? I don't see him in bed. And I wouldn't thank you to, either", Annie replied primly.

"I'm not accusing you of anything, don't worry. The way things are with you at the minute I think even a civil conversation with him would be too much to ask from you".

"Hey, get off wi'ye!". She punched him playfully in the arm.

"What has been bothering you, anyway? We've been friends all our lives Annie, I know something's up".

She shrugged, feigning bewilderment. "Don't know, just got one on me perhaps".

"Is it anything to do with whatsisname, your beau? Haven't heard much about him recently".

"He's away for a while, that's all. Just tired, aren't I?. I'm tired and I miss Lottie". The last part was not strictly a lie, she did miss her sister terribly.

"Aye", whispered Abraham, gazing at the reigns held loosely in his hands. "You and me both girl".

She squeezed his knee affectionately. "I know you suffer without her here", she whispered, almost too quietly even for Abraham to hear. He kept his eyes trained on the road and gave her a tight-lipped smile, signalling the end of the conversation.

"You would tell me though, wouldn't you? If he's hurt you or upset you?", he pressed.

"Yes, I promise", Annie croaked. How she wished she could unburden herself there and then. To confide her deepest secrets to Abraham and see if he still wanted her friendship once he knew.

"I would kill him Annie. As God is my witness, I would kill him".

"I know Abraham. I know".

~

"And here's the cobbler, he's moved from King Street – if you recall?", Abraham gestured to the shoemakers new premises, delighted to show Edward how the nearby town had changed.

"Oh aye, yes, I do remember. James Hillyard, wasn't it?".

"Aye that's right, Hillyard".

Edward was much brighter now that he had had a sleep in the carriage on the way there. It felt good to be back in Keighley. A lot had changed over the last twelve years but the bones were the same of course and this was great comfort to Edward.

"So what are we're here for again?", he asked the pair.

"Abraham needs to collect a couple of tools and I'm after some ribbon from the market. Jenny's making me a dress for the summer dance", Annie said as she fell into stride with Edward. She had decided to make some effort with him that day. Like her and Jenny had discussed, he offered too much to the family for her to drive him away. She may as well try to tolerate him better for the time he was there.

Annie was fretting about the dress fitting too, although Jenny had promised her they could let it out a bit. She was determined to go to the dance and enjoy herself like she did every year. She doubted whether she would be welcome at the dance the year after anyway, not with a baby in tow.

"Why don't I go up and fetch these tools and you pair can go over to the market. We can go to see Mrs Furber afterwards for some pies and such. Get Tab an egg custard. What do you reckon? There could be a wait, is all", Abraham suggested.

"Aye come on Annie, you can show me all the best places". Edward winked at her cheekily and nudged her in the arm. She didn't like it when he was flirtatious like that, she was too hurt and too stung to laugh along with it.

"Right, fine", she said flatly, jerking her head in the direction of the market. "It's still down this way here past the church, come along with me". The two left Abraham to go about his business and walked slowly in step down the narrow street.

"You like coming 'ere then, do you?", Edward said, trying to make conversation.

"Yeah it's alright, isn't it. Although I expect you're used to a lot more down in London. Bit more *refined* I would imagine".

"No not really, it's not what people expect. Especially not on camp anyway. And I'm not there all that often, moved all over these last few years".

"Have you got a wife hidden away down there wondering where you are?". He was taken aback by Annie's question, she had not been interested in his personal life much at all and when she was, she expected the worst of him.

"Eh, fancy your chances, do you?", he asked raising his eyebrows. "I see you looking at me, girl", he teased. Annie didn't join him in his laughter.

"Not particularly Edward. You're not the sort of man I'd be looking for". A few months earlier, Edwards attentions would have made her giggle and fawn. She would have joined in with the good-natured jokes and perhaps flirted a little bit. Maybe they would even have become fast friends. But her spirit was crushed after William; she still pined for him, still held on to a shred of hope. Now it was almost as if she hated Edward for highlighting just how much she had changed, how dead she felt inside.

"Well, I don't have someone waiting for me, no", his eyes locked on hers and he stopped walking for a moment. Without thinking, she stopped too and looked into his face as he towered over her. "What is it you are looking for then, Annie?". People hurried past them in the street as they stood at close quarters. Annie felt her face redden and she was cross with herself that her body betrayed the feelings that stirred deep inside her.

"I'm simply, *not looking*", she said so quietly Edward almost missed it.

Sensing her discomfort he backed away from her. "Come along, let's go and get those ribbons you're after", he said.

Edward stood tall with his hands behind his back, watching Annie comparing the ribbons. She picked them up and put them down repeatedly while the stall holder became more impatient.

"What sort do you want exactly?", he demanded.

"I'll know it when I see it", Annie said, not even bothering to look at him. Edward admired her confidence. She wasn't rattled by the stall holder and seemed to take even longer when pressed.

"The green would look beautiful on you", Edward said trying to be helpful. Annie screwed her nose up and shook her head.

"No, that's not it, green won't go".

Edward shared a look of solidarity with the market trader.

"What about…", he leaned in close to look at the hundreds of ribbons on their spools, clueless but ready to try.

"It's this one. This one's perfect. Two yards of it, please", she passed the royal blue spool over to him and he began to unravel it and hold it against his wooden ruler.

Then, Annie's face dropped and she gasped audibly, *it couldn't be*. She stared over the trader's shoulder, through the back of the stall and into the next row of the market.

"What's wrong?", Edward asked, trying to grab at her arm as she walked off in a daze.

"'Ere! I've cut it now, it will have to be paid for!", the trader held the ribbon out to Edward insistently.

"Bloody hell", Edward muttered as he fumbled in his pockets. "'Ere, take it", he said dropping a few pennies onto the jumble of spools and grabbing the ribbon from his hand. He didn't want to lose sight of her at the busy market place.

"Annie!", he called out to her over the bustle and noise, but she didn't stop.

Annie was walking towards a flower stand. She felt like she was dreaming, *he's away*, she thought, *it can't be him, because he is away.* There was a man there with a woman, and he looked awfully like William, but of course it couldn't be William because he was away in North Yorkshire. How could it be William when this man was whispering into this woman's ear, holding her around the waist and laughing, then letting his lips graze her neck. She chose a posy from the stand and he paid for them, grandly.

"William?", she called out. The man looked up at the sound of his own name and caught Annie's eye. His face contorted in shock.

"Whatever's the matter with you? You look like you've seen a ghost". Edward had darted through the shoppers and joined her at her side.

Annie didn't respond to him. "William!", she shouted again. William grabbed the woman's arm and led her away quickly, confusion etched on her face. Annie tried to push past some people dawdling at a stand so she could give chase and confront him, but they were already gone, winding through the stalls and away out of the market square. She felt like she was wading through treacle, her legs were lead weights. The terrible feeling was back, she could hear water rushing in her ears and then, nothing. Just the cold hard ground.

~

"Back away, give her some air". Edward shoved the gathering crowd aside and knelt down next to her eerily still body.

"Annie? Annie?", he said loudly into her ear and shook her hard by the shoulders. "Can you hear me? What's the matter?".

"I've got some salts", a voice in the crowd called out. A woman held a small open bottle over Edward's shoulder and under Annie's nose; she slowly opened her eyes, blinking hard.

"Get away, move, I've got her". He scooped Annie up into his arms and climbed to his feet, grimacing. He used to be able to lift fully grown men in one fell swoop, but now it was not so easy with the sharp pain in his side. He steadied himself and began to carry her out of the market square towards the stone bench and the water pump.

"I'm fine, put me down", Annie mumbled. He knew she was most definitely not fine, her face was ghostly pale and her eyes unfocused. She pressed her face into his broad chest and breathed him in. The last thing she wanted him to do was put her down, she felt safe in his arms and gripped his shirt tightly, her head swimming.

As he lay her down on the stone bench she let her head rest there, knowing if she raised it she may be sick. Edward sprinkled droplets of water from the pump onto her face and fanned her. "Don't get up, lie there for a minute. It's alright, no one's looking". Folk were indeed looking but he warned them off with a menacing stare, not wishing for her to be embarrassed any further by meddling do-gooders.

"I'm so sorry", she mumbled. "I feel sick, Edward".

"If you need to be sick, bring it up, I don't mind". He stroked her hair reassuringly, then caught himself and snatched his hand away. She leant over the edge of the bench and vomited there quietly, near his boots. "That's it, good job", he soothed, holding her long plait out of the way. He laughed, trying to break the tension. "I've seen much worse than this, anyway". He pulled his handkerchief out of his pocket and crouched down near her face. "Here", he said, wetting the handkerchief under the pump, "let me". He wiped her clammy brow and hot cheeks and sour mouth. "How do you feel?", he asked with concern.

"I'm fine, I'm fine now. I don't know what's the matter with me, I'm sorry". Annie couldn't bear to meet his eye, pushing herself into a sitting position and letting his outstretched arm take most of her weight.

"You're going to have one hell of a black eye there I reckon", he said with a sharp intake of breath. "Do you want a drink?".

"God, yes please".

He cupped a large hand under the pump and dribbled some cool water into it. He held the hand to her lips and she looked up at him, uncertain at first. But she couldn't resist the clear refreshing water on her dry lips. She sipped from his hand, leaning into him and moaning with the pain in her jaw and cheek where she had landed. The moment felt intimate, far too intimate. She was closer with Edward right then than she had ever been with William, even when they had made love. The closeness struck her and she moved away from his hand, embarrassed.

"More?".

She shook her head. "No, that's better, thank you. Oh – my ribbon", she said sadly.

"Don't fret, I've got it".

She nodded, relieved that she did not have to return to ask again.

"Who were you calling for? You were looking at someone – who was it?", he asked, his brow furrowed in curiosity.

"No one", she said, staring at the floor with hunched shoulders.

"No one called William?".

"Aye, no one called William".

As Annie was recovering herself Abraham rounded the corner and spotted the two at the pump. As he approached his smile dropped. "What the hell has happened here?", he asked Edward crossly. He noticed Annie's already swollen face and sickly demeanor. "Who's done that?", he demanded.

"Abraham please, it's nothing", she tried to reassure him.

"She fainted, she's not been well", Edward replied, turning to face Abraham with squared shoulders. He did not much care for his tone and what it implied.

"Fainted?", Abraham asked, confused. He looked at Annie and back at Edward. "Why what's the matter? Are you alright?", he started to fret. "I said you've not been right Annie, did I not? Only on the way here I'd said it!".

Edward caught his eye and shook his head urgently, willing him to stop talking. He would be able to explain to him about the man, this William, but not now. Not with Annie still fragile. Abraham seemed to catch on and left it alone.

"Should we get you some food, or do you need to go home now?".

"Perhaps best get something to eat for her, ey? She's lost breakfast", Edward said gesturing to the vomit on the floor near their feet.

"Aye, would you go and fetch some tea loaf or bread for her?", Abraham asked. Edward nodded slowly and walked off, worried about leaving Annie despite knowing she was safe with her trusted and dear friend.

~

After eating some tea loaf, Annie felt much better and had been able to walk back to the Devonshire Arms, where Abraham's horse and trap had been hitched. She had lain down in the back of the little open carriage, behind Edward and

Abraham upfront, under an old blanket for the journey home. She had dozed on and off, the right side of her face and jaw throbbing from the impact with the floor.

When they came to a halt outside the farm, Edward jumped down and rushed to the back, offering Annie his arms to steady herself as she climbed down. "Careful, careful", he coached her as she stepped to the floor.

"I'll come and have a word with Tab", Abraham said to them and started to hurry ahead.

"No!", Annie cried after him. "Wait until I get there".

Edward offered to carry Annie, but she shook her head wordlessly and brushed him aside. Edward took her arm firmly and guided her up the pathway to the door.

"What the bloody hell happened, Annie? God, your face looks sore, sit down here quick!", Tab said as she turned the rocking chair around and steadied her as she sat. "Let me get some tea on".

"You'll never guess", Annie said with a false smile. "My foot got caught when I was climbing down from the cart and I fell. Don't fuss me, it's been fine all day! Looks worse than it is, I imagine".

Abraham and Edward exchanged a look, but neither betrayed Annie. The two men sat down heavily at the kitchen table, exhausted by their trip.

"You ought to be more careful", Tab chided her, "shouldn't she, Abraham?".

"Aye, more careful", he replied, coolly.

Tab shook her head and pursed her lips, "Clumsy girl".

Annie stared into the fire in quiet contemplation. Her stomach churned as she replayed the market trip in her mind;

his laughter, the kiss on her neck, the flowers, the woman. She leant her head back and took deep breaths, willing herself not to cry. The heartache was almost unbearable before it was interrupted by Joseph, carrying two large bundles down from the attic bedroom.

"What are those?", Annie questioned him. Joseph and Tab looked at one another for a few moments, then Tab took a deep breath.

"I'm glad you're all back because we wanted to speak with you and this really can't wait". Joseph propped the bundles up next to the door and joined the two men at the table, looking serious.

"We've had word from Cliff Top Farm in Whitby today. My uncle is not in a good way and they doubt he will last much longer I'm afraid", Joseph explained. Tab perched on the arm of his chair and squeezed his hand supportively. "The thing being", Joseph cleared his throat somewhat apprehensively, "Tab and I need to travel there. Urgently".

"Right..?", Annie said from her rocking chair, confused. "That's alright, isn't it? Will only be a few days I'm sure".

"No. It won't", Joseph said firmly. "It may be much longer. As it turns out, I'm the sole benefactor of my uncle's will. When he dies, which will likely be very soon, I will take ownership of the farm".

Annie sat up tall and swivelled to face him. "Cliff Top Farm? At Whitby? Joseph – it's 1000 acres or more!".

"It will be worth a fortune!", Abraham chimed in.

"Please, settle down a moment. There will be a lot of administration. We would need to seek legal counsel there and secure the right buyer. These things do not happen overnight, they take months. And Cliff Top will have to be managed in the meantime. We couldn't risk such an asset going to rack and ruin".

"This is the answer to our prayers", Annie gasped.

"It *could* be, yes", he replied, nodding. "But I am no fool, I wouldn't place all our eggs in one basket just yet. Things here need to remain steady, and that's where I need your help. The money isn't ours until it's in our pockets".

"What do you mean?". Annie was puzzled. Going away with Tab and Joseph to Whitby would be ideal. No one in Haworth would need to know her secret, she would be away from reminders of William, a fresh start with her dignity intact. They could return with a tale of a little orphan baby that Annie and Tab were good enough to take in.

"You and Edward would need to run things here until the matter is resolved and the money is in our hands. We couldn't risk losing this farm *and* business in Whitby turning sour. I'm not ashamed to say that funds are very low right now".

Tab turned to Edward in desperation, "What do you say Ed, will you do it? Should not be longer that six months of course, we know you'll be returning to the south then".

"Look, I don't know about all this...", Edward hesitated.

"Hear out my offer, Ed. We intend to return with the proceeds of the sale, and expect it to be a sizable sum. We would ensure you receive your fair share. Wouldn't we, Tab?".

"Aye, we would reward you generously", Tab nodded in agreement.

"I want to come with you two though!", Annie cried. "I don't want to stay here without you for that long". She gripped the handles of the rocking chair until her knuckles turned white.

"I want nothing more than that too, Annie. But this farm needs two people to work it, more ideally. We simply can't afford to bring you I'm afraid. You and Edward would just about manage it together", Tab reasoned.

"I can always pitch in when I'm not working myself", Abraham offered. "I'd do anything to help".

"Thank you, Abraham", Joseph said, relieved. He sensed the mood was becoming favourable in the kitchen.

"Right", Edward stood and shook Joseph's hand, "I'll do it. For you and Tab, I'll do it".

"Annie?", Tab prompted, chewing her bottom lip. Her eyes pleaded with Annie to agree.

"Of course Tab, of course. For you and Joseph I'll do *anything*. You've been so good to me over the years, how could I refuse?", Annie nodded enthusiastically and smiled, despite her eyes filling with tears that threatened to spill down over her cheeks at any moment. "I'll help in any way I can".

CHAPTER TEN

The following morning, Tab let herself in to Annie's room and perched on the end of her bed. "That's us packed up", she said with a tight-lipped smile. She balanced her steaming cup of tea on her lap as she gazed around the room at nothing in particular.

"You'll be off shortly then, I suppose?" replied Annie, keeping the blankets pulled high up to her chin.

"Aye, just now". Tab looked at her with what seemed to be concern, although whether it was concern for Annie or for the great task ahead of her in Whitby, Annie didn't know.

She bent over and cuddled Annie where she lay, like a mother would a small child. "I know it's a lot to ask, staying here with, well, pretty much a *stranger*, but you know we wouldn't unless we had to. I know you can do it Annie, that's why I suggested it to Joseph". Annie was glad she didn't mention anything the night before, it might have scuppered the whole plan. What if they decided they could not go to Whitby with her in such condition? Or worse, sent her away from them to an unknown place for unwed mothers, away from everyone she loved, away from her moors and comforts.

"I'll make you proud", Annie said into Tab's shoulder, still in her embrace, "You'll see how well I can run this farm. I promise".

"I've no doubt", Tab said as she stood up and made for the door. "Get up now and come to lend a hand. We're loading up – Abraham is taking us for the coach at Keighley".

Annie dragged a heavy trunk stuffed full of her sister and brother-in-law's belongings from the bottom of the stairs to the door of the cottage, but could not lift it over the threshold.

"'Ere, let me Annie". Edward jogged over to her from where he had stood talking with Abraham, who had brought his horse and cart. Between them they lifted the trunk through the doorway and up onto the back of the cart. Edwards eyes settled on Annie's as they both pushed the luggage further inwards.

"You look better today", he said quietly, not wanting the others to overhear him.

"Thank you, Ed", Annie said humbly.

"That's your lot!", called Joseph from the cottage door, "That's all of it loaded". Annie turned to Tab who was wrapping her shawl tightly around herself to ward off the cold wind that was sweeping off the moors and buffeting them in the yard.

"I'll write to you shortly, let you know what's happening up there", Tab said. "Oh Annie, don't get upset!". She wiped away the tear that rolled down Annie's cheek. "It will be over before you know it, then we will be back and in a much better standing. Remember why we're doing this. Oh, and be civil with Edward, won't you?". Tab gave her a knowing look, urging her to be compassionate.

"If you have a problem you can't solve between yourselves, write to me. I'm counting on you both", Joseph shouted over the wind as he hauled himself up into the seat at the front of the cart.

"I will", Annie replied, but the wind swept the words away before Joseph could hear her. With that, the horse began to draw Annie's beloved Tab and Joe away and with it, the pressure of her secret.

She and Edward were left there at the cottage, finally alone.

"What now?", she said vacantly.

"We better attend to the animals", Edward said, unsure of himself.

"Aye. Let's do that". The two remained in awkward silence for a moment or two longer before they both started to walk toward the store.

Annie could sense Edward's discomfort. He sighed a few times, wanting to speak, but stopping himself. Eventually he stopped in his tracks and turned around to face her, blocking her way.

"Look Annie, I know this isn't what you wanted, and believe me, it's not what I had in mind either. But Joseph has been a very good friend to me over the years and I intend to do him this favour and then I'll be gone. Rest assured; I'll not be a bother to you after that. I'll be taking my money and returning to London".

This confrontation took her by surprise, his firm tone and jutted chin made her feel like a chastised child.

"That would be your choice, wouldn't it Edward", she shrugged, but her burning face betrayed her discomfort. He turned on his heel and once again marched forward towards the small cluster of outbuildings. She followed on with a huff, the tension between them unbearable.

"I'm not sure what it is that's displeased you so much about me coming here; if I have offended you in some way Annie, then say as much but I'm not spending the next few months stuck here, in the middle of bloody nowhere in some unspoken quarrel with you!". His chest heaved as if he had run a great distance. He stood tall and serious staring her in the eye, frustrated by her lacklustre response.

Her shoulders sagged and her bravado left her all at once. "I'm sorry, Edward. I have not been myself recently and I know we have got off on the wrong foot. It wasn't my intention but my thoughts have been elsewhere", she said matter-of-factly.

Edward was somewhat satisfied by her stilted apology, so he nodded and gave her a thin smile, wishing to put the matter to bed.

"Right well then. Let's try to make the best of it, ey?".

At that same moment, his attention was stolen by Jennifer strolling up the pathway towards them.

"Good morning! Have I missed them?", she called out. "I saw Tab yesterday, she said she was leaving early". Annie and Edward eyed each other tensely, both sensing there was something left unsaid.

"They've just gone now Jennifer".

"Oh blast it, I've brought your dress up. I wanted to show Tab before she left". She dropped her arms to her sides with a dull slap. "Seeing as I'm up here though, you may as well try it on".

"I don't know as I'm in the mood, we've got an awful lot to get on with, as you can imagine".

"Aye, an awful lot I imagine", Jennifer said. "It won't take long Annie, what if it needs *altering*? Come on inside with me – now please. Edward won't mind, will you love?". She grabbed Annie firmly by the arm and ushered her inside, leaving Edward no time to protest before he was left to get on with the vast amount of work he had inherited.

Jen closed the cottage door firmly behind them and tossed the dress in its paper packet onto the table.

"Did you get chance to tell her?".

Annie rolled her eyes, she didn't want to talk about the baby today and had planned to avoid Jennifer until church on Sunday.

"No I haven't", said Annie, staring at the floor. "I was going to tell her last night when I got back from Keighley. But then Tab and Joe told us about Whitby straight off. How could I have said anything after that? It would spoil everything".

"Oh Annie", Jennifer shook her head in resignation. "Right, don't fret. You can give her a couple of weeks to settle Joseph in and then write to her. She can either send for you or come back here".

"I'm not going to do it Jennifer", Annie mumbled. For the first time, she felt like she had some say in the matter. "I've made my decision; I'm going to stay here and do what they've asked of me. It's the least I can do".

"You're not", Jennifer laughed in disbelief.

"I am. Tab and Joe need time to concentrate on selling the farm at Whitby, not on me and my mess. I'm going to be a mother Jennifer – I need to start looking after myself for once". She spoke slowly and quietly, although her body trembled.

"What about when she comes back though? What then?".

Annie shrugged "Well, she'll have a shock, won't she", she replied in annoyance. Jennifer raised her brows, unimpressed at her nonchalance.

Annie relented, "Soon after she gets back the baby will be here anyway and there'll be nothing to do but get on with it, we won't be worrying about money anyway. I will spend my days on the farm, repaying them for their kindness. Not like I'm going to be getting wed now anyway, is it?".

"Oh Annie". Jennifer exhaled, defeated. "You're not a child any longer, I can't stop you. And I do agree there is too much at stake for Tab and Joe. They deserve some good fortune after everything they have suffered". Jennifer shook as a chill passed over her, as if Samuel's ghost had entered the room, summoned by her thoughts of him.

"I know that", said Annie, "But I won't be changing my mind", she said with finality. She thought for a few moments, wondering if she should mention it. "I saw him yesterday, in Keighley", she blurted out.

"Who? William?".

"Aye", Annie's voice cracked as she spoke. "With another woman – the pig!". She took a deep breath and puffed out her chest. "He's had the last tears that he'll ever have from me. He's dead to me Jennifer, I hope never to see him again as long as I live".

Jennifer shook her head in disbelief. "What do you *mean*, with another woman? His sister?".

"I'd hope not his sister. They were at a flower stall in the market, stroking her cheek and whispering sweet nothings to her". She sniffed, feeling foolish. "I called out his name and he saw me, but he just took off with her". Annie deliberately didn't include her fainting in the retelling of yesterday's events. She did not want to cause Jennifer any more anxiety than she already had that morning.

"What a beast! I'll have his guts if I see him around here again. I'm going to tell Mr Hague that he is to stop business with him. It's plain wrong what he's done".

"It's done now, we're better leaving the past behind".

"So be it", said Jennifer, impressed by Annie's resolute attitude. "Suppose it's you and me then. Unless you have some other midwife lined up for the job?".

The little joke lightened the mood and made them both giggle. It would be unthinkable for anyone else to deliver her baby. Jennifer had attended the birth of all the girls; Tabitha, Annie and Charlotte. She had delivered Tabitha's baby Samuel, she had delivered both Edward and Abraham. There were not many people in the village that Jennifer hadn't greeted into this world.

Annie picked the dress up from the table with curiosity, the relief letting her think of something else for a moment.

"While you're getting undressed to change, I may as well have a look at you", said Jennifer.

Through in Annie's little bedroom at the back, she slipped out of her clothes while Jenny watched on. She pulled the under slip over her shoulders and dropped it down by her feet and set about unwinding the lengths of cloth from around her middle.

"I don't recommend you do that much longer", said Jennifer, "not as the baby gets bigger anyway".

Once the bandings were off and around her feet, she turned around to face Jennifer, who gasped audibly. She cast her eyes over Annie's swollen and taught belly and darkened nipples.

"How far along did you say you were? Didn't you tell me it was three months?".

"Yeah", Annie replied, staring at the floor.

"It's not though, is it?"

"No, I don't think so".

"Just lie on the bed for me a moment".

Jennifer rubbed her hands together furiously to warm them before she pressed firmly around Annie's belly.

"Does that hurt? How about that?". Annie shook her head no. "You've probably got four odd months left". She sprang up nervously. "Annie, that baby will definitely be here by the time Tab returns".

"Oh bloody hell, I thought I had longer than that".

"Well, it's a first baby", said Jennifer cynically. "Late sickness, carrying very small like that, I'm not surprised. I'm shocked myself to be honest, I should have known!". She pulled Annie into a warm, tight embrace. "I promised your mum I'd look after you, and I've let her down".

"Don't be silly", said Annie, "You've been wonderful. It's my own fault for being easily led. I was stupid. It's done now though".

"We'll manage together". Jennifer held her at arms-length and smiled sympathetically.

"'Ere, slip this on for me then, let's see". She draped the dress over the back of the chair in anticipation and helped Annie back into her bindings and underclothes, once again reminding her to soon stop wearing them, and fastened the dress on.

"It's beautiful", she nodded in approval. "You look radiant girl", Jennifer said, her voice heavy with emotion.

She was right, Annie did look glorious. The dress was a simple empire line style that let Annie's beauty sing, rather that overshadowing it. The sky-blue taffeta had been repurposed from a matching jacket and skirt set that one of the Reverend's daughters-in-law had grown tired of and given to Jennifer. The short sleeves and low neck line showed off Annie's alabaster complexion, a truly modern design that would be the envy of every girl at the dance.

"I love it!", Annie breathed. She ran her hands over her belly, trying to gauge how obvious her pregnancy would be under the binding and the flowing dress.

"You wouldn't know". Jennifer said, reading her mind. "But I'll give it a bit more room, if you like?"

"Aye, please, just a margin for error", she replied, satisfied. "I've got the ribbon for the waistline", she handed the folded length over, which Jennifer slipped into her pocket before she helped Annie back out of the dress.

As the pair left the cottage and walked back down the path, Jenny said gently, "May I suggest you go easy on Edward? I think you have a lot to learn about him, that's all I'll say. Treat him well and it will pay dividends Annie. Speaking of which, I'm going to go see him now. I didn't get chance to talk with him much at church on Sunday".

Annie felt a tinge of guilt about her recent behaviour and nodded in agreement.

"Aye you get off, I must get on now anyway. Much to do". They both gave a 'hmm' in agreement, neither a stranger to hard work.

~

Jenny found Edward in the cow shed, the cows had been taken out to pasture and Edward was scrubbing furiously at the floor and walls. This pleased Jenny. He had never had an ounce of laziness about him and some military discipline might help to keep Annie's mind from drifting too much over the coming months.

"Well then", she said loudly to catch his attention over the noise. He turned around grinning and tossed the soapy brush back into the pail at his feet.

"Hello, old friend", he said warmly. They had not seen each other since Edward had left the village all those years ago. The short and joyful greeting at the church service on Sunday had not afforded Jennifer enough time to study his face, and only now did she realise how much he had aged and hardened. His hands were as large as shovels and his face was lined, with a scar that interrupted his left brow. He had become a man in his absence.

"I've truly missed you Jennifer, it's been a long time, hasn't it?", he said, almost whispering as if he was frightened to be caught in such an emotional reunion.

"Aye, that is has", she said, placing a motherly hand on his arm. "How are you getting on here then? Happy to be back?".

She smiled up at him and he towered over her small frame, but there was no mistaking he was the young boy she remembered.

"It's not so bad", he said glancing through the doorway and out to the moors. "Nowt's changed like". They both laughed in agreement.

"And what about her?", Jennifer said, gesturing towards the cottage in a tone that suggested she knew of the difficulties between the pair.

"God only knows", he replied. "I've turned up at a bad time, what with Tab and Joe being called away. I don't know what I've got myself into". He wiped the sweat from his forehead with the back of his arm pensively. She nodded in sympathy.

He took a step closer to her and said in a low voice, "I've said to her just now Jennifer that I won't have it. I don't have grown men speak to me the way she's spoken to me at times".

Jennifer tried to temper his frustration. "I know Ed, I know. Look, I've had a word with her and told her to mind herself – and she will. But let me say this, that girls not had an easy time recently. Please try to have patience with her, she would be very grateful".

"We'll see", said Edward, thoroughly unconvinced.

"Anyway, enough of that, I want to hear about you. Have you seen your mother's grave yet?".

"Aye, Annie pointed it out to me the other day".

"I do try to keep on top of it for her".

"It was in good condition Jennifer, I'm grateful".

"Well, she deserved it".

Edward's smile faded. He was full of regret at not being able to say goodbye, at not having spent more time with his mother. There were so many occasions in his family that he had missed while overseas, or in London, or in a pub worse for ale.

"How are you coping with the work?".

"What are you implying?", he said jokingly, "That I'm not fit for purpose any longer?".

She smiled but persisted, "Could I have a look?".

"At what?", he said puzzled, looking about the barn and confusion.

"Your side?" Jenny said calmly. Her brief meeting with him at church that Sunday had told her all she needed to know about his physical condition.

The silence hung between them for a moment, but he knew it was futile to deny it.

"It's nothing really", he said.

"I think it's something. Lift your shirt for me".

In defeat he made his way over to a hay bale where he sat down and untucked his shirt from his trousers. He looked her straight in the eye and warned her firmly; "Don't make a fuss".

He lifted his shirt and twisted to present his side.

"Oh Lord!", Jenny exclaimed, tracing the wound delicately with her fingers as Edward winced. "How did it happen?".

"Bayonet, at Bayonne".

"It's made a real mess of you lad". Jennifer stared at his exposed torso. On his left side, starting just beneath his shoulder blade was a deep, still-healing scar, red in colour and angry looking, five inches long. Just holding his shirt up was pulling at the injury and making Edward wheeze.

"So that's why your back, is it?". Edward dropped his shirt and hung his head.

"They discharged me", he said quietly, unable to look at her. "Wouldn't even consider keeping me. As soon as I was awake again, I was done for. Sent back to London straight away". The bitterness radiated from him. "I had no choice but to beg anyone I knew and Joseph Naylor answered me, he's a true friend".

"He's a good man", she agreed.

"I need to get back, I won't last out here, coasting from farm to farm. I've no other skills, I need to go back!", his voice was desperate, Jennifer could sense his fear.

"Edward, I don't know if that's going to happen. Something like this, it affects men long after it's healed. Their strength, their breathing…".

"It's all I'm good for, I was born to serve, I was born to fight, being a soldier's all I know".

He stood up and buttoned his shirt. "I'll get back in, they'll have me back. You mark my words, once I've built my strength up here, they'll be begging me to come back and sort out Napoleon's men".

"So that's why you're only here for a season?".

"Aye, and please Jennifer, don't betray my trust will you?".

"You're not out of the woods yet Edward. I'm not happy with it at all. It looks painful and inflamed!".

"Ere, I've no choice now. Joseph and Tabitha are counting on me, and not to mention the sum of money they've promised me – I barely got a penny from the army. I'll have to see it through now".

Jennifer shook her head, "There's not going to be a farm for them to return to at this rate. Let's pray they manage to sell the farm at Whitby for a decent price, or you'll all be destitute".

Edward had no reply.

CHAPTER ELEVEN

By the time July arrived, Edward and Annie had fallen into a comfortable routine around the little farm. The weather had warmed, the crops grew thick and fast and the animals were fed and content. They were surprised to find themselves making a reasonable profit and the cheese, butter and produce Annie took to market in Haworth sold surprisingly well. The villagers were not discouraged by Tab's absence, they found that Annie's wares had their own charms. Even the fruit pies and preserves she made were much sought after by the wealthier locals. The more money they were able to sequester in the little tin in the dresser drawer, the more confident she grew in her abilities.

Annie did not worry as much now about people finding out about the baby. Her sickness had finally subsided and she felt reinvigorated despite the baby growing bigger in her womb. The bindings had been cast under the bed and she was reassured that no one had confronted her about her rounding belly, but her skirts hid it well and she remained small for her established stage of pregnancy. She sometimes wondered how long her ease about the situation would last, whether the terror would return when people started noticing or when Tab returned to Haworth, but for the time being, she was determined to enjoy the last days of her freedom and pushed the worry out of her mind.

Edward too noticed his stamina was building the longer he worked on the land and in the barn. His injury still troubled him, the scar tight, fresh and nagging, but it was bearable now – not like when he had first arrived back in England. Annie too had softened somewhat, they existed together in their little kingdom like a man and wife who married decades ago. They toiled hard and conversed little, most of their time passed in comfortable silence, both of them working towards the return of Tab and Joseph and the rumoured fortune that they were to bring with them.

Annie had only received one letter from Tab since she had left to confirm that Joseph's uncle had indeed died and that there was much to do at the farm. A buyer was yet to be secured and there was a large body of staff to manage in the meantime. Annie felt more certain that she had done the right thing then, it was a task too great for just Joseph to handle, he would be strengthened by his wife's presence no end.

It was on a particularly warm late afternoon that Lord Balfour sent his cowman, John Jeffrey, to the home farm tasked with buying up Joseph's livestock. He had heard of his and Tab's absence and, true to his nature, was seeking to take advantage of Annie. Lord Balfour owned Low Moor Farm, which sat a few miles south of the village. It was the most profitable and expansive farm for miles around. Along with a great number of sheep, he also produced grain by the barnful which commanded a high price at market. He had been a military officer before inheriting the estate at Low Moor, which he ran with the arrogance and carelessness that only the extremely wealthy ever could. Joseph's humble farm was merely a small holding in comparison, and never considered by the Lord to be of legitimate competition. But the rumour of Cliff Top at Whitby had irked him somewhat, and he intended to make his power known.

Annie was in the milking shed, attending to the cows before supper time. The sweat trickled down the back of her neck as she straightened up and pressed both hands in the small of her back for relief. She was not startled when she heard the footsteps on the straw strewn floor behind her, assuming it to be Edward, but when the unfamiliar voice called her name, a shiver came over her.

"Good afternoon Miss Crossley".

She turned around recognising the mocking tone at once. John was leant against the shed door with one ankle crossed over the other, savouring her confusion at his arrival.

"Mr Jeffrey", she said warily, looking past him to see if he had fetched any other men with him. "Can I help you?". She stood up from her stool, but didn't move to greet him with a handshake.

"On the contrary, Annie, I am here to help you". He pushed himself from the door frame and came to inspect the cow she had been milking. "Fine few creatures you have up here, so I heard. Good breeders." He stared lewdly at Annie as he said it.

"What do you want, Mr Jeffrey?", she said firmly. Being alone with him made her heart race with nerves and she silently prayed Edward would interrupt them.

"All right, I'll cut to the chase. I'm here to buy your livestock, on the request of Lord Balfour. We're always in the market for decent animals and seeing as you have been abandoned here by your dear sister and brother-in-law, I figured you would be desperate for the income. I know you can only manage this for so long all alone, so I'm going to lighten your load". He grinned and awaited her agreement.

"They're not for sale".

"I don't think you heard me", he said coolly, leaning towards her. He was so close she could see his rotten teeth and pox marked cheeks. She recoiled slightly.

"The cows aren't for sale, and neither are the sheep, or the pigs, or the chickens, for that matter", she said, with a slight quiver in her voice.

"You don't even want to know the price?", he snarled,

grabbing her wrist with a filthy hand.

"She said, they're *not for sale*". Edward had appeared in the doorway of the milking shed, blocking it with his broad frame.

John dropped Annie's wrist as though it were red hot and looked at Edward incredulously. "Who the hell are you?".

"I'm Edward Brigg. And I'm here to manage this farm in Joseph Naylor's absence".

"Well then, maybe it's you I should be talking business with", John said with a submissive smile. He was intimidated by Edward and despite his efforts to conceal it, it was obvious. He backed away from Annie quickly and straightened his cap.

"The lady has already told you - none of the livestock here is for sale. She would thank you to leave now, if you have no other business here?". Edward's voice remained low and measured, almost a growl.

"I've been sent by Lord Balfour, do you know who that is?!", John replied insistently. Edward had grown tired of niceties and took the man roughly by the shoulder.

"I know, and I don't rightly care. Now let me see you to the gate". He frogmarched John through the door and away down the pathway as Annie watched on in amazement. She sat back down and resumed her milking with trembling hands.

When she saw Edward coming back, she couldn't help but rush over to him. "You didn't need to...", she began indignantly.

"I know", he interrupted her without breaking his stride.

"I was already sorting it!", she huffed, trotting beside him to keep pace.

"Yes, seemed like you had everything under control", Edward smirked, which infuriated her all the more.

"And what was that about you managing the farm in Joseph's

absence? That's me that's doing that!".

"Just a simple thank you would do Annie, no need to flatter me like this", he teased as he strode on ahead. In spite of herself, Annie couldn't help but laugh in astonishment as she watched him walk away.

~

Later that evening, Abraham joined them at the farm. After they had eaten supper together around the rickety wooden table, they decided to build a fire outside like they used to years ago, and as it roared away Annie and Edward sat on a log as Abraham lay nearby on a thick woollen blanket. As they chatted and laughed together, they shared a bottle of port that Abraham had brought along, a gift from a grateful customer of his.

Edward took great delight in recounted the events of that afternoon, exaggerating wildly much to the other's delight.

"... and then I lifted him clean up and threw him from the cow shed!".

Annie choked on her port, "Mr Brigg! You shameless liar". Abraham guffawed in amusement.

Edward was thoroughly enjoying Annie's attentions. Her face was illuminated by the fire and her bright green eyes twinkling as she laughed. Her laughter was all the sweeter for him having to work so long and hard to hear it.

"Annie! I would not tell a lie to Abraham!", he shifted on the log to face his friend with mock urgency. "Trust me when I say, I saved Annie's life today, the brute was like a wild animal!". Abraham grinned, his eyes were closed while he savoured the warm fire, the drink and the company.

Annie was shaking her head and rolling her eyes with a wicked smile. "Were you always like this?", she teased. Edward just smiled in reply. For the first time since he left the army, he had the feeling of purpose again. He was beginning to enjoy the camaraderie and the pace of life had started to suit him. Each day he worked hard, he went to church on Sundays, he ate supper with Annie every evening. *If I were to consider a marriage again, I would want it to be like this.* He stamped the feeling out quickly, the mere thought felt like a betrayal.

"It will give you something to talk to Lord Balfour about when you see him at the dance, won't it? How you beat his most trusted cowman within an inch of his life!", Abraham laughed. They sound carried away across the moors and they heard a fox cry out in reply.

"What's this dance all about then? I've heard people talking about it…", Edward replied, his interest piqued.

"The summer dance, it's held every year up at Low Moor Farm. Annie and I always go, don't we?". Abraham kicked Annie's foot to get her attention.

"Oh is that still going?", said Edward in reply, "I remember that as a lad".

"Oh aye, everyone in the village goes now, it's the biggest event in the calendar – apart from Christmas at St Michaels of course. We all help set it up the day before, it's loads of fun", Annie nodded enthusiastically. "I look forward to it every year. My dress is really something this year Abraham, just wait 'till you see it!". She eyed Edward next to her hoping he would ask about the dress, but he didn't.

"Is Lottie coming back this year? Would be nice for you to have your sister here…", Abraham ventured.

"She's not I'm afraid", Annie gave him a thin-lipped sympathetic smile. "Hadn't you asked her?".

"I've not heard from her recently", he replied quietly.

Edward shook his head, "Why don't you just bloody ask her

anyway? What are you doing – waiting for some other man up there in Scarborough to ask for her hand? You'll miss the boat at this rate friend".

"It's not like that", Abraham protested.

"It is", Annie giggled. "Did you hear what Joseph said?", she smirked with glee.

"What is it that Joseph said?", he replied, exasperated.

"He's fetching her home. Once Cliff Top is sold there will be no need for her to be in service, so she'll be coming home", she said smugly.

Abraham tried to hide his surprise but he did not manage it well, Annie could see the satisfaction on his face. For the rest of the evening there was a delight in his eyes that did not diminish.

"So are you coming? To the dance?", Annie pestered Edward.

"No, no. I doubt it. It's not my sort of thing any more", he shook his head and took a swig from the port before handing it back to Annie.

"Come on! You never know, you could meet a nice young lady there, get a wife to take back to London with you!". As he mentioned it, Abraham was sure he saw a flicker of disappointment and jealousy pass over Annie's face. He dismissed it, certain he must be mistaken.

"And what about you?", Abraham continued turning to Annie, "Now you've got shot of that bastard". She was surprised by his disdain. She was hoping he had forgotten all about William, between having Edward around and so much work to do and thinking of the baby, she had almost forgotten about him herself.

"No, I'm not interested", she replied abruptly. "There's no one in this village that would catch my eye anyway. I'm happy on my own".

"What went wrong with him anyway? You were so glum when all that was going on. I must admit I felt very protective of you, like someone was bothering my own sister".

"Abraham! Don't go on about it in front of Edward", she admonished him as she crossed her arms.

"Why not? You're as good as friends now, aren't you?". Edward and Annie looked at one another and Annie shrugged.

"I'd like to think so", ventured Edward. "You probably don't agree though", he elbowed her gently in jest. "You don't have to say anything like, ignore Abraham, tell him when you're alone, it's not my business". She gave him a grateful smile for not revealing what had happened at the market in Keighley.

"There's nothing to tell. It's all over and done with and I won't be seeing him again. I'm just happy as I am".

Abraham held his hands up in surrender, "That's good enough for me".

The evening drew on and the three remained outside around the fire. They ate some bread and cheese once the port began to affect their senses, and Annie soon felt drowsy. When Abraham got up to use the privy, she lay on the blanket in his place. The warmth and sound of the crackling fire comforted her, and she fell silent as she half listened to the conversation between the men, drifting in and out of sleep.

Not long after, Abraham stood and stretched, and decided by the height of the moon that it was time to get going.

"Shall I wake her up?", he asked Edward.

"That's alright, I'll go through and light the rush lamp first and tidy the things away, saves her having to do it".

"Fair enough. Well, I'm away then, see you soon Ed". The two men shook hands firmly and Abraham wandered off homeward towards the church.

Edward went through and lit the lamp, gathered the empty plates from outside and placed the empty bottle of port on the dresser. He hesitated, but before he knew it he had gone through to Annie's room and thrown back the blankets ready for her. She was still sleeping soundly when he returned to the fire, her shoes had been kicked off long before then; he admired her sleeping form for a few minutes as he sat deep in thought.

"Annie", he whispered. She did not stir. "*Annie*", he repeated, slightly louder. No reply came. Instead, he knelt beside her and scooped her into his arms like a baby, then stood with some difficulty. He had to rest on one knee before he was able to stand while carrying her. *Blasted thing,* he thought, *I'll soon be back to my old self.*

He carried Annie through to her bedroom and tucked her into her bed, not wanting to put her down when the time came, but to hold on to her and squeeze her and bury his face in her neck. It had been so long since he had felt the warmth of another person. The ladies in France had been impersonal and brisk, but then again Edward appreciated that business was business. No, it had been a couple of years since he felt true warmth and affection. The lump in his throat only subsided when he put her down and turned to walk out of the bedroom.

As Annie watched him retreat through one squinting eye, she willed him to turn around. To shake her awake, to kiss her, to pick her back up again and just *hold* her. She wouldn't even mention it the next day, she just wanted to feel something *now*. But he didn't. He blew out the rush lamp and closed the door quietly behind him and Annie was left in darkness.

CHAPTER TWELVE

"I'm going out for a while", Annie mentioned casually. The work for that day was almost done, Edward was tugging the last of the sprawling weeds out from between the neat rows of crop. He leant on the hoe, snatched off his cap and wiped his forehead with it. He was spent and wheezing. "Are you alright?", she screwed her nose up in concern. "You look beat".

Edward feigned confusion, "I'm fine! It's hard work this, you know".

"I know", she nodded. There had been a curious atmosphere at the cottage since Edward had carried her to bed a few nights before. It wasn't thoroughly unpleasant though.

After a moment's hesitation Edward added, "Where are you off to?".

"I promised to pick dandelion and some other herbs for Jennifer. I need to go out on the moors for them though". Edward looked pointedly at the swathes of dandelion that covered their entire meadow just next to where they stood. Each day most was eaten by their cows just to spring up in even greater quantity the next morning.

"I need other things as well, Edward. I want to check the rabbit traps too", she added defensively. "I'll see you later, I'll be back to make supper".

Edward had finished up the last of his work and spent some time tidying away all the tools that were propped up against walls all around the farm. They were fine instruments, all of the newer ones made by Abraham, and Annie had warned of rain that night. Edward did not want them to rust and be spoiled.

When all was shut away, he went through to light the range and brew a pot of tea ready for Annie's return.

"Damn it", he muttered. "No wood". Since being at the farm it was an unspoken agreement that Edward would fetch the firewood from the copse a short walk away. It was the most loathsome of his tasks, a gruelling walk back loaded up with logs that threatened to wind him beyond recovery at times. He certainly slept well at night nowadays, anyway.

Once he had gathered a manageable amount of wood, he began to trudge back along the dusty path through the low-lying heather, the old wound in his side nagging at him constantly. The sun was orange and seemed to take up most of the horizon, it was cooler than earlier in the day but the walk was still demanding. He stopped to lean against the tall jagged rock that stood at the edge of the ridge, beyond that lay a steep drop and the pools and waterfall that he used to play in as a boy.

As he caught his breath, he saw her. It was Annie. He had not noticed her before then, she floated on her back silently in the middle of the pool, covered only with a sleeveless cotton slip, her discarded clothes lay on the bank furthest away from him. He ducked quickly back behind the rock so as not to be caught watching and cursed himself for invading her privacy, yet he couldn't seem to take his eyes off her.

Soon after she swam lazily to the bank, and after being satisfied she was alone, climbed out into the late afternoon sun.

Edward gasped and pressed his back firmly to the rock, out of sight. It all made sense.

The wet cotton slip clung to every inch of her body. Even from this distance, it was unmistakable. Annie was with child.

He knew it was wrong and he urged himself not to, but he looked again, heart pounding, willing her not to look up and spot him. Her arms and legs were slender but her breasts were heavy and pointed and her belly was swollen and round, in the way only expectant mothers were round. He ducked out of sight once more feeling confused. Why hadn't Joseph told him this? Or Tab? How had he not noticed each day on the farm? Granted, she wasn't that big yet, but he was certain. She wasn't the first lady he had seen in that condition.

He cast his mind back to when he arrived. Annie's quick temper, the constant sickness that seemed to have abated altogether now, her complaints of heartburn and candied gingers. Just like the wife of his dear friend Jack, during that filthy winter of 1810 on camp. *And what came after,* he thought. He shuddered as he recalled the screams that drifted down to where he and Jack were huddled in a tent together drunk on brandy, far from the women folk. Edward had to hold Jack's arm to stop him from running to her. *It's not right,* Edward had insisted. *It's not your place lad, let her have her dignity at least.* Jack had never been that fearful waiting for battle. He wasn't even afraid when Edward cradled him there in the mud while he died, one leg blown to pieces. His hands were still gripping Edward's jacket even after he had slipped away.

He stumbled to his feet and gathered the wood as quickly as he could, eager to get home before Annie. As he walked across the moor, much more quickly than on the outbound journey, he tried to decide what to do. He concluded there was no way Tab or Joe could know. What sort of woman would leave her sister behind in trust of a man without so much as mentioning she was with child? Not Tab, that was for sure. He knew Joe well; he would surely have insisted she went with them, or he would have gone to Whitby alone and left Tab here at the farm. *No, no one else knows about this.* He felt most sorry for Annie, what a burden to have carried alone, what fear and worry she must be suffering without her sisters to support her. Or her mother.

Edward threw the wood into the store without stacking it and made straight for the Black Bull. He had already drained his second tankard of ale by the time he came to his senses again, until then he was deep in thought. The pub had filled up quickly, the men of Haworth had finished their labours for the day and were gathered there, chatting and laughing as their wives prepared suppers and tended to the children at home. He sat with his back to the bar, tucked tight into the corner, and he was fortunate enough not to be bothered by anyone.

He was suddenly struck with the responsibility of watching over Annie while they were alone at the farm together. Edward felt so protective of her, so furious with this William character that he had caught a mere glimpse of in Keighley. *I should get Abraham to take me back there now, we should hunt William down and give him a damn good hiding,* he thought. But he knew he couldn't betray Annie's confidence by going to her friend directly, first he must settle it with her.

As he left the Black Bull and paced through the church yard, he felt another weight in the pit of his stomach, one he could barely bring himself to acknowledge. He was jealous.

~

The mood was subdued that evening at the cottage. Supper was eaten in near silence and Annie could sense something was bothering Edward. He sighed a few times as he smoked his pipe while Annie sewed in the rocking chair next to the fire. On the fifth sigh, she grew irritated.

"Is there something the matter? You've been distracted all night".

Edward looked down, embarrassed. His knowledge of women was limited at best, but with another draw from his pipe, he knew he had to grasp the nettle.

"Annie, could I ask you something?", he began. He couldn't bear to turn to face her, so remained in his seat looking out of the window into the twilight.

She stopped rocking immediately, somehow she knew what the question would be and cursed herself for abandoning her bindings.

"Yes", she said cautiously.

"Is there anything you want to tell me?". He had planned to ask her outright, but just couldn't bring himself to say the words to an unmarried woman he barely knew.

"Not that I'm aware of". Annie busied herself with her sewing, hoping he would drop the subject.

"Annie, I don't want to have to ask you…", he mumbled.

"Then don't", she snapped. His head remained bowed.

She wondered what had given her away. Could he tell? She found it surprising seeing as even the women of the village with vast experience of these things had never mentioned it. Maybe it was the fatigue, the sickness… he could have put two and two together over time, especially after the run in with William and her distress. She doubted it though. Then it occurred to her, the jumbled pile of wood spilling out of the store when she returned from the moor – there hadn't been any left that morning.

"Did you follow me today?", her voice was accusatory.

"No, I didn't follow you! I went out for wood Annie, I …".

"So you looked at me, when I was swimming!".

"It was a mistake Annie, I wasn't expecting to see you – I just looked down at the pool and you were there", he exhaled in frustration and shook his head. "Are you going to have a baby?", he said in a low, measured tone. The only sound in the cottage was the crackling in the fire. He turned to look at her, and the compassion on his face broke through her resolve.

"Aye", she whispered.

"Well, I had to find out sooner or later, didn't I?", he smiled at her in sympathy, but his eyes betrayed the worry in his heart.

"I suppose so", she nodded and swallowed hard.

"Do you, erm, know when?", he probed, his cheeks were flushed in embarrassment – he felt clumsy, he didn't know how to word all the questions he wanted answers to.

"I think it will be in three months or so. That's what Jennifer said anyway".

"Bloody hell Annie, that's not very long at all... that's September". His brow was knitted as he made the calculation. "We don't even know Tabitha and Joseph will be back by then". Annie didn't reply. "They don't know, do they?".

"No", her voice cracked. She didn't think she would cry but the lump in her throat was persistent and she felt tears gather in her eyes.

"I think we should write to them, don't you?".

"I'm not going to do that", she shook her head as she spoke. "I was going to tell them the evening when we got back from Keighley, but I couldn't. Not with the business about Whitby. Edward, we can't ruin this for them. They deserve this good fortune. And *please...*", the tears spilled over and her voice quivered as she urged him, "I'm asking you not to betray me. This is none of your affair".

"Now come on Annie, we can't just carry on like nowt's wrong here!", Edward was outraged by the suggestion. He stood up and was pacing across the small kitchen in front of her, but Annie was resolute.

"Don't forget your money...".

"I don't give a damn about my money!", Edward shouted and slammed his hand on the table.

"You should. Buyers are hardly beating down their door, are they? There's not many with such a huge sum at their disposal. That farm is *huge*, it will take at least both of them to manage it in the meantime. *Plus* advertising it's sale across the length and breadth of England. What if one cannot be secured? Cliff Top will be run into the ground by Joe's lack of experience. What will they come home to if we don't fulfil our promise? *Complete ruin*, that's what!". Annie was stood up too now, releasing all the fury that had built up over the months and pouring it all out at Edward. She panted, spent by her tirade. They were face to face, Edward started down into her narrowed eyes, his jaw jutting out in contained aggression, so close their bodies were almost touching.

She spoke to him again through gritted teeth, "Maybe you don't give a damn about *your* money, but you should give a damn about Tab and Joe's".

With that, Edward grabbed his cap from the hook and stormed out of the cottage, slamming the door behind him. Annie sat back down heavily in the rocking chair and dissolved into tears – but not tears of despair. These were tears of sheer relief. After a few quiet moments, she heard the dull repeated *thunk* of the axe on the wood from the yard. *Seems like we're in agreement,* she thought.

CHAPTER THIRTEEN

Annie milked the cows the next morning in a subdued mood. Although her speech the previous night seemed to have done the trick with Edward and persuaded him not to reveal her secret, he was clearly unhappy with the arrangement. Annie couldn't blame him, this wasn't exactly what he had signed up for when he sent that desperate letter from the docks in London. He had woken early that morning as usual, and by the time Annie got up to boil water for the tea, he was already on the far side of the farm.

Just as she was leading the cows to meadow and preparing herself to go to work, he broke his silence.

"Can I walk you to the parsonage?", he asked her formally, testing her mood after the way things were left between them the previous night.

"Why? If you want to tell me you're leaving then tell me now Edward".

"No, I have no plans to leave or to write to Joseph, just in case that was the impression you were left with last night. I heard somewhere that walking is good for women like you, erm, in your condition I mean like". His thoughtfulness confirmed that he wanted to bury the hatchet and Annie was terribly grateful.

"Alright, yes. I would like that. It might do you some good too", she teased, easing any tension that remained between them, "you're left panting after walking across the yard". Edward grinned and rolled his eyes, but deep down it stung him greatly that she had noticed.

As they walked leisurely towards the parsonage in the fresh morning air, Edward couldn't help but to question Annie further, as he had intended to do the night before.

"What about the... the father. Is it that William?". He didn't look at Annie, but instead feigned intense concentration on the nearby robin singing loudly as they passed.

"Yes, it is", she said, feeling ashamed of her circumstance.

"Will you tell him?".

"I can't even *find* him, Ed. He's run off, I have no address, and I don't imagine him showing up around here again. I think he already knew".

"Bloody *fool*", Edward cursed, but inwardly he beamed at the nickname she had used for him. *Ed,* he liked the way it sounded from her – a symbol of their budding friendship. "Any man would be over the moon to have a girl like you Annie". His cheeks reddened.

"Not any more. Not now", she pressed a hand to her stomach briefly as she spoke. Edward shook his head and furrowed his brow but he did not argue with her.

As they drew nearer to the parsonage, Edward walked ahead of her through the church yard on the uneven flags and through the jumbled and jutting headstones. "Annie, mind your step", he repeated, pointing at perceived hazards all along the route. This gesture made her heart flutter, it was everything she had wanted from William, little shows of consideration for the mother of his child. But alas, it wasn't to be.

He walked with her right up to the open side door where Jennifer was hovering. She watched the pair approaching, smirking to herself in amusement. The army had not changed the boy she knew, he was still a most loyal companion.

"I see he's worked it out, finally", Jennifer giggled after she had waved him off, amused by his attentive manner.

"Aye, seems like it, doesn't it", mumbled Annie, as she rushed off to begin her jobs.

~

After the work at the parsonage was complete, Annie and Jennifer settled in the kitchen to sip their tea and discuss the happenings at the farm and Annie's baby, but the sound of the door opening shocked them into silence. The Reverend had returned unexpectedly and was stood in the doorway of the kitchen, having undoubtedly overheard their quiet chatter.

"Reverend! Oh, I was just uhm…". Annie had turned white.

"We weren't expecting you back…", Jennifer trailed off. A thick silence hung in the kitchen.

The Reverend Charnock shifted from foot to foot and swallowed audibly. He began to speak but the words caught in his throat, so he coughed and began once again. "I do apologise for intruding ladies", he said gently. He was looking at Annie's middle, although very discretely. "I want to let you know Annie, that you can confide in me about anything, should you feel you would like to. Be the matter spiritual or, well, practical".

He regained his composure and turned to Jennifer. "Should Annie need anything, any *personal items,* please purchase them from the rectory's household fund, we don't want her going without, do we? Good afternoon, ladies". He turned on his heel and retreated to his study, closing the door firmly behind him.

Annie looked at Jennifer aghast. Before she could start, Jennifer held a hand up to silence her. "Just be bloody well grateful Annie. People are going to find out sooner or later anyway". Annie knew she was right, she was lucky to have such a kind and generous employer, but she still felt humiliated at the thought of him knowing *how* she had ended up with child.

"I'm going home, I'm needed at the farm", she said sulkily. She picked up the dress that Jennifer had completed for her the night before and left through the side door, wondering how much time she had before the entire village found out.

~

Annie was glad to be alone that night while Edward was at the Black Bull. They had had supper together as usual before he left, but she did not mention what had happened at work that day, or that she had brought the finished dress back. The dance felt somewhat spoilt now that the Reverend knew, as if it was all becoming real – an inescapable fact instead of some small secret that existed only in her heart. Jennifer would be upset with her if she didn't go though, after having worked so hard on the exquisite blue dress that now lay redundant on her bed.

She busied herself with her sewing, and then once she had grown tired of that, she counted the money in the tin that sat on the dresser. She had considered asking a young lad from the village to work on the farm, just for a couple of weeks after the baby arrived, in return for a hot meal and any meagre wage they could offer. Annie had begun to think seriously about how her growing baby would affect her work at the farm. She knew most women had barely any time off at all - even Tab only stayed in the cottage for a few days after Samuel was born before returning to light duties alongside Joe. She wasn't frightened of being confined to her bed, more that soon she would be so slow it wouldn't make a difference if she worked or not. *Still,* she reassured herself, *that's a worry for another day.* Satisfied that she could offer some pennies to outside help, she returned the tin and took her seat in the rocker.

Try as she might, she could not resist the call of the dress. It beckoned to her from the bedroom, just *begging* to be tried on. Annie had never owned such a fine garment, the dress she had worn the previous year may well have been a potato sack in comparison. Before she knew it, she was slipping out of her clothes and pulling the rich fabric over her head. She let her hair down from her bonnet and arranged it to frame her face, then smiled into the looking glass, remembering what it was like to feel herself again.

"Annie?", the cottage door slammed behind Edward as he returned. As he looked through her open bedroom door he saw her. "Bloody hell", he muttered, eyes wide.

"I was just checking the fit, that's all". She was cross with him for catching her, although she wasn't sure why. She crossed the room and went to close the door, but he was already there with a foot over the threshold.

"That's a very fine frock indeed Annie". She could smell the alcohol on his breath and his speech was almost, but not quite, slurred. "Will you come into the kitchen and show me proper?", he backed away, beckoning her out into the open room of the cottage. In spite of herself, she followed.

He let out a low whistle and sat down slowly at the table. "Annie, you look bonny as 'owt, you really do".

"You're worse for ale, I don't trust you", she said, embarrassed by his attentions. She remembered when William used to talk to her like that, the memory made her resentful.

"I'm sober as a judge!", he said, in mock indignation. Annie didn't laugh. Her looked her in the eye for a few lingering moments. "What's wrong?", he asked softly, sensing her low mood.

"I'm not going to the dance, I feel ridiculous". She pulled at the fabric the draped over her waist. "I feel like you can tell", she huffed.

"You can't. Not one bit. And I know to look for it, too", he reassured her emphatically. "You look bloody *radiant*. Besides, you can't stay home, Abraham won't be brave enough to talk to any lasses unless you go along to mind him". She sniggered and Edward's shoulders dropped as he relaxed. He gazed at her with barely disguised adoration. "I reckon you deserve it, Annie. You know, to have some fun like, to think about summat else for once". He leant across the table to where her hand rested and took it in his. "I changed my mind anyway, I really want to go and I haven't any one to go with". She took her hand away, embarrassed by the gesture.

"Go with Abraham then".

"Get off, I'm not dancing a bloody jig with him! Had enough of that in the army". They both creased with laughter at the thought.

"Go on Annie", he said with wink.

"I'll come for a couple of dances", she huffed. "And *only* because Jennifer will be short with me for months if the dress goes to waste. And you'll have to walk me home".

"That's settled then", he said, his voice hoarse with fatigue and smoke from the pub. He leant back in the chair, observing her through half closed eyes, drinking her in. "Go to bed now Annie, the hour is late". She felt him watch her until she closed the bedroom door and pressed her body against it. She listened to him get up and start to undress, then the creak of the bed under the window as he sat down to take off his boots. Annie fought the urge to throw the door open with every fibre of her being, her hand still tingling from his fleeting touch.

CHAPTER FOURTEEN

The morning before the dance was glorious and it seemed the whole of Haworth was out in droves to help set up for the occasion at Low Moor Farm. The doors of the most imposing and cavernous barn were flung open and men and women from the village swept out the straw and dust that was strewn over the floor while others busied themselves hanging ribbons and paper decorations around the entrance. Inside, in front of a long, low table, Annie pieced together stunning displays of flowers, many of them brought from her own garden at the cottage and hoped they would last through the warmth until the following evening.

Abraham and Edward were loading up Abraham's cart with barrels of ale and cider from the store at the 'big house', as they called it, all of it a generous donation from Mr Balfour himself. The locals could not fault his generosity and many women in the village fawned over him like blushing maids, but the men seemed much more wary of him. Abraham and his brothers were no exception. There was something about the man they just couldn't trust.

"Damn hard work this, isn't it?", Abraham laughed, as he eyed Edward wiping his brow with his handkerchief, already red in the face and panting. Abraham expected Edward to be much more of a work-horse, due to his size and soldiering, but was quite taken aback by his lack of stamina.

"Aye, just a bit". Edward rose from where he had perched on the back of the cart, spat sharply on to the dirt at his feet, and braced himself to pick up another barrel with Abraham. He managed his half, but with great strain. As they loaded it, Edward noticed a figure striding towards them from across the courtyard. He judged the man to be in his mid-thirties, well dressed and groomed, with an air of confidence only a gentleman of high birth can be blessed with.

"Good morning Mr Eccles", the gentleman called out, his voice sharp and exacting like cut glass. Edward noticed Abraham muttering exasperatedly under his breath and rolling his eyes before he turned to face him.

"Good morning, Lord Balfour. We've certainly been blessed with the weather, haven't we". Abraham's polite tone amused Edward and he watched on in interest. "This is Edward Brigg; he is running things up at the Naylor's while Joseph is away on business". Edward proffered a filthy hand and Lord Balfour shook it firmly and enthusiastically, unperturbed by the grime.

"How do you do Mr Brigg. On business you say? I had heard something of a farm on the coast, Whitby if I recall correctly, is it?". He sniffed sharply, awaiting a reply.

"That's right sir", Edward nodded cautiously, reluctant to give too much away.

"Word travels fast at the corn exchange". Lord Balfour smirked at the pair and continued, "Quite the plot I heard, will fetch a tidy sum. I shall be keen to speak with Joseph upon his return. I am sure we can be of mutual benefit to one another in the near future. I doubt Joseph will have any idea how to handle business and finances, never having *had* any to speak of". Lord Balfour gazed across the rolling farmland that unfolded in front of them, lost in thought momentarily. "He can't be doing too badly though, to take you on to assist with the management of his *smallholding* full time, can he?". His tone was playful, but the invasion of Joseph's private family matters made Edward prickle.

"I am not privy to his personal affairs sir, I am here on

leave from the military and lodging at the cottage, it is not a permanent position", he replied flatly.

Abraham had grown weary of the Lord's snide demeanour and had returned to shifting the barrels around, dragging them to the edge of the cart with some effort, an unspoken gesture of the work they still needed to do. Edward could sense he was listening intently though, Abraham was loyal to the Naylor's and couldn't stand the gossiping about their new circumstances.

"Ahh, a soldier!". The Lord's eyes lit up at the news. "I'm a Royal Dragoons man myself, an officer for some years, until I came back here of course to take over the family estate. What was your regiment?".

"The Coldstream footguards, sir".

"Ah, I see". He wrinkled his nose in distaste. "I doubt you are an officer though, if you're having to lodge at the Naylor's cottage while on leave!". He gave a loud belly laugh at his own joke and Edward allowed him his glee.

"No sir, just a sergeant", he said with a calm smile. He was well practiced at dealing with the bloated egos of the higher-ups, but never ceased to find their arrogance incredibly irritating.

"Oh dear", Lord Balfour replied matter-of-factly. "Still, I'm sure the fresh air and good food will fortify you before your return". He leant close to Edward and added, "A few rides on that filly wouldn't go amiss either, I'm sure". He gave another booming laugh and slapped Edwards shoulder hard in laddish camaraderie. Edward narrowed his eyes, his fists clenching and unclenching as he turned the words over in his mind. He felt heat prickle on the back of his neck, rage bubbling in his belly at the crude way he had remarked about Annie, comparing her to an animal.

Sensing Edward's displeasure, Abraham hopped down from the cart and landed with a thud next to his friend, placing a protective hand at his elbow.

"Well then!", he exclaimed, "we had better be getting on, plenty more to load".

"I certainly would if I were you, old chap...", Lord Balfour said with a wink as he began to stroll away.

By the time the two men had ridden the cart back to the meadow where the preparations were taking shape, the sun had become noticeably hot on their backs. Edward squinted against the brightness, still consumed by Lord Balfour's remark, surprised at the strength of feeling that Annie had stirred in him. Abraham failed to notice Edward's sour mood, busy laughing and bantering with the other men from the village who had gathered there as they collected the unloaded barrels one by one. They seemed not to recognise Edward and did not try to engage him in conversation, content to be chatting and joking amongst themselves.

"'Ere, Abe!", George Godfrey called out, a thought suddenly occurring to him, "How's your Charlotte gettin' on up there with Lord Saunderson?".

"She's not my Charlotte George, don't start this again", Abraham replied.

"Abraham's got himself a sweetheart lads!", George announced to the group, enjoying the laughter from his friends. "Only took me six weeks to get Laura to agree to marry me, how long have you been working on Lottie now?", he teased.

"I'm not *working on her* George, she's in Scarborough, I'm here getting on with things. There's nowt to it, so leave it well alone", Abraham stated firmly, which only served to encourage George further.

"Oh aye, says something that she would rather go into service working for that heartless old bastard than marry you, doesn't it!". There was no more laughter from the group, and Edward, listening in from where he stood on the back of the cart, could sense it had gone too far. Still, he said nothing. Jumping to his friend's defence might betray him further, drawing everyone's attention to the slight and making it grow in significance.

Abraham's cheeks were red and his jaw jutted as he threw the next barrel down with more force than necessary.

"Touched a nerve Abe?", George said, uncertain.

"Why don't you bugger off, George?", Abraham replied aggressively. The mood amongst the men had shifted dramatically, and the others looked on at Abraham and George in anticipation, excited for the possibility of a fight. Edward felt obliged to intervene.

"Come on old friend", he said sternly to Abraham, steering him to the front of the cart where the horse whinnied and snorted with boredom. "Cart's empty. Let's move on".

The pair climbed on to the bench up front and Abraham shouted for the horse to walk on, snapping the reigns much harder than usual. They sat in awkward silence, the glares of George and the confused crowd of men boring into their backs as they drew away.

"What was all that about?", Edward questioned him as the cart passed over the threshold of the estate and into the narrow country lane back towards the village. "You can't let them get at you like that, you're showing them a weak spot".

"A weak spot?!" Abraham laughed incredulously. "You're not in the army any more Edward. Not everyone has to be a hard man like you".

"That's not what I meant", Edward replied gruffly, stung by Abraham's words. "Just, don't let them have a go at you like that. If you get your breeches in a knot they'll be on you like wolves".

"Oh and thanks for your support too, *old friend.* You could have said something instead of standing there like a spare part".

Edward bristled. "I didn't want to draw attention to it any further, you were doing a great job of that for yourself". He rubbed at the stubble on his cheeks roughly, staring across the fields. "Lottie's going to be coming back once Cliff Top is sold. But you already know that don't you. And when she does, Abraham, you will have to piss or get off the pot!". The comment hung heavily in the still summer air between them, Abraham's knuckles were white on the reigns as his breath quickened.

"And *you*, Edward!", he began, shifting to face him on the bench, "You would know all about that wouldn't you! Why are you even here? On extended leave, was it? For a bonus? Why don't you tell everyone how the army has seen sense and booted you out because even at 27 you are haggard and useless!" Spit gathered in the corners of his mouth as he jabbed the air with his finger. "I've *seen* you working on the farm and I've *seen* you loading them barrels today, and by God man, you're slack! So why don't you *piss or get off the pot* and admit it!".

The pair stared at one another in shock. Abraham's mouth opened and closed silently like a fish in disbelief at his own aggression. The horse had dawdled to a stop and Edward lifted himself up from the bench and stood over Abraham momentarily, who flinched in anticipation of a beating that didn't come. Edward savoured the small gesture of fear from his companion and fought the urge to punch him square in the jaw. Instead, he hopped from the cart and wordlessly walked back towards the estate, leaving Abraham alone.

~

Damn Abraham, Edward cursed to himself as he re-joined the group at the barn. The short walk back to the estate had done nothing to quell his anger, in fact his thirst and the heat from the midday sun seemed to have fuelled it all the more. On the other side of the meadow he could see Annie arranging decorations on a ladder and noticed the strange feeling of protectiveness bubble in his chest once again. He had to fight the urge to hurry over and demand she get down for her own safety, intervening would only raise suspicion. He shook the thought from his head and turned away in resignation, *she's not yours Ed, it's nowt to do with you.*

"Lend a hand Edward?", George asked him, spotting him standing idle. Edward wandered to meet him, his mind still focused on the altercation with Abraham. "Where's madam got to?".

"I presume you mean Abraham?", Edward snapped. George had the decency to look somewhat embarrassed. "You know George…", Edward continued in a low tone, their faces close, "It's as valuable to know when to stop as when to start". Their eyes met for a moment before George looked away.

"Aye, I got away from me'self before. I'll buy the lad a pint of ale tonight and smooth it over".

"See that you do", Edward replied.

By three o'clock, the preparations had begun to wind down and the villagers were returning to their homes to tend to their own chores and settle in for the evening. Edward was preparing to leave too, hoping he may catch up with Annie for the walk back to the cottage, when he was called back by a tall lean man with ginger hair, who's trousers were comically short in the leg.

"You there! Can you take a rope?", he cried.

Edward looked behind him and noticed a large piano dwarfing the horse and cart it was loaded on to. It had been fetched from the main house at Lord Balfour's insistence for the occasion, to accompany the many hobby musicians from Haworth on their fiddles and pipes.

"We need a tenth…", he ventured, gesturing to the ropes. Edward had been staring but not given an answer. His side throbbed from the morning of heavy lifting, even worse than usual after his farm work. He grimaced, uncertain of himself.

"Oh, get someone else Frankie, come on! I've got to get back soon!", interrupted one of the others impatiently, waiting to lift the colossal instrument via its pulley.

Abraham's words came flooding back to him in humiliating waves. *I'll show him*, he thought, puffing out his chest. Edward gazed up to the hay loft where the ropes met and had been fed through a large iron hook, the end of each one affixed to the piano, with the other end grasped by a waiting man.

"No, no, I'm here. I can do it", Edward assured the men, jogging over to the last remaining rope and grasping it between his calloused hands. The ginger man nodded in approval.

"Right men!", he called out. "On my count, we winch the piano up into the air, high enough for the horse and cart to be driven out clear. Then again on my count, we lower it *gently* back down to the floor. Any damage comes to this and Lord Balfour will have my neck, so watch it!".

As they began to lift the piano, Edward was surprised. He could just about manage it, although the other men were taking much of the weight.

"Heave! Heave!", the leader called out rhythmically. Edward leant back into his haunches as he pulled, strong and smooth. "Hold!". The horse drew away without incident and the men were left holding the piano aloft, awaiting instruction. Edward panted, sweat forming on his brow as he began to feel the strain.

"Now lower!". The men began to feed the rope back through, inch by tentative inch, until an almighty cry came from the hay loft.

"Frankie, the damn things going to drop! The rope's wearing through! Frankie!". On cue, three of the ropes snapped at the hook causing one end of the piano to jolt up sharply and another two men to let go. An ungodly pain ripped through Edward's middle, right where the bayonet had speared him. A great tearing could be felt across his side as he was left trembling and holding much of the weight. He couldn't help but cry out in shock.

"Jesus Christ!", Frankie exclaimed, as he grabbed the rope just above Edwards hands, his own rope coiled on the floor in two. It was lowered quickly to the floor with a thud, the keys inside making a dull musical thunk as it landed. The men rushed towards it, and once satisfied it had survived, they turned their focus to the men who were left bearing the weight.

"Bloody hell", one of them said slapping Edwards back in camaraderie, "You did well there boy!". Edward was bent double, panting, certain he would vomit at any moment. The pain made it difficult to speak, so he gave a nod in reply and waved his hand in dismissal as an older lady came to check he was alright.

"Just a shock, that's all", he managed to mumble, wiping his brow and straightening up breathlessly.

"Are you sure? You look white as a sheet", she badgered. He did not reply but shuffled urgently out of the barn and into the hot afternoon, away from the gaze of the remaining villagers.

The water pump down the side of the barn was deserted, so he made his way over tentatively and lowered himself on to the edge of the granite trough beside it. Gritting his teeth he pulled his shirt from his breeches and forced himself to assess the damage.

The wound had opened. The sudden jolting strain of holding the piano aloft had reopened his bayonet wound. Pinkish-clear fluid leaked from it and Edward dry heaved with shock. He splashed cool water in his face from the trough which helped the nausea somewhat, but the searing feeling remained. He sat there, bewildered momentarily before shaking himself back to his senses. He had been through much worse, he reminded himself, he could patch this up no bother. All he needed was some boiled salt water and a stiff drink or three. The pain began to die down to a throb and he gulped fresh air and steadied his nerves on the trough. *No way in hell is this going to stop me from taking Annie to that dance,* he thought. *She'll go alone over my dead body.*

CHAPTER FIFTEEN

"Oh, blast it", Annie muttered to herself as she saw Margaret Bartle approaching her through St Michael's graveyard. Annie was hoping to rush home quickly and splash her face and neck with cold water where she had caught the sun. It had been a long day decorating the barn and meadow at the estate, made longer still by her daydreaming of Edward. She was desperate for the next evening to arrive, when she would wear the dress and they would dance together and he would look at her full of longing again. Something about the way his eyes had lingered on her the night before gave her butterflies in her stomach. It made her feel *alive* again.

"Good afternoon, Miss Crossley", Margaret hollered across the graves, waving her arms aloft as if Annie might not notice her, despite being only yards away.

"Good afternoon, Margaret", she replied with a sigh. Her insistence on addressing everyone by their last name really grated on Annie, after all, they had known each other for many years. Sadly it was only one of her many unpleasant and irritating habits.

"I've seen your Mr Brigg today, riding with the blacksmith", Margaret smirked, her voice was high pitched and shrill, almost accusatory.

"*My* Mr Brigg?", Annie replied warily.

"Yes, Edward Brigg. Well, who's else is he? He is living under your roof, isn't he?".

"Well, he's living under Joseph's roof I suppose. He's lodging and working on the farm Margaret, that's all". Annie made to pass her and continue home, but her path was blocked by the thin, drawn woman.

"Is that *really* all, Annie? I can't believe for one moment that a wandering soldier like him could be trusted alone with *lovely* girl like you", Margaret sneered.

"I don't know what you mean, I'm afraid. It's purely a business arrangement".

"Oh of course", she continued, "I've heard all about men like him. Doing *all sorts* with any girl low enough to let them!". She had begun to enjoy Annie's discomfort, her eyes bulging in earnest as she stepped closer and closer. "Do you know, they often marry here in England and then abandon their wives in France once they grow tired of them? Truly heartless. They're riddled with diseases too, brought from far away continents".

"Margaret, I wouldn't know!", Annie snapped in frustration. "I am not aware of his private life and have no need to. He's here at Joseph's behest".

"Mmm". Margaret pursed her lips, taken aback by Annie's outburst, and looked her up and down slowly. "Watch he doesn't lead you a merry dance like he does all those whores in London...". She leant in close to Annie's face, almost giggling with glee. Annie tried to turn away from her sour breath but it was impossible to escape. "...although, I heard someone already did". Margaret jabbed a bony finger hard into Annie's middle as she spoke.

Annie was too stunned to speak. She had not been publicly confronted before, and it was the moment she had been dreading. At least the Reverend had been kind and discrete, but here in the church yard, unexpected and with no support, she felt vulnerable. She batted Margaret's hand away and pushed past her, stumbling on the uneven slabs as she made for the south gate. She didn't turn around as Margaret goaded her cruelly from down the pathway. She didn't want her to see the tears.

Slamming the cottage door behind her, Annie sat down at the kitchen table and sobbed with humiliation. It was inevitable that people were going to realise, that the villagers would be gossiping behind her back and there would be cruel remarks, admittedly - but it still hurt her deeply. The truth was, her affection for her unborn child was growing by the day and she felt fiercely protective of the baby she carried. Annie couldn't bear the thought of people's cruel rumours and whispers when her little child was innocent in all this. There was another reason she was hurt though, she admitted to herself. She cast a glance at the trunk at the foot of Edward's bed, and with some hesitation, made her way over to look inside.

It wasn't locked, which didn't surprise her. Edward seemed trusting of her well enough not to dig through his belongings. She felt a pang of guilt at the realisation that she was betraying him but opened it wide none the less. There was nothing immediately of note in there, some medals in a small wooden box, some papers - the handwriting on which she could not decipher. His small collection of clothes were rolled up at the bottom, but there was no more time to pry as she heard footsteps crunching up towards the cottage, and the handle of the water pump groaning shortly after. She dropped the lid shut and scurried through to her bedroom without waiting to greet him.

Annie was unsure what it was she was looking for in the trunk. What evidence could be found between his things that would prove Margaret's words right or wrong? There would be no evidence of these *whores* she spoke of so glibly, and he was unlikely to have a wife stuffed down under his greatcoat. She shook her head, cross with herself for allowing Margaret's gossiping and cruelty to take residence in her mind. She knew Edward – well, she was *getting to know* Edward. And she trusted him, after everything that happened with William she knew he was different, which made his inevitable departure back to London all the more distressing. Annie cradled her swollen belly under her skirts as she sat on her bed and sighed. *He won't want us both, just like William didn't. He'll be gone soon,* she thought to herself. *It doesn't matter though,* she told her child silently, *because I would choose you anyway.*

~

"Are you alright, you look a bit pale", Annie asked Edward that evening over supper. "You've not eaten much either". She used her knife to nudge another piece of bread across the table towards him.

"Aye, think I had a rough ale at the Bull, that's all", he smiled. "Don't you worry about me". Edward found that the tight bandage he had wound around his middle and the stiff few drinks at the Black Bull had relieved his pain somewhat. The pressure of the cloth felt supportive on his wound and Annie's concerned face in the candlelight stirred him so, that he was sure he would not miss the dance the next evening, not at any cost.

"I bumped into Margaret Bartle in the churchyard today", she ventured. "Do you remember her?".

"Rings a bell", Edward replied curiously.

"She, uhm, she had some very unpleasant things to say about you, Edward", Annie continued, sadly, staring down into her plate.

"Did she, aye?". Edward was indifferent. The opinions of others never weighed on his mind. "What have I done now?".

"She was telling me about soldiers and what they get up to on camp. And at whorehouses".

Edward was taken aback by her language. "And old Mrs Bartle would know, would she? Strange, because I've never seen a medal on her breast".

Annie shrugged and stuck her bottom lip out, she already felt silly for bringing it up - it was none of her business she supposed. But she really did want to know about Edward's experience of women, even if it hurt her feelings. It was a paradox in her heart that she couldn't make sense of.

"Annie, you would do well to listen to your own opinion before that of others", he said with an air of earnest that seemed out of place coming from him. Their eyes locked across the table. "Have I not been a good friend to you?", he continued.

"That you have, without a doubt", she nodded truthfully.

"Well then". He stated. Annie sensed from his tone the matter was closed.

~

Later that evening, Annie lay in bed wide awake, staring at the ceiling. She thought of all sorts, mainly her baby arriving and how surprised she was at managing the farm so well. The fear had dissipated now, she had had months to get used to the idea and the pregnancy was no longer terrifying in its enormity. She comforted herself knowing that Tab and Joseph's good fortune would be so monumental that nothing could spoil it, not even returning home to a new niece or nephew. She sometimes thought of William, he felt far away now and she was no longer sure what it was she loved about him, or why she had ached for him so.

And in amongst it all she thought of Edward, night after night, she thought of his words and his body and his quiet and masculine tenderness. He was everything she had wished William would be, just a few seasons too late. She dared to dream of him staying there at the cottage alongside her. Loving her and her child, working on the farm with Joseph, turning his back on soldiering for good and choosing her. She knew it was futile - he never would. His first true love was King and country, not her, but she would let herself dream it now and again. What harm could it do anyway? Her heart was already broken. Annie was determined to allow herself the last few months of sweetness she would ever taste, before her baby came and before Edward would leave for London once more, when no man would ever look twice at her again.

Her thoughts were interrupted by the sound of footsteps outside her door. Annie shifted on to her side to notice a pair of boots breaking up the candlelight that flowed into the room through the gap at the bottom. Edward was stood outside, listening.

She screwed her eyes shut as she heard the iron latch lift and the oak door open a few inches with a creak. The boots did not move. Annie tried to steady her breathing but her heart was pounding in her chest, every inch of her ached with desire and she felt a pleasant wetness between her legs that she had never felt with William. After what felt like hours, the door closed again quietly and Annie was overcome with a sense of yearning and bitter disappointment. Before she could stop herself, she sat up in bed and called after him.

"Edward?", she half whispered into the darkness. The retreating footsteps halted and the door opened once more. She felt drunk with desire as he walked in tentatively. She laughed to herself in bewilderment, she had never seen him so unsure of himself before, but now he was nervous - his whole body hummed with it. "Come over here", she said, her mouth dry with anticipation.

Wordlessly he crossed the little room and she stood up eagerly to greet him. As their lips met, Annie felt as though she might faint. She was trembling in her nightdress on the flagstone floor, but she was not cold. He wrapped his arms tightly around her and she felt dwarfed by him, his arms were strong and hard and safe, almost lifting her from the floor. His stubble scratched her cheeks slightly as he kissed her softly, he pulled away for a moment and asked, "Do you want this too?".

"Yes", she whispered hoarsely, "I want *you*".

As he pressed his body against her she felt his hardness on her front, straining against his breeches. She fumbled with the buttons, her hands still shaking with anticipation. Finally they were undone, and he kicked his boots off and stepped out of his trousers all together. She stared at him through the semi darkness, heart beating so loudly she was sure he would hear it.

He pulled his shirt over his head swiftly. "Annie, are you alright?", he said, caressing her chin in his hand as he stood over her. She nodded and pulled her nightdress down over her shoulders, letting it drop to the floor, exposing herself to him completely. He stepped forward and traced a hand down over her breast and across her rounded belly. "My God Annie, you're beautiful", he breathed. He smelt faintly of whiskey and new sweat, the aroma was intoxicating.

She reached her hands out to steady herself and grabbed hold of him at the waist as his fingers drifted lower still. Her feet stepped apart as he reached the golden curls at her most intimate place. She gasped into his chest, then looked up into his face. "What's this?", she asked, running her fingers over the bandage around his middle.

"It's nothing, forget about that", he chuckled as he guided her down on to the bed. And so she did.

CHAPTER SIXTEEN

Annie and Edward strolled through the narrow lane past the fields and out towards Low Moor Far in amiable silence, neither one knowing quite what to say. The night before had been exquisite, although Annie nor Edward had made reference to it since this morning, when they woke up in each other's arms, both sharing Annie's small bed.

Edward felt alive again. Since France and the bayonet and his unceremonious discharge, he felt like his life had ended, and he was just existing day to day until his next opportunity to go back to London and beg the army to reconsider. There was a moment that morning that unnerved him, when he was lying in bed with his hand resting on Annie's belly as she slept, feeling her baby move gently in her womb. A moment where he wished it were his baby inside of her, and that they were married and living at the cottage, waking every morning in bliss. He hadn't been tempted like that since Bridget and merely imagining it felt like he was betraying her, so he had shaken the desire from his heart and risen to start the farm work without looking back. He chided himself for getting side-tracked when he was here for one purpose only - to build his strength and then get straight back on the London coach.

Music was already filtering out into the summer evening as Annie turned to him and asked,

"Excited?".

"Can't wait", he smiled in return. "Are you feeling any

brighter?".

Annie had taken some coaxing that afternoon to get dressed, upset by Margaret's snide remarks the previous day but eventually had agreed to still come along.

"Aye, I am now I'm here like. Can't miss my last opportunity to dance for years because of some interfering old hag, can I?", she shrugged.

"Why, won't you want to come without me next year?", he teased her.

"No, just... I doubt I'll be welcome once I'm an unwed mother. Things might be a bit different once the baby's actually here", she said with a tinge of sadness.

"Oh. Annie I'm sorry, I didn't think". He reached out and took her hand, but she pulled it away swiftly gesturing to onlooking villagers with a nod of her head.

"Don't worry about it, I can cope with it. I'm going to be alright, you know?".

"I know you are Annie. I know you are".

The two passed through the main doors and separated off, Annie over to Jennifer and her husband, and Edward towards Abraham and Pip. The barn looked like a different place, illuminated by hundreds of candles and lamps, an orange glow cast over everyone as dusk arrived outside. The church organ player sat at the piano tracing the keys deftly with his fingers, playing beautiful music that bounced off the high rafters in the barn, while locals tuned their fiddles and pipes nearby, ready for the dancing to commence. The long low table at one side groaned with bottles of spirits, wine and ale alongside a bounty of summer food ready to refresh the partygoers.

"Annie! I haven't seen you for weeks!", Jennifer's husband Bramwell exclaimed with a warm smile from where he sat in a wooden chair, leaning both arms on a walking cane in front of him.

"Good to see the both of you", Annie replied, kissing the pair of them in greeting. "How does it look?", she grinned, giving a twirl in her new dress.

"'Ere, you look a right bobby-dazzler in that! Jenny's done such a good job for you, 'ant she?".

"She always does", Annie replied as Jennifer fussed over her as one would a child, picking imaginary flecks of lint from her skirt and rubbing a smudge from her face with a handkerchief.

"You'll do", Jennifer declared. "Now go and enjoy yourself!".

Meanwhile, Edward had smoothed things over with Abraham, both men apologising for their hot temper a day earlier. In a moment, the quarrel was forgotten and they were friends once more. Friends enough for Abraham to share his concerns with Edward.

"How's Annie getting on at home?", Abraham asked, straining his voice over the music and laughter.

"Aye, she's alright. Same as usual", Edward laughed. Abraham narrowed his eyes, seemingly wrestling with his next question.

"Are you getting on well now then, the two of you? Must be hard being alone together if you're not getting on well like?". He was doing his best to remain casual, but the way he could not meet Edward's eye betrayed him.

"What are you asking me, Abraham?".

"Just that!".

The men looked out across the crowd at Annie, who was laughing with some other girls they did not recognise.

"Edward...", he eventually continued, "Annie's heartbroken over that William fellow. You're a good man, I do believe you are - but I worry about Annie. You're leaving in a few months and it wouldn't be right for her to start depending on you. For anything except the farm work, if you catch my drift?".

"I understand", agreed Edward, taking a long draw on his clay pipe. "It's not my intention to mislead anyone. But she's a grown woman, she knows I'm off soon and I reckon that pleases her to be honest. You know what she's like, she prefers things the way they were, just her, Tab and Joseph and you and Pip". He leant down and with his free hand rubbed the dog's head affectionately.

"I don't know", said Abraham, "she's different recently. Have you heard the things people are saying about her? I wouldn't ask her to her face Ed, it wouldn't be right, but…".

"Abraham", he interrupted sharply, "don't listen to them. I've heard no rumours and I would pay no mind if I did". It was enough to stop Abraham's questioning, but the young man's face was still etched with confusion and as Edward moved away to chat with others, he was still left deep in thought. Edward couldn't bring himself to break Annie's trust, not after last night, especially - which he was beginning to feel rather guilty about thanks to Abraham.

Soon enough, the barn was packed, and the improvised band began playing much to the crowd's delight. Annie and Edward joined in the group dances with much enthusiasm, she would see his face pass by every so often, their eyes meeting briefly. Each time, Annie's stomach twisted into a knot of desire. He wasn't her only admirer there at the dance that evening, but she did not notice the others, she only saw Edward. The dance had been everything she had wanted it to be, for the first time in many months she felt carefree and truly happy.

"You're a surprisingly good dancer", she complimented him, as she reached past him to take a handful of strawberries from the table during a lull in the music. Despite having made love to one another only the night before, she flushed pink as she flirted with him. "Perhaps we could have a dance just you and I shortly?".

"I aim to please", he replied with what he intended to be a smirk, but probably came across as a grimace. The dancing had exhausted Edward and he could feel the sweat trickling down his back, which was unusual for him. The bandage felt stuck fast to his wound now as it had wept through the evening, and the pain was back in waves again, giving him chills.

"You alright?", she asked, cocking her head to one side, popping tiny strawberries into her mouth one after the other stalk and all.

"Aye! Yes", he assured her with false enthusiasm as he wiped at his brow with his sleeve. "I might just, erm, just nip outside for a moment Annie. Just get some fresh air". He rushed off unsteadily without waiting for her reply.

As soon as the night air hit him, he knew he would be sick. He leant against the outside wall of the barn with one arm and promptly vomited, again and again, while the heat from his wound seemed to spread through his body and up to his head.

"Wahey! Someone's had too much ale", someone close by called over, but when Edward tried to reply his speech was quiet and slurred. He recognised this feeling from the field hospital in France. He needed to get home *urgently*.

As he stumbled back into the barn, the music and chatter sounded distant, as if he were hearing it from down a hallway. His shoulders bounced off other partygoers as he made his way unsteadily to Annie and Abraham as they fussed over Pip who was now hiding under the drinks table.

"Ed?", someone, probably Abraham, called to him. But he did not have time to work out who was speaking, as before he knew it, he was falling with a hard thud to the barn floor.

~

"I'll fetch the cart round! Bring him to the doors". Abraham ran out into the darkness to his horse as Annie knelt by Edward, shaking him by the shoulders and calling his name again and again. His face was pale but he felt burning hot.

"What's the matter with him?", she shouted at the faces looming over them, no one answered. The music had stopped and a sober atmosphere had settled in the barn.

"Annie, mind out", said Bramwell as he appeared at her elbow, "let them lift him". Two of the men who had gathered at the scene lifted him unceremoniously under the arms and at the ankles and carried him to the waiting cart.

"Where's Jenny? Jenny!", she cried out frantically, scanning the room for any sign of her.

"She's just gone to fetch her bag, she'll meet you at home", Bramwell assured her. "Just get him back and cool him down. Go on, quick!".

Annie hurried on ahead of the men and jumped into the back of the cart, ready to pull Edward's limp body on carefully.

"What's the matter with him?", Abraham called over his shoulder as he steadied the horse.

"I don't know! I thought he was just drunk!", she cried out. Her hands had begun to shake as she shifted his body further up the cart. "Just go, Abraham, we need to get him home quickly!".

"He's not just drunk though, is he? Look at the state of him". They trotted quickly through the lane towards the cottage at such speed that Annie had difficulty staying upright as she crouched in the back. She stuffed some sacking under Edward's head to stop it bouncing on the wood and gently stroked his cheek.

"Well, I think he has something wrong with his side, he had a bandage wrapped around it last night and I'm sure I noticed it when he first got here too".

"Oh Lord, I thought he was just haggard and worn out from the war... why didn't he damn well say something the *bloody fool*. Is Jennifer on her way?".

"Aye she's coming up now with her bag". Despite the mild summer night Annie's teeth were chattering hard and her baby kicked and writhed inside her with the stress.

As soon as they had carried Edward inside and onto his bed in the main room, Annie set about lighting a fire in the grate. His breathing was quick and shallow and his clothes were drenched in sweat. Abraham was ready to go out searching for Jennifer when she threw the door open with a crash and opened her bag on the kitchen table.

"Abraham, get his shirt off!", she barked. Annie had seen her like this once before, when Tab was giving birth to Samuel. Abraham hurried over and started to pull Edward's shirt from him like a ragdoll.

"What on earth...", he gasped as he uncovered the yellowish sodden bandage wound round his middle. He turned to Annie with an accusatory look in his eye. "Didn't you know about this? How could you let him get in this *state*?".

"I didn't... I didn't realise", she stammered, her eyes wide and affixed to the open wound now exposed by Jen snipping away at the covering.

"Just look at him, Annie, he's going to bloody well die!", Abraham had never before shouted at Annie with such hurt and anger. She didn't respond as tears began to spill down her cheeks.

"Just stop that Abraham, right now. I'm going to do what I can, it's not going to help anyone talking like that is it?". Edward moaned in pain from the bed and Annie rushed to his side. "Make yourself useful and fetch some clean water, then put it on to boil". Jennifer thrust the bucket towards Abraham who dutifully did as she asked.

As soon as the door shut behind him, Annie began to grab at Jennifer's clothes, twisting them in her hands and begging her to save him.

"Jenny *please*", she sobbed, "I cannot lose him, not yet. Not like this".

"Annie, listen to me". Jennifer held her so hard by the shoulders her fingertips dug into her skin. "I am going to do what I can, but you need to hold your nerve, for your sake and your baby's".

Annie nodded wordlessly and swallowed a sob that threatened to overpower her. She rubbed her tears away harshly, dipped a cloth in cool water left from that morning, and began to swab gently at Edward's contorted face.

"I'm here Edward, I'm here", she whispered. "Don't you dare leave me now".

~

Jennifer worked on Edward until the small hours, giving him a tincture to drink at regular intervals that made him sleep and regulated his breathing. She cleaned the wound thoroughly with boiled salt water and packed it with a herbal preparation pulled from the depths of her midwifery bag. She was no doctor, but folk were usually safer with Jennifer anyway. Finally, as the first birds began to sing outside, she began to pack up the remedies into her bag, save the tincture that Annie was instructed to continue when he seemed in pain or if his temperature didn't start to reduce.

"Jenny, do you really have to go?", Annie asked in desperation.

"There's nothing more for me to do here love, his fate rests in God's hands now. Abraham will be here with you". She gestured to the dozing figure on the mat in front of the fire. "I will be back before lunch tomorrow, but now I need to go home and sleep. I am old, remember". She smiled lovingly at Annie in gentle humour, before closing the cottage door behind her.

Exhausted, Annie quickly went through into her bedroom and slipped out of her evening dress, which in the circumstances felt ridiculous, and pulled her nightdress over her head. It felt good to be freed from the tight constraints of the frock, and in her tired and emotional delirium she neglected to cover herself with anything other than the thin fabric. She pulled the heavy rocking chair next to Edward's bed and collapsed into it, falling to sleep in an instant.

Next to the fire, lying on the mat, Abraham had awoken. He peered over to Edward and saw him unconscious and quiet, his chest rising and falling rhythmically and was satisfied he could rest further… until he noticed Annie asleep in the chair. Annie in just a nightdress – and very clearly with child.

CHAPTER SEVENTEEN

After a couple of days of tireless nursing from Annie and twice daily visits from Jennifer, Edward was beginning to feel human once more. The heat in his wound had subsided and the pain had lessened again to almost nothing but a constant, manageable hum.

"You really gave us a fright", Annie said to him softly as she washed his tender and weak body down with warm water and her lavender soap, usually saved for special occasions.

"I know, I'm sorry - I really don't know how that could have happened", he replied; just speaking a few words was an effort. "My fault entirely".

"Don't be daft", she reassured him, "'tis just one of those things, isn't it. Besides, we fixed you up alright, didn't we. Although, you really should have said something about it". He smiled serenely in agreement. "I've to see to the animals now, but I won't be long, I promise. And then I will make you something to eat, if you can manage it today…".

As she slung the pig food over the sty wall, she had to fight the urge to hurry back and check on him, despite only a short time having passed. The night of the dance had shaken her to the core, and although she wouldn't admit it to anyone, lest they took over the nursing of her patient, it had left her feeling quite unwell herself. She had started to have dizzy spells and found even the lighter jobs at the farm quite exhausting, let alone the heavy work - that Edward was not presently able to do - which forced her to take regular breaks, panting and wet with sweat.

As she trundled over to the milking shed, bucket swinging casually at her side, she heard approaching hooves bouncing around the walls of the outbuildings.

"That's never Abraham, is it?", she muttered to herself, disappointed that he had not yet been to visit after his sudden departure while she was asleep. As she rounded the corner to the front of the cottage, she was surprised to see Lord Balfour, mounted on a beautiful chestnut stallion awaiting her.

"Lord Balfour!", she cried, as she attempted to smooth her frizzy hair down and straighten her skirts. "Whatever brings you up here?". She kept her hands hidden behind her back, embarrassed by their rough, chapped appearance.

"Just here to visit your patient", he replied as he dismounted smoothly from his horse and approached Annie with a disarming smile. "Are you managing this place all by yourself Miss Crossley?".

"Aye, I am sir. Just while Edward is a'bed".

"I'll have some of my farmhands sent over first thing tomorrow". Annie started to protest but he lifted a gloved hand in the air, "Please, I insist. I cannot see a damsel in distress and not rescue her now, can I?", his voice dripped with charm.

"Thank you sir, that would be very much appreciated".

"How is he then, our little foot soldier? Fever was it? Or has he brought some nasty disease with him from London?". He grinned, but Annie felt ill at ease with him.

"No sir. It appears he had an injury- from the war in France. He strained himself moving the piano on Friday morn and it had reopened the bayonet wound I'm afraid".

"He didn't mention that when I spoke to him, he said he was here on leave?". Lord Balfour was perturbed.

Annie shrugged, "He didn't tell anyone. Jennifer knew of course – she always does".

"Oh yes, her and her... *witchcraft*", he scoffed in disdain.

"Follow me, if you would like to see him. He is awake today and may be tired of my company". Annie gave a nervous smile before leading Fitzwilliam Balfour inside of her modest, rundown little home.

Once inside, the Lord looked around the room and wrinkled his nose.

"Good Lord", he muttered in distaste, but not so quiet that Annie did not hear him. His judgment stung her, but she did her best not to acknowledge it.

"Edward, Lord Balfour has come to visit you", she announced, rousing him from his sleep by sitting on the edge of his bed and placing a hand on his shoulder. He opened his eyes groggily, regarding his visitor with confusion.

"Oh, good morning sir. I do apologise, I am not dressed". He made to get out of bed but was unable to lift himself from the pillow.

"No, Sergeant Brigg, please do not rise on my account", the Lord said in his loud, commanding voice. "I am just here to satisfy myself that the dance hosted at my estate has not killed a man!". His laugh echoed off the low ceiling, but Annie and Edward did not join him.

"You can't dispatch of me that easily", scoffed Edward, his voice hoarse and distant.

Annie left the two men to talk amongst themselves, feeling out of places in the kitchen, listening in. She returned to her work on the farm, periodically fussing over the Lord's Stallion tied up in the yard, straining to hear snippets of the conversation through the door. After a while she grew impatient and returned to the cottage.

"Well sir, if you don't mind, perhaps we should let Edward get back to his rest?", she interrupted.

"Yes of course, I don't want to delay the recovery of your patient", Lord Balfour sniffed, sensing his time had come to leave. "Tomorrow morning, remember Miss Crossley. They will be here first thing", prompted Lord Balfour.

"Aye, and I am very grateful sir, I won't forget".

"See that you don't", he said coolly, picking his hat up from the wooden table and slamming the cottage door behind him.

~

"He's looking better", Jennifer said quietly as she crept about the cottage, helping Annie with the household jobs that had been overlooked during the crisis.

"I thought that too", agreed Annie. "Are you sure The Reverend doesn't mind me missing work for a while? I feel terribly guilty leaving you on your own there Jenny".

"Oh Annie don't worry about that! Besides, you'll be finishing soon for good won't you, and then I suppose I will have to find someone else".

"Aye, I suppose I will, won't I", Annie confirmed glumly. She would be terribly sad to say goodbye to her job at the parsonage when the baby arrived. "'Ere Jenny, guess who paid us a visit today?".

"Abraham?".

"No, Lord Balfour can you believe it? Came alone on his horse, said he would send some farmhands first thing tomorrow to help us catch up here". Annie had finished brushing the cold ash from the gate and began building a fresh fire ready to boil some tea for the three of them. Edward still wasn't eating, but she resolved to try again later that evening with some soup that Jenny had brought along.

"Well lah-di-dah!", Jennifer teased her. "A personal visit no less. And what was his Lordship after?"

"I don't rightly know, seems he just came to enquire about Edward's health".

"Well… that's kind, isn't it? Out of character like, but a nice gesture all the same".

"Aye, I left them to it, not sure what they were talking about. Probably the war and such things – perhaps Edward's return to the army". Annie could not hide the disappointment in her voice.

"That's bothering you, int' it?".

"No, why would it? I just don't want him to be disappointed if his health doesn't recover that's all", she said defensively.

"The Reverend gets the papers from London, the Great French War is still raging and Britain is taking any man they can to send to France. He will probably end up right back where he started, fit or not. But it remains to be seen". Annie nodded in agreement, although the news had troubled her greatly. She had treasured every moment she had spent nursing Edward, treasuring him like a wife would treasure a new husband. But ultimately she knew he would leave her in time, just as William had, and so would not dare to hope the situation would end any differently.

"Have you grown fond of Edward, Annie? You were very upset the other night, quite distraught in fact. And you have not accepted help from any other woman in the village with his care".

"Aye, I have. He's been a good friend to me Jenny".

"Just remember what's important right now. This farm, your baby and Tab and Joseph. Don't go getting your heart broken all over again Annie, I couldn't bear it".

Annie stirred the tea into the boiling water, hiding her sadness. "I won't, Jenny". She couldn't bring herself to confess they had already made love. Now she thought about it, it seemed such a stupid thing to do and she had let her hopes grow beyond reason. She stamped out the flickers of hope in the pit of her stomach and fetched the cups for their tea.

Later, once Jennifer had left and dusk had settled over Haworth, Annie heated up the clear soup for Edward. The fire roared in the grate and the cottage was peaceful, Edward watched Annie go about her work through half closed eyes as he lay on the bed.

"Do you feel like you could eat?", she asked him.

"Aye, I'll come to the table", he nodded.

"No, stay in bed, it's no good for you sitting in a cold wooden chair". She took his hands and pulled him up, placing a pillow and rolled up blanket behind him for support. She lifted the spoon to his lips again and again as he drank the soup compliantly. After a while, he cleared his throat and asked, "Do you think we should write to Tab now and let her know?".

"No Edward, I do not", she replied flatly.

"How long do you have left though? Do you know or… do babies just come?".

"Probably around two months. Jenny says I'm carrying small, so I've got away with it up until recently".

"You look bigger now though. It won't be long".

"I know. Don't worry, it's all in hand". She continued to bring the spoon to his lips with great patience, savouring their closeness.

"What if I don't survive? Have you enough money to bring in

help to bridge the gap?".

She dropped the spoon into the bowl with a clatter. "Don't be stupid, of course you'll survive". Their eyes met, there was so much left unsaid, but neither could muster the courage to say it.

"I mean it Annie", he coughed hard and groaned in pain, "What if I were to die and you were left alone here? You would need your family".

"You mean to say, what about when you grow tired of working out here in the middle of nowhere and you decide to go back to London - don't you?". Her voice cracked as she spoke, rejection once again tugging at her heart. "Don't feel guilty about me, this is my mess and I can bloody well deal with it". She slammed the still half full bowl down on the squat little table nearby, the soup sloshing over the side. "And don't feel guilty because of what happened the other night. I'm not expecting marriage Edward, don't worry about that". She rose from the bed where she was perched and busied herself washing the cups and pots from that afternoon.

"I didn't think you were Annie. 'Ere, are you upset with me? I'm sorry if I've caused you offence. I should never have done it, it was wrong of me. I should have thought about your condition".

"I'm not sick or stricken with madness. I can make my own decisions! We both wanted it, even if it meant nothing to you". Annie stood with her back towards Edward in shame, unaccustomed to talking about such intimate matters openly.

"Annie, that night meant everything to me", Edward assured her, emphasising each word in sincerity. "Me leaving has nothing to do with the way I feel about you, please believe that. But I have nothing to offer here".

"What if you weren't fit enough to re-join? Then would you come back here?". She had stopped washing the crockery and a tense silence descended on the room.

"I don't know Annie. I don't want to lie to you when I don't know the answer".

"Is that because you have someone waiting for you or is it *really* just the Great French War you're rushing back to?".

"Someone? Are you asking me if I have a sweetheart hidden away somewhere Annie?". Edward was crestfallen that she would think so little of him.

"Aye, a girl wondering where you are".

"No, Annie. I don't", his voice was tinged with regret. "I would never have misled you like that. It's just me, there's no one else".

"I understand", she replied glumly. But Edward feared that truly, she didn't.

CHAPTER EIGHTEEN

As promised, the farmhands arrived from the Balfour Estate at the crack of dawn. Annie jumped when the knock came at the door, having forgotten the agreement entirely, as one often does when they have more on their plate than they can manage. The three of them set to work eagerly and Annie boiled water on the fire for their tea, feeling like a spare part compared to their fast and efficient labour. The farm was such a hive of activity that she didn't notice Abraham meandering up the lane with Pip at his side.

"Is there a cup going for me", he asked with a strange air of distance about him, while Pip pressed his wet and eager nose into her boots. Annie called across the small field to where the men were cutting spinach and courgettes and pulling carrots, and they started to stroll over for their drinks before she replied.

"I'll see what's left when they've had theirs", she shrugged noncommittally.

"I heard you were getting some help today – that's good isn't it?". She only nodded in reply and smiled sweetly as she handed the men their brews, but Abraham could sense the smile was not meant for him too.

"Good job I wasn't relying on you for help, wasn't it? Took you long enough to darken my doorstep", she snapped when they were left alone once more. "I haven't seen you for three days and Edward nearly died. You left without a word before dawn on Sunday and you haven't troubled yourself since!".

Abraham sighed, "D'ya know something, Annie? I really thought we were best friends. I thought we told each other everything – had done since we were bairns. But then I find out you're hiding something from me. Something very important". Annie had never seen Abraham look so hurt, so she let him continue. "I've heard all sorts from people saying you had got yourself in real trouble – but I would never have asked you about it direct because I would never believe you would keep something like that from me. I thought you trusted me like a brother, but you're keeping a *baby* from me?".

"How did you find out?". Abraham could detect a hint of relief in her voice.

"I saw you in your nightdress, didn't I? I might not be that sharp but I could pretty well work it out then".

Annie's shoulders dropped. "I truly am sorry. I've been so embarrassed about it and worrying about everything here too – I was scared you would write to Tab and Joe. Then time kept passing and it got later and later and… it got harder to come up with a way to tell you".

"I would never have done that Annie. I would have kept your secret to the end, you *know that*".

"I know, I know. You are my dearest friend, even though I haven't been the greatest friend to you recently".

"I assume Edward knows?". She turned to the cottage where Abraham gestured, half expecting to see him in the doorway watching them, instead of in bed asleep where she left him. Her face was creased with regret.

"Aye, he does. I didn't choose to tell him though, he found out. He saw me from the moor path when I was swimming".

"But we always go swimming together…?". Abraham's hurt was almost childlike. "Is it William's then?".

"Aye, it is". She placed a protective hand over her belly as Abraham looked down wide eyed.

"Oh Annie, what a bastard he is, ey? There's nowt to be done about it now, anyway. We'll just have to get on with it. For what it's worth, Tab's a good sort – I don't think she'll be too hard on you. It might be nice for her after... you know", he trailed off.

"After Samuel you mean?".

"Aye, after Samuel. She might be happy to have another baby in the house. It will take some getting used to but, in the end you can't help but love a baby, can you?".

"That's true enough", she smiled.

"Is there anything else you want to tell me then Annie, only you were hysterical the other night over Ed. Am I to expect to hear you two are courting soon or... what?".

"No!", Annie replied defensively. "I hardly think so. Doubt he came here to find himself a young lady who's already with child, do you?".

"Who knows? Stranger things have happened I suppose", shrugged Abraham. "A good woman is a good woman, after all. You have to hold on to them when you find them".

~

Later that afternoon the farm was starting to look a little more cared for, and after Annie had fetched good bread and cheese and pieces of pie for the workers, she decided Edward would benefit from some fresh air. She carried the big rocking chair outside with substantial difficulty and then helped Edward to his feet, gently walking him into the herb garden as one would an elderly relative.

"Mid your step, Edward", she prompted as he shuffled squinting into the relative brightness after days spent in the low light of the cottage.

"Feels good to be outside", he said, drinking in the summer air and savouring the warm sun on his face.

"Well, be grateful you're still around to enjoy it!", she chuckled. They both remained quiet for a few moments, savouring the birdsong and fragrance from the garden.

"A letter came from Tab this morning", she said softly after a while. "The farm was sold three weeks ago and they hope to return home soon". She gave a tight-lipped smile, a gesture of resignation. "You're growing stronger and I know you will want to make plans soon. It shouldn't be long at all now".

He nodded thoughtfully. "Thank you, Annie". She placed her hand on his thigh and he closed his eyes peacefully, enjoying the peace. "I can't believe you've managed to keep it all going, what with me being useless and you in your condition. I'm so impressed, I've never met another woman quite like you".

"I can't quite believe it either", she replied, as he gave her hand a squeeze. She watched a swallow take flight from a branch nearby and followed it with her eyes, further and further across the moors until it was nothing but a fleck on the horizon. *That will be Edward soon,* she thought, choking down a lump in her throat.

"I had better start cooking, you look like you could eat". She stood up and brushed off her skirts, distracting herself from the tugging in her chest. "But if you need me, just call me. I will come straight to you, alright?". She gave his shoulder a squeeze and turned on her heel back to the cottage as a single tear rolled down her cheek.

CHAPTER NINETEEN

Edward tugged the stiff collar at his neck. He felt as though he was being strangled by it, but he pushed it from his mind and pressed on up the lane and towards Low Moor farm. It had been a fortnight since his accident and he had recovered well, thanks to Annie's patient nursing. He had returned to light labour on the farm and bolstered by Abraham, he and Annie were coping. But only just – harvest season would soon be upon them.

His side nagged at him dully as it tended to do with any exertion, but thankfully Low Moor loomed in to view and he knew he would soon be able to sit down and rest. The invitation had come as a surprise to him and no sooner had he read it his suspicions were raised. What on earth did Lord Balfour want with him?

"Sergeant Brigg! So good to see you again, and on your feet this time". Lord Balfour shook his hand vigorously in the splendid drawing room of the sprawling manor house. The housekeeper who had brought him there made discreetly for the door, and as another two men greeted Edward he felt an urge to call after her like a child would a nanny. He wanted her to guide him back to the stone gates and out once more into freedom.

Despite the mild summer evening a fire burned in the grate, a necessity due to the height of the ceiling Edward guessed. A room like this could quickly become chilly, especially at night, but the heat only served to make Edward more uncomfortable. There was a distinct sense of airlessness in the room.

The light from the fire illuminated Lord Balfour's face giving him a comically evil quality, which reminded Edward of the tapestries one would see in churches – warning of the dangers of sin with its lively depictions of hellfire. He laughed to himself at the comparison and returned the handshake. Lord Balfour introduced Edward to the two other men who were sunk deep into opposite ends of a large leather settee, quaffing brandy and smoking what Edward wouldn't doubt to be extremely expensive cigars, Lord Connell and Brigadier Hutt.

"Please, have a drink old chap", the red-faced Brigadier insisted, straining to reach the decanter from his chair, his round protruding belly hampering his efforts. Edward thanked him warily and sat in the plump velvet armchair next to Lord Balfour.

"So glad you could join us", Lord Balfour's voice echoed around the room.

"I must say, I was surprised to be asked again after the dance", Edward laughed nervously. He admired the imposing military portraits of Lord Balfour that hung around the room. He had no proud records of his service like this, only his sad little kitbag back at the cottage.

"Not at all", dismissed Lord Balfour with a wave of his hand. "I almost feel responsible for the accident. I should have had the men who set the piano up flogged!" There wasn't a shred of sincerity in his voice. "I wanted to invite you here to make amends, wouldn't want you leaving Haworth on a bad note, would I?".

"No harm done", smiled Edward tentatively as he raised his glass with the others.

"Balfour here tells me you were in the guards?", Lord Connell asked, surveying Edward with a critical eye.

"That's right sir".

"Ah! Us military men must stick together, mustn't we", he smirked, glancing at Lord Balfour.

"Yes sir, I agree, sir". The men were amused by Edward's formal tone.

"You're not in the company offices now, old chap – I'd like to imagine the respect in this room flows both ways", Brigadier Hutt reassured him generously, but Edward felt it was insincere.

"Your injury, Battle of Bayonne was it? Nasty business on all accounts. I believe I know your Captain… Captain Stanier?", the Brigadier continued.

Edward shifted in his seat, his brow knit in confusion. He noticed that the velvet felt prickly through his shirt, and beads of perspiration gathered on his forehead. His eyes fixed momentarily on the large painting hung above the fireplace. Seven men on horseback chasing down a fox with a pack of dogs leading the way. Even from high up on the wall, Edward could read the terror on the fox's face as the hunters closed in.

"Captain Stanier, yes", he replied after a few moments, "a truly great leader. It's been an honour to serve under him".

"Yes, he's a decent sort. He and I were together in Mysore, with Cornwallis. He's a talented man". Lord Balfour listened to the other men talk with great interest, uncharacteristically quiet.

"And you intend to return to the army?", enquired Lord Connell. He was a tall and lean man, unlike the Brigadier, with broad, perfectly groomed mutton chops across his cheeks. Edward believed him to be around the same age as Lord Balfour – late thirties at most.

"Of course sir, as soon as I am fit and well enough I will be returning to London to re-enlist. Well, once Joseph Naylor returns to the farm of course". Edward looked towards Lord Balfour, unsure how much of his circumstances the other men understood.

"A fellow man dedicated to King and country! Very admirable", Lord Balfour toasted. "Loyal like a dog to his master". Connell and Hutt guffawed into their brandy.

Edward grit his teeth. He glanced at the carriage clock on the side table close by – half past nine. He wanted his bed, or at least to be back at the cottage sipping tea with Annie in front of the fire.

"Well Sergeant Brigg, that brings me to the purpose of my invitation tonight. I'm afraid I had an ulterior motive, inviting you here today".

Edward leant back in his chair, listening warily.

"Nothing sinister Brigg, don't be alarmed. After your accident I took the liberty of writing to Captain Stainer out of...", he looked around the men as if for inspiration, "call it a healthy interest in you". Edward narrowed his eyes, regretting his attendance.

"Seems to be the case that Captain Stanier does not believe you to be returning to the guards at all".

"No, sir. I have not sent any correspondence to my regiment yet, they are most likely unaware of my intentions. But the Great French War rages on and they will find use for me yet". Edward's tone was low and measured.

"Seems like we may have a use for you as well. We three have been discussing our need for... how could one put it? Private security. Captain Stanier did me the courtesy of sharing your records. I'll admit Brigg, it's impressive stuff. His character reference was also good, he thinks of you as a loyal and courageous man". Lord Balfour paused to give Edward chance to thank him, but no thanks came. Edward remained silent, watching and waiting. "We have personal affairs across Britain, sometimes overseas. They can often be confidential in nature;

sensitive, *delicate* affairs. And as it seems that you will not be returning to the guards, we wanted to offer you a position".

Edward went to protest, but Lord Balfour raised a hand to silence him. The smiles of the other men had dissolved, and he got the distinct feeling that *no* was not an option the gentleman had anticipated – or would accept. "Please, before you decline. You would be based here in Howarth with a very generous wage. We would call on you as and when you were needed; to pay visits to our business associates, collecting any debt, travelling overseas *etcetera*. You wouldn't have to stay in that grim little cottage any longer, I'm sure we could find you a much more fitting residence here. Connell owns a house on Main Street, which he is happy for you to use". Balfour smirked, "This offer is more than a man like you could have ever dreamed of, no?".

"It's certainly a very appealing offer sir, but please understand that I must return to the army". There was a knot in Edward's stomach. Something about the meeting made him feel deeply uneasy.

"Oh dear", Balfour said with a sigh. "I didn't mean Captain Stanier was unaware of your *intention*, but instead that you will not be welcomed back to the regiment at all. You're finished there". Lord Balfour's smile had contorted into a snarl, the reflection of the flames dancing across his face.

"That's not true". Edward's voice was barely more than a whisper. "Captain Stanier would not refuse me. I'm the best soldier they've ever had in Coldstream".

"You've been put out to pasture Brigg, accept it. And after your performance at the summer dance, rightly so. You would be a liability to your fellow soldiers. And now here I am, offering you a lifeline – and I highly recommend you take it".

"He wouldn't do that". Edward gripped the velvet arms of the chair. His knuckles blanched with the strength of his grip and there was a pain in his chest. "You don't have the authority to tell me this".

"He already has", Lord Balfour replied with an air of finality. He looked at his nails casually, then with a sigh stood up from the chair and walked over to the drinks table to pour another brandy. He gazed into the glass in contemplation as he swirled the spirit around inside, and then said, "He mentioned something about your courage erring on the side of recklessness over the last year".

Edward stood up, whether to strike Balfour or to leave Low Moor, he wasn't sure yet. "You know nothing" he stated flatly, as he drained the last of the alcohol from his glass was an audible gulp and slammed it back down onto the table.

"Oh, I do Sergeant Brigg. Granted leave for your wedding and your poor little bride dead not seven months later. Captain Stanier feels you perhaps went *off the boil* at that point. Suggested you had been reckless with your own life. Since then, no, I think your chapter in the British army is closed. But your fearless, there's no denying that, and you get the job done. I've done a lot of research on you, Sergeant Brigg – you should be flattered!", Balfour said with mock indignation.

"You leave my wife out of this", Edward threatened. He started to cross the room but was stopped in his tracks by Connell's hand on his chest.

"Think very carefully about your position boy", Brigadier Hutt urged from the settee, his voice thick with smoke and booze.

"Oh aye", Edward laughed in derision, "I've done nothing *but* think about my position for the last five months". His chin jutted, so close it was almost touching Connell's. "Find yourself another *loyal dog* to do your dirty work men, it won't be me".

With that, he strode to the door and slammed it behind him. Rage bubbled inside him as he marched down corridors, searching for the main door. Once he was back out into the moonlight, his fury overtook him and he punched his fist hard through a wooden outhouse door, wishing it was Lord Balfour's face.

~

As he threw the cottage door open with a crash, Annie jumped in her chair where she had been dozing.

"Bloody hell Edward, I just jumped out of my skin". He didn't answer her but instead went straight for his pipe on the dresser and lit it, pacing the room as he puffed.

"What's the matter with you? Did it not go well?". He took a long draw on his pipe smoke billowing from his nose. "What did they want?", she pressed.

"Nothing, just a drink", Edward snapped.

"For what though? Was it just him?".

"For God's sake, it was just a drink to make up for what happened with the piano, that's all. You know he's a snake Annie, he's only invited me to show off".

"I'm only asking Edward. I wondered if you'd had a nice time that's all". The hurt was clear in Annie's voice as she turned back around to stare into the fire glumly.

"Well you were very keen for me to go, weren't you? You should have gone in my stead if it were such a good idea".

"Something's happened tonight", she said, narrowing her eyes. "You've come home in a foul mood".

Edward clenched his jaw, staring vacantly across the room. "Did you know why he invited me? Have you heard some rumours around the village?".

"No...", Annie replied truthfully. "I haven't! Only what you've told me of it".

"He's asked me to be his monkey, stay here and work for him doing his dirty work". He took another long drag on the clay pipe held between his gritted teeth.

"What do you mean?". Annie pulled her shawl around her more tightly, feeling strangely vulnerable. She had never seen Edward angry like this before.

"He said I can forget about going back to the army because he's written to my Captain – to put a bad word in for me no doubt. The meddling BASTARD!". His shout echoed around the room. "I could tell he was up to something when he came to visit here".

"I think you might be overthinking things…", Annie scoffed.

You don't *know* men like them Annie. This is what they do! We are just pawns in a game to them. They tread and climb on others for their own benefit".

"He's bluffing, he won't have written to anyone", she dismissed.

"He has Annie, he knew things no one here does".

"Like what?". She leant in towards him, intrigued. "What things? Secrets?". Her face contorted in confusion.

"Just… service records and things like that". Edward would not meet her eye. He couldn't bring himself to talk about Bridget. Not now, not to Annie.

"Maybe it's a good idea though? If things don't work out in London, or you change your mind and want to stay here… at least you know you would have income?".

Edward rubbed his face in exasperation and shook his head. "No, Annie".

"Well just think, you could…".

"Annie, *stop!*" She was stunned into silence. Tears of

indignation threatened to spill down her cheeks.

"Goodnight, Edward". Her voice trembled but she remained steadfast. "I'm going to bed". She closed her bedroom door heavily behind her and Edward dropped onto his cot, head in hands. The walls of the cottage felt as though they were closing in on him, he was desperate to get out, to run – but where was there left to go?

CHAPTER TWENTY

"It really is a beautiful piece of furniture", Jennifer said, gazing at the oak cradle.

"Well, I doubt I'll have any use for it in the future", Reverend Charnock chuckled. "I'd rather somebody get the use out of it instead of it just languishing in the rafters". He smiled contentedly at Annie. "There's no one I'd rather give it to. Such a happy occasion, welcoming a child".

Annie and Jennifer had finished their work, not that Annie contributed very much these days at the parsonage, but nevertheless, the routine of going there helped to pass the time and she always felt brighter for a day spent amongst old friends. The cradle, which had once been used for the Reverend's now grown-up sons, had been brought down from the attic and cleaned and polished until the wood shone like glass. It was a rocking cradle with a frame above it, suspending rich red curtains around it. Annie was surprised when she had first seen it, it was much more extravagant than she would have imagined – the Reverend tended to have more simple tastes.

"It's very grand, just beautiful". Annie said gratefully.

"Yes", the Reverend sensed her surprise at the extravagance of the piece. "My wife chose it. It was made specially when we were expecting our first son. It has rocked all our children to sleep over the years, and now it's ready for a new home and a new life". Annie beamed, feeling extremely lucky.

They were in the kitchen, waiting for Edward and Abraham

to come and collect the cradle and carry it back to the cottage. While they waited, Jennifer and Annie finished up some embroidery on the baby clothes that they had been making over the last few months. Delicate bonnets and blankets lay scattered across the table, along with long white linen baby shirts and quilted bed gowns.

"These are very fine garments ladies". The Reverend held one after the other up to the light streaming in from the window and admired the delicate craftsmanship. "I think other women would be delighted with them too. Have you ever thought of taking them to Keighley to sell at the market? A lot of the more well to do families would purchase them for a good price, I am certain of it".

"Gosh, no. I've never even thought of that!". Annie flushed, she was not used to such high praise. "Besides, it's Jenny's skill really, not mine".

"Don't be so modest!", urged Jennifer. "That's not true at all and you know it. I've only added little bits to some of them. She's made them up very quick too, Reverend. Just a couple of hours here and there, plus everything else she has to attend to at the minute".

"Hmm", pondered the Reverend. "You really have come into your own recently Annie. Perhaps your sister and brother-in-law being away has forced you to find your resilience? You're like a different girl to the one I knew but six months ago. It's wonderful to see".

"Oh *really* now. I've just done what I've had to do".

"No, no. It's really quite something. And you must consider pursuing this craft Annie, I mean it. It would please me to see you have independent income, especially as a mother. Not that you won't be welcome back here of course, as soon as you're ready. I do miss having children around the place. Their joy really is good for the soul". Annie gripped his hands and gave him a heartfelt thank you. Had it not been for the Reverend's discretion and unwavering kindness Annie would have felt cut adrift, bobbing around in the sea of confusion and fear, without her job at the parsonage to anchor her.

"Speaking of which Reverend, I think Annie might be taking over from me one day soon. She's done brilliantly with Edward and I won't be around forever. Someone else will need to train in healing and midwifery, the village needs it – and these things take time to learn".

"Oh don't talk like that Jenny, you have years in you yet! I can't bear this sort of talk".

"Comes to us all though Annie, eventually", added the Reverend in his calm, singsong voice. "And Jennifer is right, you have shown a great intuition for healing and care".

"People are happy to pay Annie, if you can reach them in their hour of need. Then you wouldn't have to fear for your security".

"I'd be honoured Jenny, I really would".

"That's settled then. After your baby arrives, I can start to teach you the ways".

The Reverend nodded, content with the arrangement. The truth was that he too was getting older, it was as if the years were accelerating past him more quickly than for others. He worried about Annie and was heartened to see how she had grown from a rather timid and indecisive girl, into a thoughtful, strong willed and resilient woman in front of his very eyes.

The clock in the hallway chimed half past four, and soon after Edward and Abraham arrived, calling out through the side door in the scullery as they let themselves in to the parsonage.

"Oh aye", said Abraham giving a low whistle, "that's a fine piece of furniture, bit too fancy for your cottage, Annie!", he teased.

Edward gave an appreciative murmur once he joined the group in the kitchen. "Annie's baby will be the most comfortable in Haworth it seems", he said, catching her eye from across the table. The argument of a few nights before was almost forgotten, but a strange tension remained between the two like a fog.

"Will you stay for a cup of tea?". Jennifer set about filling up the pot and placing it over the fire on the range.

"Don't mind if I do", said Abraham sitting himself at the kitchen table in anticipation. "I've got the cart outside, I didn't want to risk this one busting his gut again by carrying it". He winked at Edward who punched him playfully in the arm.

"I'll have a brew n'all Jenny, if it's on offer", agreed Edward. "If I might use the privy first though…?".

Jennifer nodded, "It's just back outside through the gardens and to the right. Annie will have to show you, I'm busy with this". She gestured to the cups set out on the table vaguely. Dutifully, Annie rose and followed Edward through the backdoor.

Outside, the gardens were fragrant and balmy. The summer had been quite mild, the nights still had a noticeable chill and there had not yet been any days one could describe as hot so the garden was thriving, more alive with colour and life than Annie could remember from any other year. As they strolled, the hum of bees and dragonflies floated toward them on the air through the parsonage's peaceful quiet, until Annie gestured towards the outhouse with an extended arm.

"I'm sure I could have found it myself", laughed Edward, feeling silly at how obvious it was.

"I don't mind", she reassured him. "It's good to stretch my legs. Before you go though, I did want to ask you something".

"Aye, what is it?". Edward waited patiently while she looked around the garden, gathering her nerve.

"I've been thinking about it for a while, you see. I just want to show how grateful I am for the last few months. Edward, would you consider being godfather to my child?".

"God Annie! I wasn't expecting anything like that, it's very flattering". Edward was taken aback by the gesture. "It's really lovely of you to ask Annie, but I have no experience of children. Besides, don't you think your baby deserves godparents who will be around to lend a hand and teach them how to go on?". Annie's shoulders sagged in disappointment. She had expected Edward to be delighted by the thought of it, being twenty-seven already and with no children of his own. She imagined it might be a comfort to him, a reason to come back to visit.

"Would it be fair on them for me to say yes, and then to disappear back abroad?", he continued. Annie looked crestfallen.

"Oh, yes. I suppose you're right". Her cheeks flushed and she looked down at the grass kicking at it with her shoes.

"Annie, it really is very thoughtful. It's not that I don't want to, of course I do!". He took her hands firmly in his. "Look at me". She lifted her eyes to meet his. "Why not ask Abraham? He's been such a decent friend to you and he'll be around to help you out – like a father figure for the little one".

"Yes, you're right. That's a better idea". She said flustered, shaking her hands free of his and turning back towards the parsonage. "Just a thought, that's all". Edward sighed, and with a heavy heart turned and carried on towards the privy.

~

Edward's refusal ate away at Annie until late in the evening. She had been so sure he would accept, would thank her and feel significant and relish his new role in her child's life. But he hadn't. He remained steadfast – he was leaving. Annie didn't go straight home after the parsonage, instead she wandered across the moors for hours until she was certain Edward would be out again at the Black Bull and she could return to the cottage alone and have her privacy. She lay amongst the long dry grass listening to the grasshoppers chirrup close by, marvelling at how far she had come since those cold winter days when she would sit out here shivering and alone, waiting to see if William would deign to show up to their meetings.

The talk with Jenny and Reverend Charnock had lit a flame inside her. The idea of learning the intricacies of healing and midwifery with Jenny was thrilling. And yes, she could make baby clothes and go to Keighley to sell them proudly on a market stall. She would get to know the vendors there, make new friends, make *money*. She wouldn't need anyone to support her. She would never have to beg again. *Look how well things have gone at the farm,* she thought, *maybe there's more to me than people knew? Maybe even I knew?*

And yet despite all that, she still wanted him. Annie didn't need anyone, but she really did *want* Edward and the feeling was only growing stronger the closer his departure came. Very soon Tab and Joseph would be coming back and he would fly away from Annie and her baby and Haworth, away over the horizon never to be seen again. The longing in her heart was a lead weight, now that there was a buyer for the farm she knew she had to decide. If she didn't speak up now she might never have another chance.

Back at the cottage, Annie waited restlessly for Edward's return, a speech had been rehearsed several times in the looking glass in her bedroom, but none of the words felt quite right. Eventually, she decided that it didn't matter how she said it as long as she was brave enough *to* say it.

When the cottage door finally creaked open, she was ready.

"Annie?", called Edward, hanging his hat on the stand next to the door. "You there?".

"Aye, you wanting a drink?", she asked brightly, emerging from her bedroom, hair brushed and plaited and face freshly washed. She had put on a clean nightgown and pulled one of her mother's shawls around her, which normally lay squirreled away in her coffer, too precious to use too often.

"Go on then", he replied kicking off his boots and placing them neatly next to his bed out of habit. "You look good tonight... what's different?".

"Nothing, just done my hair", Annie replied, delighted that he had noticed. "Do you want a drop of this?". She held up a bottle of port that William had given to her early on in their courtship. The bottle was dusty, having remained untouched on the dresser ever since.

"Why not, little nightcap ey?". He stoked the fire in the grate and drew up a rickety kitchen chair. "You get sat down in the rocker, I'll pour the drinks".

Annie sat down gingerly, every fibre of her being felt like it was humming and her nerves were making the baby fidget and kick with great strength. Edward noticed her grimacing as he fetched glasses.

"What's the matter? You alright?", he asked nervously.

"The baby kicks me much harder now", she giggled. "Sometimes she gets my ribs".

"She?".

"Well that's what Jenny says, that I'm having a little girl".

"Is that what you wanted?".

"Oh aye, definitely. I think I'd be pleased as punch with a bonny little daughter. Tab would like that too I reckon".

Edward beamed. "Any daughter of yours would be the most beautiful baby Haworth has ever seen. She'll be perfect". He joined her near the fire.

"Do you want to feel it?". Annie stood up to proffer her swollen belly to him without waiting for a reply.

Edward hesitated, unsure if he could. Memories flooded back to him in waves that crashed over his head and stunned him, leaving him short of breath. But Annie was nodding enthusiastically and before he had chance to protest, she took his hand in hers and pressed it firmly to her baby.

Edward's eyes opened wide in anticipation. He didn't speak, just allowed his hand to be held there.

"Just wait a moment", Annie whispered, staring deep into his eyes. She felt his pulse quicken in his wrist, his shallow breaths barely audible in the silent kitchen. Then he felt it. The fluttering and writhing inside her womb. He pressed in further, trailing the baby's kicks as they moved upwards.

"Good isn't it?", she asked giddily. Edward simply nodded. Before she could stop herself, she tilted her chin up and pressed her lips firmly against his and brought her free hand up to his cheek where it lingered, tracing over his sideburns and down to his jaw. He opened his mouth slightly and moaned, a deep echoing moan that made Annie's bones tremble with longing. For a brief moment they were one again, as she had dreamt of, before he pulled away from her lips abruptly and snatched his hand back as if he had been burnt.

"Annie, I...I...", he stuttered, shaking his head. He stepped backwards into the kitchen table away from her, making the glasses tinkle and judder with the force.

"Edward, please? Just listen to me...".

"Annie, I really shouldn't be doing this, it's not right".

"It is right, though". Annie smiled broadly, which made the tears threatening to spill from her eyes look almost comical.

"Don't fight it".

"No, that's not what I mean".

"I want you to stay. I don't want you to re-enlist and I feel like if I don't tell you this now while you're here in front of me, I'll never forgive myself. When we went to bed together it was so special, so different to William. It felt right Edward, I know you felt it too". She panted, eyes wide and pleading. "Just say something".

Edward sat down heavily next to the fire and cradled his head in his hands.

"Oh good God Annie, what have we done here? I've made a right mess of it all, haven't I?".

She shook her head so vigorously her plaits danced against her back. "No! We both wanted it. I've really fallen for you. I feel I've fallen in *love* with you Edward".

"Oh Annie, no you haven't".

She took him firmly by the shoulders. "But I know you feel it too, don't you?". He didn't reply, only nodded his head, still unable to look up at her. "So stay".

"I can't Annie. I have nothing to offer you. I'd be a terrible husband to you. I'd only end up letting you down. I can't stay here, I have no skills, I barely know a thing about farming. There's no other work I'm skilled in. Soldiering is all I know. You deserve more than that".

"Then take me with you".

He laughed in disbelief. "You don't want that, believe me".

"I do, more than anything".

"I would never, ever do that to you and your baby. Could never even *think* of asking that".

"Why not? Plenty of others do. I hear of wives going along with children to the camps in London and all sorts of places".

"Oh God, no". He lifted his face up to the ceiling and bit his lip to stop it from wobbling. Visions of Bridget swept over him. The bitter cold, the wet and the mud that got into your very marrow. Her pregnant, still body and blue lips in that rancid tent. His sobbing that was so loud and unnatural he thought it came from someone else entirely. "I would never allow it. It's not safe for you".

"I don't understand, I really don't. I thought you... felt the same way about me".

"I do. I just can't give you what you deserve". He leant forward to her, elbows on his knees and hands clasped together as if he were begging her to understand. "I wish it were different Annie, but it's not. I should never have come here".

"Maybe in that case you shouldn't have", she said. Her arms dropped from his shoulders and fell to her sides.

"I'm sorry, Annie. I wish things were different".

"Why be sorry when you got what you wanted?". With that, she walked slowly to her bedroom in disbelief, leaving Edward alone by the fire.

CHAPTER TWENTY-ONE

The few days following Annie's confession passed in a blur at the farm. Neither Annie nor Edward spoke more than a few words to one another, passing like ships in the night in the cowsheds and meadow. Edward would retire to the Black Bull each evening, sensing his presence unwelcome at the cottage. Annie preferred it that way, it was less humiliating.

"Are you coming to church?", Annie asked on Sunday morning, which was the most interest she had showed in him for days.

"Not today. I'm going to stay here and finish some jobs I've been meaning to get to".

"Suit yourself". She picked her linen bonnet up from the stand by the door and left, not giving him any time to reconsider.

The sermon was short that Sunday, the villagers had plenty of work to return to in the fields across Haworth. Harvest time was almost upon them and the toil felt endless, so the Reverend tried his best to accommodate his rural flock by keeping services short. Even so, Annie could barely concentrate. The words flowed from the pulpit and up into the rafters too quickly for her to catch them. There was something else that morning too, one too many faces turning to look at Annie with sneers and looks of derision. Whispers in the pews between women who nudged each other to turn around and steal glances from behind their bonnets.

Annie turned to Jennifer, sat next to her in the pew. "They're talking about me", she mouthed, trying not to draw any further attention to herself.

"Bloody *shrews*", Jennifer muttered in reply, loud enough that some of the gossiping women might hear her.

"They know, everyone knows now".

"They were going to work it out sooner or later. Forget them. There will be someone else to gossip about soon enough. Besides, they'll all get bored when the baby is here and you've got Tab and Joe back. They won't dare do this when you have family around you again".

Jennifer's husband Bramwell placed a gentle hand on his wife's knee, a request for the two to stop whispering back and forth while the Reverend was in the pulpit. Jennifer pursed her lips and narrowed her eyes, disappointed in but not surprised by the unkind attitude of the parishioners.

"I know there is much to attend to in our little village. We may come to church with hearts and minds full of worry and doubt about the harvest, our families and friends and even our own spiritual direction at this time of year. We neglect our bibles and often our Sunday services in order to attend to the land". Reverend Charnock raised an eyebrow at the disturbance in the crowd and the ladies soon settled down. "But let us not forget that we can also praise God through our labours. Our everyday tasks and interactions can serve as a time of quiet reflection and obedience in the Lord. The way we treat others in our church, or our village, demonstrates our holiness and Christian values". He spoke sternly and directly, at odds with his usual calm and flowing delivery. "It would please me to see this Christian kindness demonstrated more often here amongst our own".

After the last hymn, Reverend Charnock wished everyone a

productive week, and as he always did, reassured his flock they were welcome at the parsonage to discuss anything that might be weighing heavily on them. Just as he was closing his bible and people were rising from their pews, he halted again.

"May I leave you all with psalm 127:3 to consider this week? Behold, children are a gift of the Lord. The fruit of the womb is a reward".

The womenfolk looked at one another aghast, shaking their heads in disbelief and rolling their eyes. Barbed whispers floated to Annie through the thick, dusty air.

"There are *no exceptions* to that. This is the word of our Lord". The Reverend said gravely.

"That's them told", said Jennifer smugly, striding over the stone flags and out of Saint Michaels, leaving Annie to trot along behind her.

"Will you be joining us for supper tonight?", Bramwell asked Annie, as the three of them stood chatting near Samuel's grave. Annie thought of the tension at the cottage and agreed.

"That would be lovely, aye. I'll come down after my work at home".

"Well just you go carefully", the stooping old man urged her, looking up through his bushy grey eyebrows. "We don't want you suffering exhaustion, do we Jennifer?".

"We certainly do not, no".

Just as Annie was bidding them goodbye, a call came from the group of churchgoers next to the main door.

"There she is! Annie Crossley!", Margaret Bartle marched across the flagstone graves towards her, face contorted in anger and finger outstretched. "Been telling tales and crying to the Reverend, haven't you!".

"I've done no such thing!", Annie insisted.

"I think it's questionable that a Reverend would keep you working in his home after everyone found out you were carrying a bastard, God knows who the father is! Could be anyone knowing you".

"He should have made an example of you!", cried another.

"It really is disgusting the way you carry on around this place flaunting it. God knows what your poor sister is going to say when she gets back. Poor baby Samuel in the ground and no other children in sight – and *you!* Knickers 'round your ankles and up the spout unwed". The other women jeered unkindly from across the graves.

"Oh Margaret, give it a rest would you", Annie said feigning boredom, although she was shaking in her shoes with anger. "My personal affairs have nothing to do with you".

"They do when we all have to see them! When we are forced to question the morality of our own Reverend. And watch you living in sin, day in day out with that... *ruffian!*".

"Mrs Bartle, *please!*". Reverend Charnock hurried over from the church, his face red with uncharacteristic anger. "If you would like to question my suitability to preach here in this parish then I encourage you to come with me at once to my study where we can discuss the matter in private".

A quiet fell over the churchyard as people turned to watch the unpleasantness unfold.

"Reverend, I am merely stating that...".

"Enough!", he shouted. "You have taken no notice of the sermon today. That also includes all of you over there who murmur and snicker as you see a young woman attacked in the place she should be most safe!", he pointed to Margaret's supporters huddled near the main church door. "If the spiritual guidance I provide here is not to your standard of holiness, I *insist* you find another church to attend".

"No! There has been a misunderstanding, Reverend. I am not questioning...".

"I insist, Mrs Bartle. You will no longer be welcome here at St Michaels".

Margaret looked as though she had been slapped. Spittle gathered in the corners of her mouth as she searched the shocked faces in the crowd that had gathered and sensing no recourse, she gave up.

She stepped closer to Annie and jabbed a finger hard in her chest. "You won't get away with this, you jumped up little *whore*". Then she turned and marched out towards Main Street, chin aloft and eyes fixed straight ahead.

Annie's legs were unsteady. She looked about at the other folk who had seen the altercation unfold, but the faces were stony and unkind. One by one they turned their backs to her and walked away, muttering in disgust. Annie opened her mouth to protest, to insist that she was a good girl, a hard worker and a faithful churchgoer who had found herself in a very difficult situation. She wanted to reason that she had nursed Edward back to health, kept countless secrets for others who stood there sniggering at her distress and had been a dutiful sister who was keeping the family farm afloat despite being with child and separated from family. But the words didn't come. The humiliation was too much to bear.

"Come to the parsonage Annie, you need a sweet tea – you've gone very pale", Reverend Charnock insisted and Bramwell nodded in agreement, holding her unsteadily at one elbow lest her legs give way underneath her.

"Yes Annie, you must. You need to sit down. Where's bloody Abraham and Edward when you need them? They would have put a stop to her nonsense".

Bramwell interjected, soothing his wife's fury. "The Reverend handled it beautifully Jennifer. A very strong message has been sent today, and Margaret has been made an example of. Well done, Reverend." Jennifer nodded in agreement.

"Thank you for doing that", Annie said, lower lip wobbling.

"I would do it all over again too. This needs to be stamped out, I've let it go on too long". The group started to walk Annie carefully over the uneven ground to the parsonage. Sweat had gathered on her forehead and she complained of feeling dizzy.

"What do you mean, too long? We've barely had any problems until now. Just a few unkind comments and dirty looks here and there. Just nasty gossip that's all". Jennifer was puzzled, sure that Annie would have confided in her if the behaviours had escalated.

"Margaret Bartle and a few others approached me last month and ask that I explain why Annie was still working for me in her condition. I assumed that it was misplaced concern about her workload, but it wasn't. They wanted Annie to leave my employ and to be expelled from Saint Michaels. I'm afraid that is not something I am willing to do, and they were informed of that in no uncertain terms".

"They wanted me removed from the church? Because I'm having a baby?". Annie's heart ached as she realised the strength of the women's vitriol.

"That's not going to happen on my watch", Reverend Charnock reassured her. "I imagine things will be better from today on, now they understand their hate won't be tolerated".

~

After a hot sweet tea and a small brandy, Annie had stopped shaking. The fierce pain in her heart that she felt in the churchyard had been replaced by a dull ache by the time she shuffled back through the south gate and up the lane towards the cottage. A hole had opened up inside her, for the first time she sobbed for Tab, missing her so much it threatened to tear her in two. The abandonment first by William, then Tab and Joe, then Edward and finally, the entire village had taken its toll. She felt angry that Abraham hadn't come to church that day, not that he could have known what would unfold and would no doubt be furious with himself that he wasn't there to deal with them. She expected nothing of Edward though, he had already disappointed her enough.

When she got back to the cottage he was working in one of the barns and emerged as he heard the crunch of her footsteps approach.

"Y'alright?", he asked tentatively. She didn't reply, just shook her head and slammed the front door behind her. "Bugger you then", he muttered, and returned to his work.

Once inside, the fury rose in Annie's chest. Months and months of resentment and fear and anger washed over her. She hated William with a passion for what he did, she hated him for the situation he had helped cause, and for leaving her to face it all alone. He had walked away without a care, but she was suffering here at the farm day in day out. She hated the villagers for their cruel and unnecessary treatment. But most of all, she hated Edward for the way he had broken her heart, much worse than William ever did.

Her eyes settled then on his bed, the beads of cold wax that had dripped down from his candle onto the window sill above and his nightclothes folded neatly in a bundle. Annie wanted him gone, seeing him every day was a stark reminder of how unlovable and unacceptable she was to him, to William, and everyone else around her. With a scream of pure frustration she began grabbing his belongings and stuffing them into his kitbag unceremoniously.

"If you don't want to be here then LEAVE!", she shouted to the empty kitchen. She threw open the trunk lid, unlocked as usual, and pulled his greatcoat out and flung it hard on to the bed, letting every ounce of hatred flow from her for the first time. His spare shirt flew into the air and floated down like a ghost, settling near Annie's feet where she knelt. Her hair escaped its pins, flying wildly about her face. His army issue knife, fork and spoon clattered down onto the wooden floor where they were tossed, and the bundle of papers were strewn around her, ready to stuff down into his bag for his departure.

That was until a little envelope escaped, falling with a heaviness that the other's didn't, making a barely audible thunk on the floor. Annie panted with the effort, her hair stuck to her lip, fixated on the envelope. As she picked it up she felt something small and hard inside, so she opened it curiously, her heart pounding.

Inside was a wedding ring and a lock of deep black hair.

Her hands shook as she held it, knelt in the kitchen amongst the mess. A cry of anger welled in her and escaped, rising to a scream that caused Edward to run to her from across the yard.

He threw the door open and furrowed his brow, seeing Annie kneeling with her back to him, his meagre belongings crumpled and strewn around her.

"Annie, what the *hell* is going on here!?", his voice boomed, startling her from her trance.

She turned to face him, her face red and her eyes wild. "You *are* married. I KNEW it!", she screamed, as she jumped to her feet with surprising agility and rushed at him, the envelope with its precious contents screwed in her clammy hand. "You bastard!".

She made to strike him across the jaw, but he caught her hand in mid-air and gripped her wrist painfully tight.

"Give me that!", he commanded, wrestling the envelope from her other hand. "That's not yours Annie!".

"I shall throw it in the fire!".

"Don't you bloody dare!". He pulled it free from her and held it tightly against his chest, backing away from her with an arm outstretched.

With a guttural scream, Annie launched the half full bottle of port they had drank from together just the other night, and it smashed against the wall behind him, narrowly missing his head. Shards of glass and sprays of red port showered down over him.

"Where did you leave her? Where does she think you are?".

"She's DEAD Annie!".

Annie's chest heaved as she tried to catch her breath. Dust fell gently to the floor around them, illuminated in the afternoon summer sun.

"She's not though, is she? Don't lie to me Edward".

"How dare you", he snarled. "How dare you question me. Bridget died, with my child inside her in the *shit* and the *mud* and the *snow* in a dirty squalid army camp out in France". His eyes were cold and unforgiving. "And I had to leave them there, in the cold earth in an unmarked grave". He grit his teeth and stared Annie down, unwavering. "And you girl, you have the nerve to tell me I'm lying?".

"Oh God". Annie held on to the chair for support as the weight of the situation dawned on her. "Edward, I am so, so sorry".

"Don't! Don't apologise. I don't want to hear any more from you". He pulled his belongings together from the floor and the bed, stuffing them into his kit bag.

"Please Edward, don't go. I've lost my senses… I must have!

Just don't leave now, not like this". She tried to pull the kitbag from his grasp but he snatched it back with such force it made her lose balance and stumble. "I'm begging you!".

"Enough! I should never have come here. You can tell Joseph whatever you like. Tell him to keep his money, I don't bloody want it".

"But it's yours, you deserve it".

"I deserve a medal for putting up with this! There's enough money in the tin to pay a labourer to do my work. You should arrange that, because I'm leaving and I won't be coming back". He took his cap from the stand next to the door and heaved his kitbag on to his back. "Tab will be back soon. Best of luck Annie, because you'll damn well need it". With that, he slammed the door behind him and was gone. As his footsteps grew more distant, Annie threw herself onto his bed and howled into the pillow, muffled screams filling the cottage, but he did not come to her. Not this time.

CHAPTER TWENTY-TWO

Edward stared at the blank paper on the makeshift table in front of him. Below he could hear the buzz of chatter and laughter from the bar at the Black Bull, but in Mr Hague's lodging room the atmosphere was solemn. He had tried to find the right words to send to Tab and Joseph, but every iteration he came up with felt like a complete betrayal of Annie – on the other hand, he felt not sending the letter would be betraying Tab and Joe's generosity and leave Annie alone and in peril.

He pushed the paper away and lay back down on the sagging hard bed, the candle on the table casting a flickering orange glow across the room. It reminded him of the light from the rush lamp in the cottage that would cast a heavenly glow on Annie's face as they chatted and laughed and bickered together in the evenings. He turned over and closed his eyes so he would not need to see it.

The room was cheap enough, but he decided this would be his last night there. He had already spent one night in the bare and uncomfortable room, coming directly from the cottage straight to the Black Bull, slipping Mrs Hague an extra coin to get the room ready in haste so he could retire up there to privacy. He kicked himself for not walking over the moors and straight to Keighley, but deep in his heart he had hoped Annie would come looking for him, but she didn't. He couldn't blame her after the way he had left things.

He dozed there for an hour or two, before a knock at the door woke him up. He was disorientated in the darkness, still believing himself to be at the cottage, peering into the darkness trying to find his bearings.

"Supper, Mr Brigg?". It was Mrs Hague outside his room. "Are you there?". He rose groggily, rubbing roughly at his face and stumbled over to the door. She presented him with a tray laden with a bowl of meat stew, potatoes and a large piece of bread with a mug of ale perched on the side.

"Thank you", he mumbled, stepping aside and she hobbled into the room, placing his supper down on the rickety table.

"Are you quite well, Mr Brigg?", she asked, eyeing the empty bottle of whiskey he had forgotten to hide away.

"Aye, quite well thank you". She took the bottle and made for the door.

"If you say so".

"Mrs Hague, before you go. Has anyone, erm, come to ask for me at the bar?".

"No, were you expecting a visitor?".

"No, just wondering, that's all". She rolled her eyes and turned once again for the door.

"Or letters? Has anyone left a message or a note for me perhaps…?".

"I'm not in the habit of withholding messages from my lodgers, Mr Brigg. My husband and I have been running this public house for over thirty years. I know my trade".

"Yes, *thank you*", he replied in exasperation, shutting the door in her face.

"And leave that tray outside when you've done!", she called

through the wood. Edward declined to answer, but hurried to the food and began to devour it urgently, until then unaware of his ravenous hunger. Once he had eaten, he felt ready to face the letter again.

My dear friend Joseph,

I am writing to you with a heavy heart. I have left the farm as Annie and I have quarreled a lot over the last few months and I fear the situation is beyond repair. Please do not blame Annie, I am a difficult man to live with and I am not used to civilian life. It's entirely my fault and I bear all responsibility. Annie remains at the farm with enough money to pay for farm labour until your return. Of course, I expect no payment due to my early departure.

I have to tell you something, and I ask for forgiveness that I have not told you until now. Annie is with child and the baby is expected quite soon, perhaps in a month or so. She kept this from you as she feared for your business dealings in Whitby, should you have to return to her at short notice. She has worked hard on the farm and as you already know, has made good profits in your absence. I know that as a trusted friend I should have written to you and Tab as soon as I knew, but I was weak and could not go against Annie's wishes. Please know that she did this for you and don't be too hard on her.

I hope we can remain friends in spite of this, you will be able to reach me through my old regiment, the way you always have. I begin the journey back to London tomorrow.

With regret,

Edward Brigg.

He folded the letter and placed it gently in the small envelope, already mourning his life-long friendship with Joseph. He would have to take the letter to the postmaster in Keighley and set three pennies on top of it ready for its charge. To ask Joseph to pay the postage on receipt would only add insult to injury.

~

The following morning, after paying his tab at the Black Bull, Edward set off to the smithy to see Abraham. As he wandered slowly down Main Street, he bid a silent farewell to Haworth – to the moors, the clean air, Joseph's little farm and to Annie.

"Didn't expect to see you here this morning! Thought you'd be busy at the farm?". Edward hovered in the doorway sheepishly, as Abraham clocked the bulging kitbag on his back. "Hang on, what's all this?". Abraham set his blacksmith tongs down in the fire and walked towards him, his brow furrowed.

"I'm off, Abraham. Today".

Abraham laughed and shook his head. "Don't be daft, no you're not". He started to walk back to the fire. "I'm stopping for a brew shortly if you want one?".

"I can't, I have to get off to Keighley. Got to catch the coach for London tomorrow and I need to find lodgings".

"You're serious?".

"Aye. Just stopped in to say goodbye".

Abraham shook his head. "You can't, what about Annie?".

"She's got enough money to pay for help there until Joseph gets back. And there's a surplus of men looking for work, you know that".

"But why? Why aren't you waiting for Joseph to come back?". A look of recognition passed over his face. "Oh. What's she done now?".

"Nothing. It's my fault. A misunderstanding that's all. But it's caused hell of a quarrel and now... I just don't know that I can ever go back".

"Ah don't say that Ed. Not with how close you are to having all this sorted and Tab and Joe on their way back. It can't be beyond repair, surely?".

Edward gave him a tight-lipped smile. "I'm afraid it is. My time here has drawn to a close. If there's any more fighting or stress for her, I think it's going to make her ill. It's best I go".

"Oh".

"It's been great while it lasted though. Great to see you again". Edward extended a hand to Abraham, who swiftly pulled his gloves off and pulled Edward into an embrace.

"It really has Ed. It's been great having you here. Don't forget us when you're back sailing the seven seas and committing acts of true heroism, will you?" Abraham laughed, but his eyes betrayed his sadness at his friend's departure.

"How could I, ey?".

"Look after yourself, won't you?", Abraham said as they released each other and Edward heaved his kitbag back on to his back.

"Always, my friend", reassured Edward, as he walked through the doors of the smithy and towards the moor path. "You too".

~

All was quiet at the farm as Abraham let himself into the cottage. Inside, Annie was sat in the rocking chair next to the fire, which had burnt out to ash the night before. The blankets on Edward's bed looked slept in, twisted about and crumpled as if somebody had been tossing and turning in them all night.

"Annie? Are you alright?", he asked sympathetically. "Edward came to see me this morning, to say goodbye like".

"Mm-hmm", Annie muttered.

"What's going on here? Looks like a cannonball has come through". Abraham looked round at the uncharacteristic mess and disorder.

"Nothing, just haven't got round to tidying up that's all".

Abraham carried the dirty cups over to the wash basin and straightened the blankets on the cot bed. "Looks like you've dropped a bottle of something?", he asked cautiously when he noticed the remnants of the smashed port bottle on the floor.

"Oh just leave it alone please, Abraham", Annie groaned. She turned around in her seat to face him. Her eyes were red and swollen, and her hair lank about her shoulders. "I'll do it later", she insisted.

Abraham huffed but left the housework alone. "Why haven't you got a fire going? Haven't you had a cup of tea today?".

"I just didn't feel like it, alright?".

"Annie, the place is a state. What are you going to do for help around here? Those crops are going to go to seed if you're not careful".

"I've already sorted it. I went out yesterday and arranged for two labourers to come tomorrow. So don't mither me, alright?".

"Have you got enough money for that?".

"Just about. As long as Tab and Joseph get home on time".

Abraham pulled a chair up towards her and sat down, reaching out for her hand. "Annie, this is not good, is it? Joe arranged Edward to come here and help you and now he's hurrying off back to London. What happened the other day?".

"Oh Abraham", Annie lent back in the chair and covered her face with one hand sighing deeply. I did something dreadful".

"Must've been bad to drive him away. He thought the world of you, Annie".

"Doesn't seem like it. Feels like everyone except you and Jenny have abandoned me. First William, then Tab and Joe. Now

Edward too".

"Well, I hardly think you can accuse him of abandoning you, if you yourself say you did something dreadful to him".

She rested her chin on her hands glumly. "This started when I asked him to stay. Made a bloody fool of myself, told him I didn't want him to re-enlist. Told him I had fallen for him".

"Ah". Edward's departure and Annie's heartache began to make sense. "Oh, I'm sorry love. Did he not feel the same?".

"No, it's not that exactly. Just said he couldn't. Couldn't stay here, couldn't marry me, couldn't leave the army. Or wouldn't, I'm not sure which".

"You can't force these things. If it's a no, it's a no, as much as it hurts. Just like with Lottie". Abraham gave her a sympathetic smile but she just stared vacantly. Then it dawned on him.

"'Ere. You two haven't been carrying on, have you?".

"Only once, but once was enough. I just...". She threw her hands up and exasperation. "I just *wanted* him".

He shook his head and sighed. "I really don't think that was a good idea, not in your condition anyway. You're vulnerable Annie, and you knew he was leaving. The two of you should have known better than that". Abraham said disapprovingly as he shook his head. He fetched the brush for the grate and swept out the old ash, then set about building a new fire. "But I would hardly class that as dreadful, would you?".

"That's not the dreadful part. When I got back from the church on Sunday, I was so angry with him for still wanting to leave I just packed all his things in his bag and told him he should go ahead and leave if that's what he wanted". She shook her head in shame. "But I was angry, so humiliated that he turned me down so I just thought – well he can go too. I can manage on my own, you know?".

"Oh Annie, what are you like? Why do you keep doing these things to yourself?".

"In his belongings I found a little envelope and inside was a lock of hair and a wedding ring, so I threw a bottle of port at the wall". Abraham gasped in shock.

"He never was! Married? Good God".

"She's dead though, he's a widower. I was *senseless* with fury and when he told me, I said I didn't believe him. And of course, he was very hurt. I accused him of lying about his dead wife for goodness' sake. And now he's gone".

The flames started to crackle in the grate and Abraham threw a log on top. "I'll boil some tea", he said in resignation. "But that really is an awful thing to do Annie. No matter how hurt you were".

"I know", she groaned. "I feel terrible about it. Worst thing is, I have no address to write to him at. I just want chance to apologise".

"Well, I don't think you should! Some things are best left in the past Annie, you've got your baby to think about now. Sometimes you know, you don't see what you have right in front of you. You've got me and Jennifer. Oh, and a Reverend who is happy to risk his public reputation in order to protect yours. Tab and Joe are coming back any time now, with a fortune in their pockets that you just *know* Joseph will be generous with. So why do you do these things? You've got so many good people around you, but you spend most of the time focusing on the bad".

Annie closed her eyes, savouring the warmth from the new fire. "I know, Abraham, I could kick myself. I've made such a mess of things. I've been so hard on people who have tried to help. And now he's gone, and we didn't even part on a good note".

"You're your own worst enemy, take my word for it". He handed her a hot cup of tea which she balanced on her knee gratefully.

"You don't have to tell me that", she said. "I already know".

"He's gone and now you've got to make the best of things as they are. I can help you, Annie. The labourers start tomorrow which is good. You can't feel sorry for yourself forever, what's done is done". Abraham looked about the place. "Do you want me to help you with some work? Make you something to eat?".

"God no – thank you though. I couldn't even think about eating right now".

"I'm going to lay something out anyway, it's no good for you not to eat in your condition". He cut a piece of the cheese and potato pie that was left on the side and put it on a plate for her, then peeled and sliced up an apple with his pen knife like one would for a child. "Here", he said, thrusting it into her hands. "Eat".

The two sat in comfortable and familiar silence as Annie ate the pie and drank the tea, finding that as she started to eat, her hunger returned, and she felt much better afterwards.

"I've got to get back to Pip – are you going to be alright?".

"Yes, yes. Of course". She dismissed him with a wave of her hand. "Don't worry about me".

"I do, though. Worry about you I mean", Abraham said with a heavy heart. "You're like a sister to me and you've caused me so much strife. It hurts me to see you in distress". Annie didn't reply but only nodded, so Abraham let himself out of the cottage. After hovering for a moment, he felt a strange inclination to look through the window discreetly and catch another glimpse of Annie before he went home. There she was, lying on Edward's bed with her face pressed into his old pillow. Then he walked away, and left her to her grief.

CHAPTER TWENTY-THREE

Annie stood watching the labourers from a distance, not wanting to appear overbearing or meddling. They worked swiftly, they were transient farmhands down from Durham where the terrain and weather could be much harder. Annie had done well to secure them, she had left an advertisement with Mr Hague at The Black Bull, but he already knew of the men and was able to send them up to the farm the same day to arrange the details. The price was relatively high but as she watched them work, she was satisfied they were worth every penny.

What's more, they did not question her about her situation despite her pregnancy being obvious now. They did not press her about personal matters or ask where the master of the farm was – they were just happy for the wage. Only months before Annie would have crumbled under such pressure, but now as she stood near the rows of herbs in the garden, she marvelled at her resilience in spite of her heartache at Edward's departure.

She returned into the cottage feeling a little brighter and set about cleaning it from top to bottom, making the most of her freedom from the responsibilities of the farm. She had been sleeping in Edwards bed since he left, but she felt the time had come to wash the sheets and fold them away upstairs in Tab and Joseph's room. She scrubbed the wooden floors and swept out the grate with a sense of finality, as if it would sweep away memories of Edward. But still, the trunk that lay open and empty at the foot of Edward's bed tormented her. If only she had a chance to say goodbye properly, to ask his forgiveness and wish him well as he waded back in to the cruel wasteland of the war in Europe. Maybe then she would find some respite from matters of the heart.

After lunchtime when her work was almost finished, she felt spent. Since the upset of the other night she had been feeling pains periodically, squeezing across her middle, that made her pause from whatever she was doing. She was certain they were down to her nerves so cast them from her mind, but now they grew more persistent. These couldn't be the pains that Jennifer had warned her about though. They were far too infrequent and mild compared to those from the horror stories she had heard, passed around the women of the village in whispers. Nothing like the agonising screams that flowed from the depths of Tab's soul when she brought Samuel into the world. No, if she went to Jennifer now she would look weak and fearful, an over-anxious first time mother so she gritted her teeth and kept her mind on her work.

As she gathered the dirty sheets from Edward's bed into her arms, she buried her face into them and sniffed deeply, savouring his scent. Annie knew that once she plunged them into the laundry tub with the caustic and powerful household soap, they would never smell like him again. Overcome, she sat on his bed and cradled them, waves of grief and sadness crashing over her. A desperate thought occurred to her but she tried to dismiss it, shaking her head as if the idea could fall right from her mind. The soap was already grated and the water was boiling rapidly ready to fill the wash tub. But still the thought persisted, stopping her from plunging the sheets in.

When does the coach for London leave Keighley?

It was futile. Abraham had already said that Edward would be catching the coach today, and if it hadn't already left, it would be going any time.

Doesn't the coach for Halifax set off at 4 o'clock? To get to London, you have to change at Halifax, don't you...?

She stared at the bubbles breaching the surface of the water in a daze, racking her brains. When Reverend Charnock's son had returned to London after his visit, he had to go to Halifax first – she was certain of it.

Her trance broke and she dashed to the carriage clock on the dresser. It was quarter to two. If she left then, she might just make it to Keighley in time. In her condition, it would take around two hours to walk there, but she had time.

"Damn it", she muttered to herself. "It's worth a shot".

Annie rushed outside and hurriedly told the farmhands that she had urgent business to attend to in Keighley, and would be back much later in the day. They seemed content with this, happy to be left to their work. So with that, she grabbed her shawl and linen cap and set off on the moor path to find Edward.

The sky was overcast that day and the weather was humid. After half an hour or so, Annie found herself wishing that she had stopped for a cup of water before she set off. Her legs were like lead weights in her boots as she trudged onwards into the great expanse of the moor. She stopped to rest momentarily on a large boulder, perching there as another of the pains came. Grimacing, she waited there until the pain had subsided, gripping and pulling at long stalks of grass with all her strength, which seemed to help.

"Annie!". The cry carried easily and clearly to her across the flat moorland, and as she shaded her eyes to get a better look, she recognised Abraham and Pip on the horse and trap, quickly approaching.

"Oh God", she muttered, embarrassed. Annie felt like diving behind the boulder to hide from him, before she realised it was futile, he had already seen her.

"What the bloody hell are you doing out here? Walking to Keighley? What a stupid thing to do".

"How did you know where I was?".

"I've just called at the cottage to see how you were getting on. Two men told me you left in a hurry, saying you had urgent business to attend to?".

"Aye, well I do".

"You're never trying to find Edward, are you?".

"I am, and there is not a thing you can say to stop me Abraham. So don't even try!".

She rose from the boulder with great effort and pressed on, forcing Abraham to trot along behind her.

"Annie, let me take you home. This is *stupid,* he's already gone".

"That coach leaves for Halifax at four. I've got time, but I need to rush".

"Annie, get on this trap now! I'm taking you back".

"Abraham!". She stopped in her tracks to turn and shout at him. "If I don't do this now, I might never have another chance. I just want to apologise and part on a good note. I don't need your permission for that". Pip whined in distress at her outburst.

He persisted, but Annie did not change her mind. Soon, he saw there was no use in begging and badgering her to return to the cottage, so he drew the horse to stop with a frustrated "Whoa there", and pulled Pip closer to him, making room on the bench.

"Well you can't walk all the way. You're already sweating and you'll only have to walk back later. Go on, get on. If you're insisting, I'll have to take you there".

~

"If I've told you once, I've told you a thousand times", huffed the landlord of the Devonshire Arms Coaching Inn. "I 'ant seen him!". He walked away from Annie down the length of the bar and she followed him from the other side, dodging stools and drunkards on the way. "The coach for Halifax left at 2 o'clock – he must have been on that".

"It's four o'clock though? That coach leaves at four", Annie reiterated.

"Not anymore love! Two o'clock that carriage left, and I assume whoever your man is, he was on it. I can't help you, now if you don't mind… buy a drink or sling yer hook!". Annie hovered for a few moments, reluctant to draw her search to a close. "Now!".

"Come on Annie, he's gone. Leave it". Abraham appeared at her elbow.

"And get that bloody *dog* out of here too!". Pip cowered as the landlord pointed at him aggressively. Beaten, the three of them made their way back outside into the light of the summer afternoon.

"So that's it then", Annie said flatly, sitting down on some stone steps to stroke Pip's ears absent-mindedly.

"Look, it was worth a try. We must have just missed him".

Another pain swept over Annie where she sat and she screwed her eyes shut tight. Short puffs of air blew from her mouth as if she were trying to whistle, but there was no sound.

"Are you alright?".

"Aye, my back hurts from walking here I think. That's all".

"Come on, lets get you home". Abraham couldn't bear to see Annie so melancholy and despondent.

Abraham and Annie walked to where his horse and trap where hitched, down the side of the Devonshire Arms. Carriages darted past this way and that and Annie peered into each one as well as she could, hoping to see Edward's face appear in the window, but she was left disappointed.

"Wonder how your two lads are getting on back home?". Abraham untied the horse as Annie mounted, then he and Pip hopped up next to her, Pip nestling between her legs.

"Fine I should expect", she answered, disinterested. She sat with her arms folded, holding herself in a protective embrace as they peeled away down Church Street. Just then, she noticed a man who looked rather familiar, stood leaning on a barrow, his eyes following Annie intently as she passed. She could not place him, no names sprang to mind as she wracked her brains for how she knew him. She turned in her seat to look back at him as they drew further away, and still he stared at her.

"Odd", she muttered.

"What's that?", asked Abraham.

"Oh, nothing", she replied, as they left Keighley behind and with it, Edward.

~

The pounding in Edward's head was unbearable. His eyes were gritty and dry as he peered around the dingy room, just able to make out a few sleeping bodies around him. He sat up with a start. His kitbag was still tied to his ankle where he had secured it the night before. Relieved, he fell back into the pillow and rubbed the sleep from his eyes. From the orange sunset filtering through the shutters, he decided it must be evening time, but where was he? He coughed, a drawn-out spluttering cough that was so forceful it caused him to wretch.

"Shut up will ya?", came a voice from one of the bodies,

huddled under a blanket across the room.

Edward searched around himself for something to soothe his throat, but there was only an empty bottle of brandy lying next to him. He heaved himself up and untied the kitbag from his ankle, then rested his head in his hands, waiting for the room to stop spinning.

Then it came to him, patchy snippets of memories from the day before… the near barrel full of ale he had drunk to wash away the thoughts of Annie, him trying to force coins into the coachman's hand and shouting and posturing when he was denied passage. Then, the sharp crack as the coachman's fist connected with his nose and made his eyes stream. He groaned in realisation. That's why he had ended up in this place, a seedy little boarding house of ill repute. The only place in Keighley with low enough standards to lodge him.

Clumsily, he stepped over the other bodies in the damp bedroom – if one could call it that – and emerged into the hallway. The light was dim, and the place stank of urine and rot.

"Jesus Christ", he muttered to himself as he hung onto the doorframe, trying in vain to maintain his balance. Next door, he could hear a working girl plying her trade, her theatrical shrieks and cries splitting his head in two like an axe.

"Good God, I need a drink". He made his way down the narrow, rickety staircase at the end of the hallway, gingerly holding onto the wall mounted candlesticks, the candle in each one burnt down to a nub and caked in dust. The walls had once been painted a fetching shade of red, but now the damp bubbled up underneath, causing it to flake off in great sheets on to the loose and crumbling steps which threatening to break his ankle at any moment. *Lodging houses were so much better on the continent,* he thought. As he emerged into the bar downstairs, he was confronted by a very angry looking woman in a low-cut bodice and comically heavy make-up, which had settled into the crater like pockmarks underneath.

"I hope you're not going to cause me any bother today!", she shouted. "Or you can bugger off and find yourself somewhere else to sleep". The handful of patrons in the bar barely looked up from their tankards, their shoulders remaining hunched over the empty barrels that served as tables.

Edward recoiled from her shrieks, squinting against the light in the bar.

"This isn't the Devonshire Arms, is it?", he asked, his mouth dry and pasty.

"I think you must be lost", she laughed unkindly. "This is my lodging house, you're on the other side of town". She wandered off back behind the bar and picked up a broom.

"Could I have a pint of ale, I've a terrible thirst". Edward mumbled as he sat down on one of the stools next to the bar. The woman rolled her eyes and dropped the broom against the wall with a flourish. "Anything else my Lord?", she asked sarcastically, as she filled up the grimy tankard.

"No, don't trouble yourself, whatever you do", he replied, placing a few pennies on the bar. She nodded, sweeping the pennies into her apron and returned to brush up a pile of sawdust that was caked with vomit on the floor. Edward took long gulps, the liquid, soothing his burning throat.

"Two more days?".

"I'm sorry?", Edward asked.

"Two. More. Days?", the woman repeated in frustration. "You said last night you wanted two more days, until the next coach comes? I'm not surprised you don't remember, what with the state of you last night".

"Oh, did I say as much?". Edward screwed his eyes shut, the effort of talking made his head pound harder. He dug his hand in his pocket and took out some more coins which he scattered dutifully on the bar. "Is that enough?".

The woman eyed the money and curled her top lip. "It'll do, but don't be expecting much for that price".

Edward gave a short laugh. "My expectations are on the floor as it is, woman".

She ignored his barb, but instead gestured vaguely to her nose. "You might wanna… clean yourself up a bit".

Confused, Edward lifted his pewter tankard up and squinted at his reflection. Dark red dried blood was caked around his mouth and nose. *That would explain the headache,* he thought.

"Don't know what you got up to last night, but you turned up here in a right state". She laughed heartily. "But, if it doesn't happen here, it's none of my business. Looks a right mess though". The woman had finished brushing up and set about sprinkling fresh sawdust on top, most of it landing on Edwards boots, but she paid no mind.

Edward leant across the bar for a dirty cloth that had been left there, stewing in a puddle of sour beer.

"'Ere, you're not using my cloth for that! Sort yourself out you dirty thing!".

"I expect the cloth costs extra", muttered Edward in annoyance as he dug in his pockets for something clean to wipe his face with. To his relief he found a handkerchief and dipped it in his ale to wet it, then rubbed at the dried blood delicately. Then he noticed it – in the corner of the handkerchief there was a small clumsy monogram embroidered in blue thread; A.C., Annie Crossley.

Edward ran his finger delicately over the monogram, his heart pounding. He looked around at the dingy lodgings, and then his kit bag at his feet.

"Ey! What time is it?", he asked the landlady, with sudden urgency.

"Just gone 8 o'clock".

Edward took a deep breath, fighting the urge with all his might. But then he caught another glance at Annie's hanky. He lifted it to his nose once more, inhaling deeply. It still smelt of her, he realised. The same scent that rose from her silky skin and golden hair.

"I... I won't be needing the room tonight", he's spluttered, stuffing the handkerchief deep into his pocket. He wrestled his bag onto his back and drained the last of the ale from his tankard.

"Well, it doesn't work like that! You can't just have your money back!". She rushed over to him threateningly, but Edward was already on his way out.

"Keep your money. I don't care for it", he said, slamming out of the door behind him.

CHAPTER TWENTY-FOUR

The two lads had indeed done good work at the farm whilst Annie was in Keighley. She had been worried on the way home about her naivety, imagining that she may return to a ransacked cottage and her farm equipment stolen, but they had worked admirably and already the farm looked more cared for and orderly. As soon as she arrived back home she thanked them profusely for their work and bid them farewell until the morning.

The later the hour got, the less Annie felt she would be able to sleep and the more restless she became. She had pulled out some baby clothes that she was working on, but was too listless to finish the embroidery on them. Instead, she sat by the fire thinking of Edward and before she knew it the sun had set and the cottage was shrouded in darkness once more. The silence was astounding , no more laughter or chatter or bickering with the strange soldier who had left her life as suddenly and mysteriously as he had entered it. He was gone for good. The pains in her belly had subsided but were replaced by a deep, longing ache in her heart. She felt like she might cry, but the tears never came. Instead, there was just an engulfing numbness inside her.

Just as she had begun to fold the baby clothes back into their cloth bag and ready herself for bed, there came a loud knock at the door. She stiffened, the hour was late and she was not expecting company. There were no neighbours who would call, no one really ventured out to the cottage after dark except the foxes and badgers.

"Who is it?", she called out confidently, hiding her fear.

A gruff and muffled voice replied, "It's me. Let me in, Annie". The knocking continued, louder and more urgent now.

Her mouth dropped open; she was sure it was Edward's voice calling to her from the dark. It wasn't Abraham's – that much she knew, he never called this late. She ran across the room without a second thought and wrenched the door open gleefully, ecstatic that Edward had returned to her.

But it wasn't Edward. Leaning in the doorway was a dishevelled William, reeking of booze. She screeched and made to slam the door shut again, but he had already wedged his foot in the frame. He flung the door open with ease, knocking Annie back onto the floor.

"That's no way to greet an old lover now, is it?", he slurred, striding into her kitchen.

"Get out, William! I don't want you here!". She clambered to her feet and tried to push him through the door, but he was unmovable.

"Just you sit down". He shoved her back onto a kitchen chair and looked at her with utter contempt.

"What the hell are you doing here? If you think you can come here and pick up where we left off, you've got another thing coming!". Annie grabbed the poker from next to the fire and waved it menacingly in his face, but even in his drunken state he wrestled it from her grasp and sent it to the corner of the room with a clatter. He paced around the room, taking in every detail of her modest home.

"God, what a dump this place is. No wonder you were clinging onto me like a limpet, saw a bit of money in it, didn't you?".

"If you don't leave now, I'll start screaming", she threatened.

"Go ahead, Annie. Who will hear you? The cows?". As he laughed he slobbered down his chin in great glistening strands, but was too drunk to notice and wipe them away. Annie had never seen him worse for drink and waves of revulsion rose in her throat.

"What do you want from me? I haven't seen you for months! Why have you come back here at all?".

He leered at her breasts, thinly veiled by her nightdress. "I'm here because of *that*". He advanced on her, holding onto the mantlepiece for support "That right there". He jabbed her belly hard with his finger.

"It's nothing to do with you", she cried, closing her arms over her baby protectively.

"Well, it's got everything to do with me when a friend tells me you're wandering around Keighley fat with child. Searching for me were you, by any chance?".

"No!", Annie gasped, remembering the man who was staring at her intensely from the road side. "I'd be happy to never see you again as long as I lived".

"Oh *give over* Annie!", he shouted, swiping the unlit rush lamp to the floor where is smashed into shards. "You've come searching for your pound of flesh, haven't you? Wanting a few pennies for your little *bastard,* weren't you. Well you won't get them from me!".

Annie was too scared to speak. Her heart raced and her teeth chattered as she held onto the arms of the rocking chair with shaking hands.

"I thought we had fun Annie, while it lasted. And that's all it was to me. You knew I had a wife and children, but you still lifted your skirts up for me, you pathetic little whore".

"I didn't know that!", she insisted, aghast. "I would never have....".

"Oh, shut up!". He shouted so loudly that Annie jumped in her seat violently. It was enough to bring her to her senses and somehow, she managed to leap up and charge for the door. Just as her hand was on the latch, he was behind her, grabbing her by the hair.

"I don't think so", he snarled into her ear, his hot, wet breath making her skin crawl. "I know your type Annie; you'd ruin everything I've got given the chance. Do you seriously think I'm going to stand by and let that happen? Let some simpleton milkmaid rip my life to tatters?". She grappled with his hands trying to free them from her hair.

"William please, I'm *begging* you! You will never hear from me again. I want nothing from you!".

"Do you truly expect me to believe that? Given a couple of months you'll be turning up on my doorstep, bairn in arms, begging for your pittance". She freed herself from his grip and darted to the other side of the great wooden table.

"This baby isn't even yours", she pleaded desperately. "I want nothing from you, not for me or my baby", she insisted.

"Don't talk wet girl, it couldn't be more obvious you'd never had a man before. I barely got any satisfaction from you as it was. And I hardly think you have them queueing up and down the street for a ride!". With that, he cornered her by the dresser and grabbed her firmly by the neck, the veins in his temples throbbing. "No, it's no good – I have to do away with you. I can't risk you running round telling tales to the magistrate, can I?". Even in her distress Annie found the regret in his voice jarring, he spoke as if he were putting an animal out of its misery.

William squeezed harder, lifting her clear off the floor. She writhed and kicked in his grip, gasping for breath as she clawed at his hands.

"Please...", she said, her voice no more than a wheeze, "...stop".

Darkness started to creep in to her vision until she could no longer focus on his red and sweating face. William's voice grew quieter and more distant, drowned out by what sounded like waves crashing in her ears until the hands were suddenly released from her neck, leaving her to drop limp onto the floor. Her throat burned as she coughed and wheezed, fighting for breath. She crawled into the corner of the room cowering, when another voice joined hers and William's in the cottage.

"I'll kill you, you bastard!".

As her vision returned she saw him. Straddling William with his fist raining down on his face repeatedly, Edward was back. A fine mist of blood sprayed into the air as he swung his fist again and again, before he stood up and stamped down with his boot until her attacker's face was unrecognisable and his body lay still. He was swollen and bloody and there was a horrible gargling sound coming from his throat that she could not bear.

Edward stood in shock over William's body, panting from the exertion, until after a few moments of blankness, Annie's screams pulled him back to reality.

"Jesus, Annie!". He rushed over to her and fell to his knees at her side. "Let me see". He lifted her trembling chin delicately with his fingers and peered at the redness around her neck. "It's alright", he soothed, "it's over now". He glanced down at her middle and placed a hand across her belly, biting his lip.

"Are you both alright?".

Her screams dissolved into sobs, wracking her whole body. She reached out for Edward, too shocked to reply, so he lifted her up and carried her into her bedroom away from the sight of William's body on the cold flagstone floor of the kitchen.

"Stay in here my love, don't look at it". He cast a glance over his shoulder at the mess, silently weighing up his options. "I'll sort it all out, don't you worry". She wheezed painfully, struggling to answer him. He traced a delicate finger over her tear-stained cheek. "How *could* he?", he said, his voice cracking at the sight of his battered and disorientated Annie.

Edward returned to the kitchen, leaving Annie cowering on her bed. He nudged William in the side with the toe of his boot, but there was no response. He bent down and held his ear over William's mouth where most of the blood had pooled. There was no warm breath on his cheek, no more gurgling. His hand rested on the man's chest, but there was no heartbeat to be felt.

"Shit", he muttered, rising quickly and sliding the bolt across the cottage door. Edward rushed to the basin of water in Annie's room, rinsing off his hands and splashing his face in the cold water, willing himself to think.

Annie sat on the bed, hugging herself and rocking gently back and forth. "Is he… is he…?".

"Aye, he is". Edward nodded gravely. He took her in his arms and cradled her like a child, kissing her forehead and wiping away her tears gently with his thumb. "I am going to sort all of this out, and you will never have to worry about that brute again, alright?". She nodded, her teeth chattering.

"I can't… I can't look at him".

"You don't have to. I'm going to take him outside while it's still dark, so I can wash the flags down and think it through".

"You can't!", she cried, gripping his elbows and shaking him. "The lads will be back tomorrow and they'll find him. I've got two lads for the farm…". She began to scream once more, and Edward shushed her urgently.

After a few moments, he spoke again. "I need you to do

something for me". He looked her deep in the eyes. "I need you to walk to Abraham's and I need you to fetch him here. Do not let him bring Pip, or his horse, we won't need it. I need you to fetch him *now*, and I need you to hold yourself together while you do it. Alright?".

"But what should I tell him?", Annie clung to Edward like a frightened child.

"Don't tell him anything about this. Tell him one of your cows has gone over and broken its leg. Tell him to hurry and I'll deal with the rest. Got it?". Annie nodded, wide-eyed with fear.

"I can't go through there". She gestured towards the kitchen.

"You can, because I'll walk you through", Edward said, already standing up and reaching for her hand. She took it and followed him trustingly, covering her eyes with her shawl. Edward led her gently around the kitchen table and out through the door into the eerie silence beyond.

"Go", he urged, and Annie took off into the night.

CHAPTER TWENTY-FIVE

Edward rocked gently back and forth in the chair next to the fire. In the corner of his eye he could see William's body lying still on the floor, but his presence didn't trouble him much. No more than if someone had brought in a slaughtered pig for butchering. Who could say how many men he had witnessed leave this life? Hundreds, most likely. There was no guilt in Edward's mind, just the sincere wish he had arrived sooner. His only regret was that his dear sweet Annie had witnessed what he was capable of. It would have been much better had he been able to do this outside, out of sight, he mused. Still, it was over now.

He glanced at the carriage clock on the dresser. Abraham and Annie would be returning any moment, he decided. The possibility of discovery crossed his mind. He would hang for this, there was little doubt, should anyone find out what he had done. The gallows didn't strike fear into his heart as they should have though, his only fear was being taken away from this place without being able to give Annie everything of himself as she deserved. That thought was unbearable.

With a sigh he stood up from the rocker and stretched, his fingers dragging across the ceiling, savouring the pull in his joints. From the pile of dirty laundry in the corner of the cottage he fished out a plain sheet, the same one that Annie had made his bed up with over the summer. He pondered how he could replace it for Tab and Joseph, wracking his brain for a place in Haworth that sold household goods, then laughed at the absurdity of his misplaced concern.

With a flourish, he flicked the sheet out and laid it over the stone flags gently, before rolling William into it and tying the makeshift shroud around him. The blood that had pooled in his mouth seeped through indecently, a crimson reminder of what lay beneath. Edward observed its spread matter-of-factly; all things considered it was a neat job, it would only take a thorough wash of the kitchen before order was restored. Just then, his attention turned to the voices outside, he ran through the speech in his mind once more before stepping out into the night to greet them.

"Jesus, Edward! What's going on here? What's this about a cow...?". Annie cast a worried glance at Edward. "What have I missed...?".

"Abraham. I need to ask a favour of you, I'm afraid". Edward was calm and direct.

"I have a feeling that you're not asking, but telling".

"Aye, that's about the measure of it". Edward pushed the door open and Abraham entered tentatively, before his eyes came to rest on the body bundled up on the kitchen floor. He staggered backwards on unsteady legs, shaking his head in disbelief. He looked away, back out through the door and into the darkness, before looking back into the kitchen as if he expected it to be no more than an apparition or trick of the light.

"My God. What have you done? Who *is* that?".

"It's William". Abraham looked from Edward to Annie, who was once more sobbing uncontrollably, trying to make sense of the scene.

"Did you fetch him here to kill him? Oh Ed... you're going to *hang* for this". He interlocked his fingers behind his head and took a deep breath, trying to calm himself.

"Annie, take that shawl off, show Abraham your neck". Edward maintained his composure.

As she pulled her shawl down and tilted her head upwards, Abraham gasped. There was a bright red mark around her neck where William's hands had gripped her. "He just turned up, out of the blue", she cried.

"I was already on my way back. Caught the bastard in the middle of it, didn't I? What else could I have done, Abraham? What would *you* have done?".

Abraham nodded wordlessly; his eyes transfixed on the shrouded body at Edward's feet.

"And now I need your help. I won't be able to carry him out by myself and I'm not about to ask Annie to do it".

"I understand". Abraham nodded and turned to Annie. "For you, I'll do it".

"You're a good man, I always knew that about you. Go outside and fetch the barrow from the barn, the one that Joseph made. Bring it here to the door and do it quietly. There's slim chance anyone's around but the less disturbance the better". Edward peered through the small window above his old bed, out into the darkness for any signs of movement. "It's now or never. By morning the lads will be back to work on the farm – it has to be tonight".

Dutifully, Abraham scurried away to the barn leaving Edward and Annie alone.

"Go upstairs and sit on Tab's bed until Abraham and I return. We will be some time, perhaps an hour or two". The clock showed quarter to midnight. "But if we are longer Annie, don't come out looking. Understood?".

She nodded timidly and made for the steps, before turning around once more. "Edward, why *did* you come back here?".

His face creased with what looked like pain, the first display of emotion since William had been killed. Tears streamed down over her cheeks as she waited for his reply with bated breath. But as Edward went to speak, the door opened once more and Abraham gestured to the barrow with a nod of his head.

"Upstairs now", Edward urged. "Don't worry about a thing".

~

"These damn rocks", Abraham cursed as he and Edward pushed the wooden barrow, weighed down by William, along the moor path and away from the scattered lights of Haworth village.

"Shut up would you, man. We've to get this done quickly and quietly".

"There's no one here, thank God", Abraham whispered, casting a glance over his shoulder. "Where are we going to leave him?".

"Up by the waterfall should do it", Edward mumbled. "Here, let me take a turn". Pushing the barrow along the uneven ground with such a heavy burden loaded was exhausting, and he was glad he had company.

"Can't see a damn thing out here". Abraham stumbled and fell, landing hard on his knee. "You want to watch you don't go over the edge with him when we get there".

Edward rolled his eyes, "I know what I'm doing, alright?", he mumbled, pushing the barrow with great effort over a clod of rough grass where it had caught. "We're nearly there".

"Don't know why we have to dump him there, it's Pip's favourite place to swim…and Annie's".

"Well luckily Annie will never know. And I'm not sure how sharp you think that dog of yours is, but I doubt he'll work it out either". Edward grit his teeth in annoyance, his hangover had not quite faded yet and the grim events of the evening and subsequent rush of energy had only given him temporary respite from the throb in his head. "Let's just get this over with. I think this is the place".

Abraham took a strike light from his pocket. "'Ere, let me get some light".

"No, we'll have to do without. No light".

He put it back in his pocket reluctantly. "I hope you're grateful the moon is full then".

On the same elevated path where Edward had first seen Annie undressed, the pair lifted William's body out, sending the barrow over with a clatter that echoed across the moor.

"If we throw him over and down onto the rocks below, they'll think he's fallen over drunk and caved his head in, alright?". Abraham nodded along seriously.

"Right, on the count of three, let's swing him over the edge then".

"Abraham". Edward dropped William's legs to the ground. "How many men fall to their deaths already in a shroud?".

"Oh Christ. Of course", he muttered in embarrassment and set about untying the sheet with shaking hands. "I wasn't thinking".

"It's alright. Just get it off".

Once the body had rolled out, Abraham caught his first glance of the bloody and mangled mess that had been shielded from him until then.

"Are you alright?", Edward asked. But Abraham had already darted away from the scene and was leaning over a nearby clump of heather, vomiting. He felt pity for him then, remembering his first time. It was a dreadful feeling – one that changed you forever – but there had been so many since, that it had very little effect on Edward at all. Even the metallic stench didn't trouble him. "I'll push him, you stay there".

Edward rolled the body over until it hung on the precipice, then placed his boot on it, steadying himself. With one kick William was over, landing with a sickening thud on the rocks below. "It's done", he confirmed, peering after him. "That will have to do".

Abraham staggered back, his pale face illuminated in the moonlight. He knelt down to gather the discarded sheet but gagged again once the foul stink of the blood reached him.

"Leave it, I'll get it", Edward assured him, stuffing it into the barrow. "You've not dropped anything, have you?". Abraham patted his pockets and duly shook his head. "Then it's over. We were never here, alright? We never saw him. He was drunk, wandering on the moors late and he fell. That's all anyone will think. Not that anyone will miss him, hateful bastard that he was".

"Aye, we were never here. I never saw you tonight".

"It's time to go back now, Abraham. We must never speak about this again, agreed?".

"Agreed".

CHAPTER TWENTY-SIX

Annie was still upstairs in Tab and Joseph's bedroom when Edward returned to the cottage, after he and Abraham had gone their separate ways at the edge of the moor. As soon as he placed his foot on the first step to go up to her, he thought of the mess on the kitchen floor and decided against it. He didn't want Annie to come back down and see it again; her distress at seeing William's body was troubling enough. He took a bucket from by the door and went across the yard to the water pump instead, hoping she stayed upstairs long enough for him to restore order downstairs.

He washed down the flags and scrubbed the legs of the table and chairs where little red droplets had settled. Once he was satisfied, he stoked the fire and threw the soiled sheet onto the flames. The sheet was damp from where it had lain on the grass in the dew causing it to smoke profusely; Edward became frustrated when it didn't burn up quickly. As he nudged it with the poker, Annie emerged on the stairs.

"Is he gone?". She twisted her shawl in her hands and glanced around the room, as if he might jump out from a trunk or behind a door.

"You will never have to fear that man again", Edward replied earnestly. She eyed the sheet smouldering on the fire and came down into the kitchen tentatively. On her hands and knees, she searched for any evidence of what had happened across the floor and furniture but found none. "I've sent Abraham home... We never saw him tonight, alright? I came back here from Keighley late on and we didn't see anybody else around".

"No, no. Of course". Annie held onto the edge of the table and hauled herself to her feet. "Thank God you were here Edward. You saved my life tonight. You should have seen him – he wouldn't have stopped until he killed me".

Edward looked away finding Annie's distress unbearable. "I did see him and I know he wouldn't have".

"I came to Keighley looking for you. Someone must've seen me and told William about the baby. I think a man was watching me, I noticed him at the side of the road".

Edward hung his head. "This is all my fault. You should've been at home, safe and sound. But instead you were chasing me across Yorkshire". He hung the fire poker back up on its stand, dejected. "I should never have left you here Annie, I shall never forgive myself. God, if I'd have lost you as well...!".

She reached out and gently took his hand in hers, "But you haven't lost me! I'm still here, thanks to you. I was praying for you to come back, as soon as I saw him I *prayed* for you. And then there you were Edward".

"Not soon enough though".

Just then, she felt the familiar squeeze across her middle once more. They had been coming quicker while Edward was out over the moor, this one being so strong it caused her to fall into the rocking chair and cry out.

Edward dropped to his knees in front of her and stroked her furrowed brow.

"Annie, what is it? Is it the baby?".

She remained silent, for another few moments, her eyes

screwed shut with concentration. "It can't be", she said through gritted teeth. "It's too soon I'm sure of it".

"Should I fetch Jennifer? You've had a terrible shock tonight. That can make a baby come early".

The tension released from her body in an instant and she opened her eyes once more. "No, they just come now and again, and then I'm fine. It's the shock, nothing more".

"You need sweet tea". Edward jumped to his feet and set about boiling water over the fire, the tattered remains of William's blood-soaked shroud reduced to ash. As he busied himself, Annie chewed her nails in nervous anticipation.

"Edward, I need to ask you something".

"Anything. What is it?". Edward looked her in the eye with deep intensity as he spooned tea into the pot, sending little black shreds all over the table where they spilled from the spoon through his inattentiveness.

"Why did you come back?".

He hesitated, wrestling with the urge to escape his vulnerability, to run away from her questioning. "I just... I just knew you needed me".

"Just for that".

"I don't mean just tonight – because of William, like. I mean, I know you *need* me. And I need you. I realised that...". Edward shifted from foot to foot, fidgeting in discomfort. "I can't be apart from you Annie". He avoided looking at her again; his cheeks flushed and he was embarrassed by the creeping warmth in his face as it betrayed him. Annie's heart pounded as she listened to Edward's confession. It was all she had dreamed of and wished for these past lonely nights – but still she was careful. His earlier rejection had stung her beyond imagination.

"I thought I would never love again", he continued. "Not after

Bridget. Now I realise how bloody stupid I've been in leaving. I've really fallen for you Annie, I've fallen *in love* with you and I cannot bear to be apart from you for another moment".

"Edward, I'm so sorry for what I said about Bridget".

"Oh, please don't. That *stupid bloody* argument, I could kick myself. I was so pig-headed and ignorant to run away like that". He poured boiling water into the pot and sighed deeply. "I didn't treat you well enough when I was here. And I should've told you about her. I shouldn't have let you find the ring, not after what you've been through. That was wrong of me".

Wordlessly, Annie rose from the chair and crossed the kitchen to him. She cradled his face in her hands, and once more drank in his masculine scent. Their lips gently brushed and she could feel his ragged breath on her mouth and chin as his heart thumped through his chest, before they gave themselves to one another in a deep, lingering kiss. He wrapped his arms around her and squeezed tightly, never wanting to let her go.

"I nearly lost you tonight. I *cannot* lose you again". He pressed his forehead to hers, awaiting her answer.

"Then don't", she whispered, so close their lips were almost touching. "Never let me go Edward". They stayed in each other's embrace for a few minutes, savouring the relief of having one another to hold. Edward cherished the feel of her warm breath on his neck, before she pulled away from him, gasping. Another pain emerged, sweeping over her back.

"I'm sorry Edward; I must go to bed. I fear I am not well at all".

"Of course my love, you should rest", Edward replied, "I'll bring the tea in for you just now".

CHAPTER TWENTY-SEVEN

The next morning, Edward awoke to a shrill scream. His eyes shot open, the cottage was bright with sun streaming through the window. He had slept in late after the activities of the previous night.

"Bloody hell", he muttered, throwing off the blankets and dashing into Annie's room.

"Annie, what is it? What's the matter?".

Annie was doubled over, crouched on the floor with her arms leaning on the bed. She looked over her shoulder at him, her face was red and sweaty and her hair stuck to her forehead in strands.

"Please!", she wailed. "Please, I need Jennifer!".

Edward was frozen momentarily, "Is it…?".

"Yes!", she screamed. "The baby is coming *now*. Please, Edward – hurry".

He skidded back through to the kitchen and pulled his boots on, just tucking the laces in – he had no time to tie them. He grabbed his cap from the hatstand, and in his haste to leave he brought the whole thing down, which landed with a crash on the stone floor. As he ran through the gardens, he cursed himself for forgetting to check the clock. Where would Jennifer be? At home, or at the parsonage? To his relief, Saint Michael's chimed half past eight, so he knew he would be best looking for her at work. He had no idea how long Annie had been awake and suffering for and felt terribly guilty for sleeping late. He wished she had woken him so he could have sat up with her, stroked her hair and mopped her brow. All the things he never had chance to do with Bridget. He had not noticed the labourers working on the farm as he bolted, but they watched him curiously running off the land and towards the church, with no jacket and untucked shirt trailing behind him in the breeze.

He hammered on the door to the scullery kitchen, but after receiving no reply, he let himself in and began shouting for Jennifer in a panicked frenzy. She came shuffling down from upstairs, her face stricken with worry.

"Edward? I thought you were back in London... whatever's the matter?".

"It's Annie", he said breathlessly, "come at once. The baby, it's coming, *now*".

"Oh good God". Jennifer opened the towering built-in cupboard next to the fireplace in the kitchen and pulled out her midwifery bag. She thrust it into Edwards chest and grabbed her bonnet and shawl from the back of the chair. "Go!", she ordered. "Take my bag on up ahead. I'll just tell the Reverend and then I'll follow on".

"Jennifer, *please* don't dawdle... I don't know how long she's got left".

"Probably longer than you think for a first baby, but don't fret, I'm coming. Just go back there and wait for me".

Edward didn't need to be told twice, he left her there in the kitchen and made for the cottage once more. He still didn't have the stamina to run all the way, so he walked with great long strides, urging himself to stay calm. He didn't want her to be alone at the cottage for too long, she looked like she was in great pain, and he couldn't bear the thought of her suffering by herself.

As he approached the front door, he could already hear Annie's groans pouring from the cottage and into the garden beyond. He threw Jennifer's bag down on the table and dashed through into her bedroom.

"Where is she?", she shouted through gritted teeth. "Lord, please tell me you found her. I *cannot* have you deliver this baby, Edward Brigg". Another wave of pain swept over her, and she bit down hard on the blanket on her bed, stifling her cries.

Edward grabbed her hand, it was wet with sweat. "Hold my hand as hard as you need to", he instructed. "Give it a good squeeze if you like". Annie did and it felt as though he had caught his hand in a vice. "That's it, good girl. Jennifer is coming, she won't be long, she's only at the parsonage. You're doing really well".

Edward had heard babies being born on camp before, it was terribly grim to listen to the women in pain. But after that, when one of the other wives would come to tell a new father the happy news, Edward always felt overjoyed. They would share a smoke and a brandy, if they had it, and would bask in shared pride with their fellow soldier. He reminded himself insistently that this wasn't *his* baby, that he wasn't about to become a father – but the pride and excitement in his heart told him otherwise.

"Edward, I can't do this… please, make it stop!", Annie cried.

"Yes, you can. You can do anything you set your mind to girl. If there's anyone who can do it, it's you".

Annie only wailed in reply, while Edward dipped a square of cloth in the basin and dabbed at Annie's clammy forehead.

Before long the cottage door flew open, and Jennifer rushed into the bedroom. "It's alright! It's alright", she soothed. "I'm here now".

Edward backed away from Annie to give Jennifer space and stood loitering in the doorway of the bedroom. "Pass me that bag". Jennifer instructed, and Edward did so dutifully, grateful for the opportunity to be useful.

As Jennifer began to undo Annie's skirts, she noticed him still hovering. "Go! Go outside, I'll fetch you when it's over".

Edward didn't move for a few moments, reluctant to leave, but he knew he should give Annie her dignity. He wandered outside onto the farm, her cries still drifting over to him, even as he tried to escape them.

He meandered over to the cowshed, where he found the two farmhands readying the cows for meadow. He watched them in confusion for a few moments before remembering that Annie had brought in outside help in his absence. There was another stab of guilt in his heart.

"'Ere, what's going on in the house? We didn't want to intrude like, but we were a bit worried...", one of the men asked as Edward greeted them with a nod.

"Oh, Mrs Crossley is having her baby. Midwife is with her now". He couldn't bring himself to call her Miss. He wasn't sure how much the farmhands knew about Annie's situation and he felt fiercely protective of her privacy. As he had already seen, folk could be very cruel.

"Right so! Many congratulations, my man", the two men both rubbed their hands vigorously on their breeches and proffered them to Edward.

"Is this your first?", the other one asked. "I remember my first. I was white as a sheet, much like you are my friend". The two men left good-naturedly.

It took Edward a moment to understand, but once he

did, he did not correct them. He simply beamed at the misunderstanding.

"Aye, my first". He said with great pride. "Glad I'm not the only one who's shaking in my shoes".

The first man spoke again. "The women told me to go to the pub, but I couldn't bear to. I waited downstairs the whole time, listening out for her just in case. It gets easier after the first though. By the time the second comes, you'll be a dab hand!".

Edward laughed. "I hope so", he said. "I'll be well practiced by then".

"Oh aye, you'll be grand. Women know what to do, just keep yourself busy until the good news comes. You'll have a healthy bairn before you know it".

Edward thanked the men and left the barn, searching for some work to do to while away the hours. He didn't know how long it would be until the baby arrived, but he hoped it would be over quickly, for Annie's sake. He scattered grain for the chickens and then set off to mend the fence on the far side of the meadow, away from the cottage. He spent most of this time gazing over the moors though, in quiet contemplation. How strange life was, he thought, and how utterly unpredictable.

He felt better where he was not able to hear Annie's pain. He found it easy to handle when it was the men on the battlefield – he could be useful there. He knew what they needed, knew how to help. But not here, not for women in childbirth. Knowing that he was powerless to do anything to relieve her suffering was what hurt him most. He praised God for Jennifer, comforted to know she was there alongside her.

~

Throughout the afternoon, Edward achieved very little in the way of work. He had spent most of the time daydreaming and dithering, his nervous excitement mounting. Finally, by mid-afternoon, he saw Jennifer walking over to him, and he ran to greet her.

"Well? Is Annie well? Is the baby here?".

"She did beautifully". Jennifer smiled. The old woman looked worn out, having been with Annie most of the day.

"And...?", Edward persisted.

"A baby girl, a big one too! It went smoothly and they're both grand".

Edward almost collapsed with relief. "A baby girl", he gasped. "It's perfect. Has she chosen a name?".

"That's not for me to tell you, is it?", Jennifer replied with a wink. "You'll have to ask her yourself". Edward began marching towards the cottage eagerly, desperate to hold Annie again, to hear it from her own lips that she was alright.

"Excuse me!", Jennifer cried. "Where do you think you're going?". She stood firm with her hands on her hips.

"I want to see her. I want to see the baby".

"I don't think so Edward, not yet anyway! Baby's only been here five minutes. Annie needs some time to get sorted out. I've just popped over to tell you, that's all. You see yourself off down the Black Bull, looks like you need a drink". She smiled. "I'm so glad to see you back, I *really* am. And so is Annie".

"When might I come back, then? How long do you need?".

"Just give it a few hours, let me settle her in. I'll stay with her until you return".

"Right so... I'll see you later then", Edward replied with good natured frustration. He set off for the pub feeling like he was walking on air.

"Edward!", Jennifer called after him. "You might want to go

and tell Abraham the good news, ey?".

"I'll do that now", Edward nodded enthusiastically. "I'll do that right now".

CHAPTER TWENTY-EIGHT

That afternoon felt like the longest of Edward's life. He had gone to share the good news with Abraham at his forge, who was initially surprised, but ultimately as delighted as Edward and Jennifer. The birth of Annie's baby was a welcome distraction from the terrible secret that hung unspoken between the three friends. Edward had invited Abraham to The Black Bull to wet the baby's head, but he was somewhat behind on his work and had to decline.

"I won't rush over – I'm sure Annie needs a bit of time to herself, poor girl. You give her my love in the meantime, won't you. I'll be over in a day or two though", he'd said.

Edward sat in the Black Bull for what felt like days, but really he had only drunk two pints of ale before he became too restless and had to move on again. He wanted to share the happy news with everyone he passed but reminded himself again and again that wasn't *his* baby and it was not for him to share the news. He thought it strange how he could forget that this was William's baby and surprised himself how much he felt like a proud new father. It was only natural, he assured himself, after watching her blossom and grow over the months and loving her the way he did.

He left the Black Bull and crossed Main Street to the apothecary. Even in his youth, he had never ventured in there.

There was never any money to spare for such frivolities at home and even back then, his mother had relied on Jennifer for any remedies she might have needed for the children or herself, like many others in the village.

As he opened the door a large bell sounded, and a middle-aged woman with a moon-like smiling face appeared from the back of the shop. Floor to ceiling cabinets towered over Edward, laden with all sorts of medications and toiletries. He greeted the woman with a nod, and then stood awkwardly before a cabinet that groaned with delicate items intended for the finer ladies of Haworth.

"Something in particular you're looking for?", she asked in a singsong voice.

"Aye, I am. Do you happen to sell lavender soap?". He didn't turn around but continued to scan the vast array of soaps stacked in the cabinet. He picked one up and sniffed cautiously, struck by the idea of the delicate scent flowing from Annie's skin.

"Oh yes, we have all sorts here. I'm certain lavender is among them. Is it for yourself, sir?". She regarded him with amusement.

"No. For a friend".

"Is he particularly fond of lavender?".

"A *lady* friend", he confirmed, bemused by the suggestion.

"Ah!". She winked at him. "A sweetheart, is it?". She came round to the front of the counter and swished over to Edward, her wide skirts almost knocking over a pile of boxes on the floor.

"These are very fine indeed. Ladies always appreciate receiving them, they make for a thoughtful gift". She laid before him a set of three delicate lavender soaps, nestled in tissue paper inside a decorative box. "She can use these for her ablutions, or leave them in draw with her shifts and nightdresses. They leave a pleasant scent on the garments, you see".

Edward nodded. "I'll take them. They will do nicely".

"Right you are", she said brightly, carrying them over to the counter. Edward paused and gestured to some intricate glass bottles on a high shelf.

"What are these?".

"They are toilette waters. Although I must warn you, they are a quite a bit more expensive than the soaps".

"It doesn't matter", Edward said, aloof. He was enchanted by them, with their intricate designs and beautiful letterings. "Would one of these please her, do you think?".

"Oh absolutely. The quality is very fine and the scent is refreshing. I'm sure any lady would be delighted to receive one from a suitor".

"Which one would you recommend? It has to be special mind".

The woman hemmed and hawed as she joined Edward once again at his side. After a few moments, she lifted a bottle from the shelf and unscrewed the lid.

"Try this one".

Edward sniffed cautiously. The scent was perfect. Light, blossoming honeysuckle – it would smell divine on Annie's neck.

"Yes, I'll have that as well, please".

"Gosh, you really are trying to charm her aren't you?".

"Seems so doesn't it", he replied with a grin.

The woman wrapped the items in paper and tied them with a lace ribbon and Edward gladly paid for them. As he walked to the door, she followed him and turned the 'open' sign that hung in the door to 'closed'. On the doorstep, he halted.

"Before I leave – do you have the time?".

"Yes it's almost five o'clock, I'm just closing now".

He thanked her and decided it had been long enough for Jennifer to attend to Annie and the new baby girl. As he walked back to the cottage he was so excited he wanted to break into a run, but instead, he savoured the sunshine on his back and the sweet scent of hay in the air. He looked down at the packet in his hand and thanked the Lord he was still here in Haworth, bringing gifts to Annie after her successful delivery, instead of back in the great grey stink of London.

~

As he walked up the front path, Jennifer was outside throwing a bundle onto a fire in the yard, and she turned to greet him.

"Just in time", she said. "I've finished tidying up inside. You can go on in now", she said with a smile.

There were butterflies in Edward stomach as he opened the door and let himself in. He did not call out for her, not wanting to break the serene atmosphere in the cottage, but instead left the gifts on the dresser and knocked gently on the bedroom door.

"Annie", he whispered. "Can I come in?".

"Of course", came the reply from behind the door.

Edward pushed the door open and was greeted by Annie sat up in bed, cradling her newborn baby. He tried to congratulate her, to ask her how she was and fuss over her achievement, but he couldn't find the words. Instead he stood there, mouth agape, astounded by her beauty.

"This is Bridget", she said, carefully holding up the bundle for him to look at.

A lump rose in Edward's throat. He swallowed against it, ordering it to disappear, but it persisted.

"Bridget?", he asked, his voice cracking with emotion.

"Aye", Annie replied. "Bridget Tabitha Crossley".

Edward stared down at Bridget's angelic face. Her eyes were closed and her clenched fist rested on her cheek as if she were deep in thought.

"She's perfect", he breathed, tears welling in his eyes. "She's absolutely perfect. Just like you Annie".

"Thank you", Annie whispered sincerely. "I didn't think it would feel like this", she continued, gazing at her infant in amazement.

"It's not as you expected?".

"I just didn't expect to love her so much. I'm so *in love* with her, Edward. So much so, it hurts".

"I don't doubt it. She's a truly wonderful little creature, isn't she?". He sat down carefully on the bed at her feet. "And how are you? How are you feeling?".

"Quite well", she said. "A bit sore, but I'm quite well. Jennifer said it was a good one. An *easy one*, she called it. Although I wouldn't agree", she laughed.

"I knew you could do it". He reached out and stroked her hand as she held Bridget close.

"Do you want to take her?".

Edward tried to protest. "I'm not sure I know how; I don't want to upset her. She looks so peaceful there with you".

"Don't be daft", Annie giggled. She held the bundle out towards him expectantly and he took it from her with great care. Bridget fussed a little at the transition, but as soon as

Edward held her close in his strong arms, she settled once more. Edward stroked her rosy cheeks gingerly with his fingertip as a single tear fell from his chin and was soaked up instantly by her blanket. He stayed like that for a few minutes, listening to Bridget breathe and feeling an overwhelming love well up in his chest.

"I haven't held many babies", he said.

"You wouldn't know", Annie reassured him. Seeing him cradle her precious daughter with such tenderness made her heart sing.

"I've got something for you", he said, passing Bridget back to Annie. "Just wait there a moment and I'll fetch them".

He brought the parcel from the dresser through into the bedroom and laid them on the blankets next to Annie. She placed the baby down on her lap and opened them with much anticipation.

"Oh, Edward – thank you! You shouldn't have". She leant down and inhaled the scent of the lavender soaps. "They're lovely. Lavender, it's my favourite.".

"Aye, well I thought when you're up to it, I could do a bath for you if you like? When Jennifer says it's alright, of course. Then you can use your soaps.".

"I'd like that very much," she said, nodding. As she opened the bottle of toilette water, she gasped.

"This must've cost you King's ransom!".

"Never you mind that", he said dismissively. "I wanted you to have it. You deserve it more than anyone. You deserve everything".

Annie took his hand and pulled him towards her, kissing him deeply. Edward's stomach turned over with the thrill of kissing her once more, he was so happy that he felt drunk.

"So am I to understand you are staying here?", she asked.

"Forever", he replied. "I'm not leaving you again Annie, or Bridget. I couldn't bear to be apart from you another minute". She closed her eyes in relief and kissed him once more, a long, lingering kiss that said everything she wanted to, but couldn't find the words to express.

"You must rest now. You'll be exhausted". Edward said once their lips had parted again. "I'll go through and talk to Jennifer. You just lie down and close your eyes".

"Thank you", she muttered with a yawn. "I may just sleep for an hour or so". He lifted Bridget from the bed and placed her in the cradle nearby, then arranged the blankets over Annie and kissed her delicately on the forehead before he left the room.

"Sleep well my darling. I'll be back to you shortly".

~

"Bonny little thing isn't she?", Jennifer giggled as Edward came back outside.

"She is that. Absolutely beautiful, just like her mother".

"So that's you back then, is it?", Jennifer asked with a knowing smile. "Didn't think you two could be apart for long".

Edward nodded. "Now I've just to deal with Tab and Joe, I suppose", he mused. "I wrote to them, you know. To tell them about Annie, when I left".

"I thought you might have done".

"Strange that we've heard nothing back though".

"Wonder if they received it?". Jennifer squinted into the low orange sunlight. "Do you know, the postmaster *is* unreliable. Sometimes the Reverend gets letters weeks after they're sent. He plays hell about it".

"Maybe not, or maybe they'll be on their way back. The sale must be complete now, they'd be due back anyway".

"I'm sure Annie is relieved not having to face it alone". Jennifer rubbed Edwards arm, affectionately. "Either Tab or motherhood".

"I couldn't bear to be anywhere else", Edward replied as he looked out across the farmland and over to the moors. "I hope to never be away from this place again".

"Anyway, I better be getting home", Jennifer said, as she prodded the last of childbed waste on the fire.

"What? Are you going?".

Jennifer laughed heartily. "Aye, that's it now lad, you're on your own! Night'll be drawing in soon anyway and she's comfortable. I'll be back first thing in the morning to see to her, but until then – they've got you, haven't they?".

Edward took Jennifer in a tight embrace, "Thank you", he whispered. "For everything over these last few months. My mother would be so grateful to you for what you've done for me".

"Wouldn't have missed it for the world", she replied, squeezing him back.

~

Annie spent some of the evening sleeping, but by eight o'clock, she was awoken by Bridget's cries for milk. She leant over to pick her up from the cradle, wincing in discomfort, before lifting her to her breast, just as Jennifer had showed her. Hearing the baby was awake, Edward burst into the bedroom, worried whether Annie would be able to reach her without straining. He was momentarily embarrassed to find Annie feeding her and apologised.

"Oh, sorry. I should've knocked". He made to exit the room,

but Annie called him back.

"It's fine!", she chuckled. "I don't mind. It's nothing to be embarrassed about".

"No, I suppose not", he agreed. "Did you manage to sleep?".

"I did thank you. I feel a bit better for it too".

Annie shifted in the bed. Her back ached from being laid down on the hard mattress all day. "I find myself hungry", she said, looking at Edward in anticipation.

"There's plenty of food", Edward assured her. "I've got a lovely fire going and I've made up the bed in the main room. I was wondering if you wanted to move into there? Then you can have the fire and it will be more comfortable. I can sit in there and talk to you, too – instead of you being cooped up in here alone". Edward looked almost embarrassed at his insistence. She nodded, sleepily.

"Would you like a bowl of hot water and one of your soaps fetching? You might feel better for freshening up", he suggested.

Annie basked in his attentiveness. "I'd love that, thank you". She stayed in the bed, feeding Bridget, while Edward hurried about bringing a warm basin and a cloth for her, and took one of her lavender soaps out of its delicate paper packaging.

"I'll drag the cradle through, shall I?". He left her to finish feeding and set up the bed under the window where he had spent the summer, borrowing blankets from upstairs in Tab and Joseph's room. He drew up the rocking chair next to it, but then pulled it away again, feeling it might be too overbearing to sit so close to her, even though what he really wanted to do was climb into the bed next to her and hold her tightly.

"Edward?", she called to him. "Can you take her while I have a wash?".

"Of course, whatever you need". Cradling Bridget in the

kitchen by the fire while Annie had a wash felt surreal. He couldn't remember the last time he felt so calm and serene, so *happy*.

~

Annie took her time washing herself and brushing her hair. When she emerged from the bedroom again, she looked angelic. She had a glow about her, despite feeling so delicate she still looked radiant with her golden hair swept into a plait and a fresh nightdress on. She sighed when she saw Edward holding her daughter, gazing down at her with love.

"Feel better?". Edward looked up at her with tenderness and affection.

"Much, thank you", she said. She made her way over to the kitchen for some food, but quickly, Edward returned Bridget to her cradle and insisted Annie get into the bed.

"I'll bring you something to eat", he assured her. With relief, she crawled under the blankets that still smelt of her sister and rested her weary body.

"You look beautiful", he told her, as he sliced bacon for the frying pan. "You always do, but tonight, there's something special about you".

"You're flattering me". She smiled to him across the room. She lay her head back on to the pillow and breathed deeply, savouring her first evening as a mother. Throughout the last nine months, she could never have imagined that things would end so perfectly for her.

"Don't fall asleep", he whispered to her. "Your supper will be ready just now. I hope you like eggs and bacon. There's some bread here too…".

She rolled on to her side and propped herself up on her elbow. "Can't wait".

"You won't have to suffer my food much longer, Jennifer is back tomorrow, she said she would bring some things for you to eat that are good for your recovery".

Annie made a face, playfully. "That means liver, knowing Jenny". Edward laughed as he plated up her food and brought it to her, balancing it on her lap.

She looked down at it gratefully, then gestured to the rocking chair. "Bring that closer and sit with me, won't you?", she asked him. Edward obliged with a smile. As she ate her supper, he watched over her and Bridget protectively, soaking up the warm, loving atmosphere in the cottage.

Annie laughed. "Do I have something on my face?", she asked. "You're looking at me very intently…".

"There's just one last thing on my mind", he replied.

She looked at him with wide eyes while she chewed, "what's that?".

Edward dropped to one knee in front of her as she sat propped up on the bed. "Annie Crossley… will you marry me?".

CHAPTER TWENTY-NINE

The first few days of Bridget's life passed in a joyful blur for Annie and Edward. They had begun to believe that their lives would forever be that way, just the three of them on the isolated farm in a bubble of pure bliss. Annie was recovering well and spent her time tending to her baby and doing small jobs around the cottage, while Edward joined the two labourers, making the most of their help to prepare the farm for Tab and Joseph's imminent return. Jennifer visited each day to check on Annie, making sure she was feeding well and was healing properly. She was very happy with Annie's progress and let her know as much, assuring her she was a natural mother.

On the fourth afternoon after the birth, as Annie and Jennifer sat in the kitchen while Bridget fed and Edward worked on the farm, a carriage rolled up the lane and stopped at the bottom of the winding garden path. Edward straightened up and shielded the sun from his eyes, straining to see who it was. The carriage was laden with a trunk and several cloth bags and was driven by a man that Edward did not recognise. It was a fine carriage, the type you could hire privately to take you off the usual transit routes, but Edward could not think of anyone they knew who could afford such a thing.

As he stared, the driver hopped down and opened the door, holding his hand out for the lady who emerged. It was Tabitha, followed by Joseph. They had finally returned.

Anxiety rose in Edward's chest, he looked quickly over to the cottage, unsure if they had received his letter. He thought about running inside and warning Annie, but it was too late, Tab was already rushing over to him, holding her bonnet to her head as the ties fluttered behind her.

"Edward! We thought you had left?". He shook his head, unsure how to explain himself.

"A... a misunderstanding", he stuttered. "You received my letter then...?".

Tab's eyes darted to the cottage. "Is she in there?". She didn't wait for a reply, but ran across the herb garden and off into the cottage, leaving Joseph trailing behind. Edward steadied himself, waiting for the wrath of Annie's brother-in-law – his life-long friend, but as he approached, he could see instead that Joseph was smiling.

"Edward. We got your letter just yesterday morning. But I see we needn't have rushed back... what happened to London?".

"A change of heart", he said, vaguely. "Anyway Joseph, about Annie...".

"I know. Tab's been breaking her heart over it. She's so upset she didn't notice before we left. Wracked with guilt the poor woman, worried sick".

"I'm so sorry, I should have written straight away. Annie was so worried you would come back and it would ruin things for you over there, and...".

Joseph held a hand up to silence him. "We would never have left you here if we had known, I hope you know that. Not you *or* Annie. *Never*".

"Of course. Although, things have a way of working out". Edward stood awkwardly in front of Joseph, unsure how to tell him that his niece already awaited him inside. "Perhaps you need a cup of tea. It's not an easy journey down from Whitby, even when you travel in the lap of luxury". Joseph punched him in the arm, playfully and began to walk up the path.

As the door opened, Edward and Joseph were greeted by a sobbing Tab, cradling Bridget in her arms.

"Oh, Joseph. Just *look* at her". The baby juddered in her arms as she shook, overcome by the news.

Joseph looked puzzled. For a moment, he failed to understand that Annie had already had her baby. He looked around for a friend of Annie's or Jennifer's, someone who had brought their baby to show off to the women, and he had just happened to walk into the middle of a visit.

"This is Bridget", Annie said, pulling the blanket down further so Joseph could admire her face. "My daughter".

"Good God", Joseph whispered, walking around the table carefully to join Tab where she sat. "I don't believe it. I can't…".

"She's beautiful, isn't she". Tab looked up at him with wet eyes, joy mixed with grief for the memories of her Samuel. "It's so *good* to hold a baby again". She held Bridget close to her and squeezed her eyes shut. "I never want to let her go". Annie stroked her arm affectionately.

"I'm so sorry I didn't say anything", she said.

"I should have known! I'm your sister, I should have realised. I can't believe you've been here all on your own, suffering – and me not knowing!".

"Well, I haven't been alone really, have I?". She looked over to Edward, smiling expectantly. "I've had Edward here with me".

"Thank God for that", Tab added. "We really are grateful you know Edward. For everything. And to you Jennifer, for sorting her out". Jennifer cocked her head and smiled at the scene, finally able to put her worries to bed.

"And what of... of the father?". Joseph found it excruciating to ask Annie such a personal question.

"It's William. But I haven't seen him for months, not since before you left. I think he worked it out and... disappeared". She glanced at Edward, but he looked down at his shoes, avoiding her gaze.

"We'll be alright the four of us". Tab held Annie's face in her hand affectionately. Me and Joseph and you and Bridget. We'll muddle along quite fine without him".

"About that", Annie said. "I have something else to tell you". Edward took her hand in his and squeezed, nodding for her to continue. "Edward and I are getting married".

The kitchen erupted in gasps and friendly cheers, even Jennifer was astounded.

"You never mentioned anything, you sly fox!", she teased, slapping Edward's legs in jest.

"We wanted to save it until Tab and Joe got back", Annie laughed. "We thought it would be nice to tell you all at once".

"I *knew* there must have been something blossoming between the two of you from Edward's letter. Only lovers argue with such passion". Tab said.

"So does this mean you're staying here with us in Haworth?", Joseph added, hopefully.

"Aye, it does. I'm done with the army – that's it now. There's no going back". He looked at Annie in adoration, squeezing her shoulder. "We're going to tell the Reverend tomorrow so he can prepare to read the banns".

"You're a very lucky girl Annie", Tab said, gazing down at her niece.

"It's me that's the lucky one", Edward interrupted. "Who

knew I would come here and find a wife and a daughter. I'm the luckiest man in England".

"That you are", Jennifer said, giving him a stern glance. "And don't you forget it!".

Bridget began to cry again, and everyone cooed over her, offering her soothing words. Tab passed her back to Annie, who began to feed her again, rocking her back and forth for comfort. "Anyway, enough of us – tell us of Cliff Top Farm!".

"Ah, yes. The news you have all been waiting patiently for". Joseph lit his pipe and held it between his teeth thoughtfully. "The sale is complete, and like we had hoped for, it's brought us a small fortune". The kitchen fell silent as they all waited in anticipation to hear more. "The estate sold to a young gentleman recently returned from Sussex, for sixteen thousand pounds". The colour drained from Annie's face while Edward looked between Joseph and Tab in utter disbelief.

"Bugger off!", he replied, astounded. "It never did".

"Aye, it's true". Tab grinned at Joseph. "It's held in a bank for us at Bradford! Imagine that".

"There's no two people deserve it more than you do", Jennifer said warmly. "Imagine if your mother and father were still alive to see you now, Tab. They would be over the moon for you both".

"So, what are you going to do with it?", Annie asked, Bridget still feeding contentedly in her arms.

"Well first of all, Edward will have his payment as promised", Joseph confirmed. "And then Tab and I will be looking for a residence nearby. We have heard of an estate that may soon come to market at Laycock. There are already tenant farmers in situ, farmland with a handful of cottages, like. There's also woodland for lumber. Makes a good income by all accounts".

"Joseph Naylor, part of the landed gentry! I can't quite believe the change in your fortune!", Annie cried.

"*Our* fortune. Ours. You didn't think I could come back here and leave you short, did you? Especially not now, Annie".

"Just as well I'm afraid. I've had to spend some of the profits on the farm hands – just while I had Bridget and Edward was, erm, away for a short time".

"That's hardly something you need to worry about now", Joseph assured her. "Besides Annie, I had been thinking – even before the news of your marriage and Bridget. Wouldn't it be nice for you to take this small holding for yourself – for as long as you would like to live here. I will have the place renovated and can add some furniture for you, if that's something you would like…? We would be close by, but it's right that you and Edward start your married life in a home of your own".

Annie squealed in delight. "Oh Joseph! I'd be delighted! What a generous offer".

Edward paced towards Joseph with hand outstretched, beaming. "We really are truly grateful. I will never forget your kindness as long as I live".

"We can discuss your money later on, when we have privacy". Joseph winked at Edward and returned his handshake, slapping him on the back in masculine affection.

"Well". Jennifer rose from the kitchen table decisively. "Perhaps you two gentlemen could give us ladies some privacy now, we want to talk babies and the like…". She flapped her hands to shoo Edward and Joseph from the cottage.

Joseph leant close to Edward and mumbled, "Bloody hours I spent in that carriage. Can't even have a cup of tea in my own home".

"Now, if you wouldn't mind. Go to the Black Bull if you want a rest", Tab chimed in.

"That's us then". The two men placed their hats back on their heads and left the women to it, secretly glad to be out of it for a while.

~

At the pub they were joined by Abraham who was delighted to see Joseph back in Haworth. "Come back to restore order, have you?", he asked him, smirking at Edward all the while.

"Aye, alright. Things did go sideways while you were away Joseph, I admit". Edward held his hands up in mock surrender as Joseph laughed into his tankard.

"I'm not bothered by any of that. You two stood in for me and looked after Annie while I was away. I can't thank you enough for that. And besides, from now on things will be a lot easier for all of us, as a family". The three men knocked their glasses together in mutual appreciation.

"And a wedding to look forward to as well. Very... unexpected", said Abraham, raising his eyebrows. "I shall have another horseshoe waiting for Annie, she'll need all the luck she can get, knowing you". Edward took Abraham's joking in good spirits, after all, he had done much more for Edward than he could ever be repaid for.

As they caught up on the events of the summer, Mr O'Leary, one of the gamekeepers from Low Moor Farm, entered the pub and called for an ale. Dragging a stool up to the bar, he said to Mr Hague, "'Ere, you know your man from Keighley. Comes to sell you your spirits and what not?".

"Who? William Black?".

Abraham and Edward exchange a cautious look over their drinks, straining to follow the landlord's conversation over the noise.

"Aye, that's him. Just found him over the moors, haven't they?

Dead for days they reckon! The magistrate and the watchman are there now... fallen over the bloody craggs, 'an't he? Worse for drink, knowing him".

"Well I'll be damned!". Mr Hague gave a low whistle. "What on earth was he doing out there, drunk?".

Mr O'Leary shrugged. "I don't know, won't be doing it again though, will he?". Mr Hague shuffled off to inform his wife of the news, while Joseph looked at Edward and Abraham in earnest.

"Jesus, did you hear that, lads...? William's dead". The two of them feigned surprise and joined in with the posturing about how he might have met his end.

"One thing's for sure", Joseph continued. "Not a word of this to Annie, she's had enough to deal with. Agreed?".

"Agreed", they replied in unison, before their talk returned to Edward's newfound fatherhood and upcoming wedding.

"Oh, and I suppose I'll have a second one to pay for before long...", Joseph mused.

"Ey? Who's that then?".

"I'm going to collect Lottie in a fortnight, Abraham. Surely you're going to make an honest woman of her then?".

Edward savoured the sound of his friend's laughter as they bickered and joked with one another. He looked out through the soot-stained window and to the horizon where the moors opened up in vast expanse and counted the seconds until he could return to his fiancé and new baby daughter, waiting for him at home.

"Anyway men, a toast", Abraham proposed. "To Joseph's newfound fortune and Annie and Edward's new bairn". He held his tankard aloft and turned to face Edward directly. "May Bridget be the first of many!".

"Agreed", Edward echoed sincerely. "May Bridget be the first of many".

THE END

JOIN MY MAILING LIST!

If you would like to be the first to hear when the next book in the Sisters of Haworth Moor series is released, then sign up to my mailing list here!

BOOKS BY THIS AUTHOR

By The Morning Light

With their beloved father dead and the family dressmaking business destroyed, sisters Helen and Ruth are hounded from their home by moneylenders. Ruth is already lost to the workhouse, but Helen, hearing whispers of a job at Lord Balfour's estate, sets off to find any shred of security she can. Vowing to send for her sister as soon as she is established, Helen is willing to put up with cruel and brutal treatment to rescue her sister from destitution.

Spirited Jack works in the stables with Lord Balfour's horses, but dreams of training racehorses and leaving his life of servitude and drudgery behind. When the headstrong and stubborn Helen arrives a passion ignites between them, the likes of which neither have ever felt before.

Helen is desperate to be reunited with her sister, but risks losing the only man she has ever loved in the process. Can she find a way to have both?

A heart-warming tale of risk, love and loss; By the Morning Light is a Victorian romance short story set against the harsh landscape of 1800s Yorkshire.

IF YOU ENJOYED THIS BOOK...

Please consider leaving a review on amazon - it really helps my work reach new readers!

I would also love to hear from you directly with any thoughts you have about Annie's Way... you can reach me at eveeverdenebooks@gmail.com. I reply to every message I received.

Thank you for reading!

Printed in Great Britain
by Amazon